*The Fat Woman Next Door Is Pregnant*

# The **Fat** Woman Next Door Is **Pregnant**

Michel Tremblay
Translated by Sheila Fischman

Talonbooks

Copyright © 1978 Leméac Éditeur Inc.

Translation copyright © 1981 Sheila Fischman

Published with assistance from the Canada Council.

Talonbooks
P.O. Box 2076, Vancouver, British Columbia, Canada V6B 3S3
www.talonbooks.com

Printed and bound in Canada by Hignell Book Printing.

Seventh Printing: October 2008

*La Grosse Femme d'à Côté est Enceinte* was first published by Leméac Éditeur Inc., Montréal, Québec.

**Canadian Cataloguing in Publication Data**

Tremblay, Michel, 1943–
[La grosse femme d' à côté est enceinte. English]
The fat woman next door is pregnant

Translation of La grosse femme d' à côté est enceinte.
ISBN 0-88922-190-1

I. Title. II. title: La grosse femme d' à côté est enceinte.
English.
PS8539.R47G713        C843'.54C81-091331-3
PQ3919.2.T73G713

ISBN-13: 978-0-88922-190-1

*to Hélène,*
*who rebelled twenty years before everyone else*
*and had to suffer the consequences*

*to Louise Jobin and Jacqueline Rousseau,*
*with all my affection and gratitude*

*E pur si muove*
Galileo

## May 2, 1942

Rose, Violette and Mauve were knitting. From time to time, Rose (or Violette, or Mauve) would put her knitting on her lap, cast a half-amused, half-severe glance at her sisters' work and say: "You're knitting too loose" or: "I'm glad Momma didn't give *me* that colour yarn!" or then again, she might say nothing at all. If she was inactive for too long, one of her sisters would look at her. "Finish your bootie, then you can daydream." And Rose (or Violette, or Mauve) would sigh discreetly and take up her work again. Silence settled in. Comfortably. But after a few minutes: "Not often you can sit outside on the second of May, eh?" "Mmm...yes.... This is the first time, I think." "Come on, you're kidding! What about..." "That's true, you're right.... I remember the year Victoire had Gabriel..." "Not the year she had Gabriel, the year she had Edouard, her second..." "Whatever you say." "It isn't whatever I say, that's the way it is. It was the year she had Edouard." Silence again. The triple clicking of knitting needles. "Well, anyway, it was the second of May." Rose, Violette and Mauve were sitting on straight-back chairs. Rocking chairs encouraged laziness. Backs stiff, elbows at their sides, eyes lowered on their yarn. Blue. Or pink. Or yellow. Or some other colour. In the morning, before they brought out the chairs, they had washed the balcony. As they would every day until the beginning of September. A pail of water, lots of Javex, three brushes. The tiger cat that had spent the night under the balcony, exhausted after three days of fasting and violent love, had awakened, spitting foul-tempered "phhttt's" and cleared out, cursing the pernickety smell of cleanliness. "That cat this morning, was it Marie-Sylvia's?" "Yes." The door behind them opened softly. Meekly, they went on with their work. In the motionless tableau, only their hands moved. And the door that was opening. The house across the street slid to the left in the doorpane, then the house next door to it, then the others. And finally, Marie-Sylvia's restaurant at the corner of the lane. With a bit of sky this time, because Marie-Sylvia's restaurant, pretentiously baptized "Restaurant Arc-en-ciel," was on the ground floor of a two-storey house, the only one on the street — a luxury in this neighbourhood where only three or four-storey houses had been built, to save space. And money. "When you're done, bring them inside instead of leaving them out on the balcony. It looks sloppy." Florence, their mother, glided out of the house and bent over the work of her three daughters. "You're knitting too loose." "I'm making summer booties!" The other two laughed. Florence smiled. "There's no season for babies." Florence straightened up, turned and went inside. The door was ajar. "I think she's going to come out and sit with us." Rose, Violette and Mauve got up, picked up their chairs by their backs and made room for their mother's chair. Before they were seated again, Florence appeared in the door with a rocking chair. She put it down on the clean floor. They all sat down. The creaking of Florence's chair blended with the clicking of her daughters' needles. Rose, Violette and Mauve were knitting booties. For the fat woman next door who was pregnant. "Tomorrow, we'll start on Madame Jodoin's." And Florence, their mother, began to rock.

"Duplessis! Duplessis!" All dolled up, though it was early in the day, Marie-Sylvia was standing on the first of the three cement steps that went up to her restaurant. "Duplessis!" Summer and winter, beginning at seven a.m., on St-Jean Baptiste Day as well as Epiphany, and even on Good Friday, Marie-Sylvia wore rhinestones in her ears and glass beads around her neck. Her lipstick, which stained her teeth and made her breath smell sugary, was famous on the whole street. The children said Marie-Sylvia smelled of candy. The women said Marie-Sylvia smelled. "Duplessis!" She was wearing her Saturday dress. Yes, she had a dress for every day of the week. Just one. They never varied. You could tell what day it was by Marie-Sylvia's dress. Some people did just that. If Marie-Sylvia had bought a new dress, not only would the whole street have known about it, some of the residents wouldn't have been able to tell what day it was. Marie-Sylvia went back into her restaurant, peeved, dragging her broken-down bedroom slippers along the hardwood floor. For Marie-Sylvia was stylish only above the knees. She'd never been able to tolerate shoes, which she called "foot-killers." "Shoes? Who needs them behind a counter? What people can't see won't hurt them! Why should I suffer like a martyr day in, day out, just to sell one-cent candies to dirty-faced brats!" She walked behind the glassed-in counter that faced the door, and slipped into the back of the shop. Her kingdom. A veritable hecatomb piled up to the ceiling with cases of soft-drink bottles, statues made of plaster or of salt, in a full range of sizes (phosphorescent or not, painted or plain), most of them depicting the Blessed Virgin or St. Joseph, as the other saints on the calendar were not very popular in the neighbourhood, odds and ends that spilled out of bashed-in cartons, from which packages of bobby pins and tangles of shoelaces escaped, and an armchair so old that even Marie-Sylvia, who knew the origin of every article in her restaurant by heart, even the most insignificant, called it "the mysterious armchair." As a matter of fact, the chair had already been there for years when she rented the premises, but Marie-Sylvia claimed she'd found it in the lane with a note addressed to her. "It's a present. A mysterious present. I never found out who it was from. Maybe a secret admirer..." Marie-Sylvia wasn't known to have any admirers, secret or not, so people let her go on about the chair, the note, the bashful lover, nodding discreetly as they took out the change for an ice-cream cone or a bag of peanuts. Sitting in her mysterious armchair, Marie-Sylvia saw everything that went on in the restaurant and, especially, everybody who walked past it. She'd never been seen to read or knit or even sleep in her armchair. No. Neck craned, she watched intently. She saw everything, and according to the neighbours' comings and goings, she could interpret their moods, their days, their lives. If they were looking for someone in the neighbourhood, a lost child or a pie-eyed husband, Marie-Sylvia would say: "I saw him at such-and-such a time. He was going in such-and-such a direction, wearing such-and-such, and he looked as if he was thinking about so-and-so." Hence, the nickname, "the neighbourhood newshen," that the fat woman had given her. Marie-Sylvia walked past her armchair without even looking at it and into the short hallway that led to the back of the

12

house. She came into the tiny kitchen that still had the lovely smell of fresh coffee. "I'll kill him! Three days now, he's been gone! Three days!" She opened the door that gave onto the lane. "Duplessis! Duplessis!" She looked in every direction, her tongue travelling along her upper teeth to erase any trace of lipstick. And to taste again its sweetness, which made her feel so secure. She closed the door abruptly, sighed and poured herself another cup of coffee. "Never trust anybody! Never!" Her hand trembled slightly. A tear sparkled through the lashes of her left eye. "But anyway, I know. . ." She returned to her hecatomb and slumped into her mysterious armchair. Her head turned automatically towards the restaurant. Towards the door. Towards the glass, always clean. The chair was placed in such a way that Marie-Sylvia could spy at ease, without being seen, and drown herself completely in other people's lives. Between the two counters with their candies, chips, cupcakes and ice-cream, a breach opened onto the world.

His dream was filled with biting and screaming. Vague images, just precise enough to excite him, appeared in his mind and all his muscles tensed, allowing him to pounce on his fantasies, lacerate them, tear them, plough them, rip them to shreds that were easy to chew, swallow, digest, forget. But he couldn't move. Other images, more provocative, replaced the first ones and he snapped his jaw at them. The voice, his own perhaps, or that of a squirming victim he hadn't yet managed to fell with a single blow, seemed to blossom from his own throat, then suddenly move away and come back so powerfully his skull exploded and he cursed because it prevented him from leaping and overpowering the chimeras that assailed him, that voice was suddenly silent. The phantoms vanished. He opened his eyes. He saw the old woman shut the door. He stretched, yawned, sighed and curled up again. Later, caresses. First, he must destroy the shape over there that was running away, crawling (Crawling? No, it was floating, but where was the sky? Where was the ground?), that he thought for a moment he recognized, but then it was transformed before his eyes, goddamn it, and it charged, almost crushing him beneath a huge padded paw. "I'm suffocating! Death is coming for me! That's it, that's it, it's death." Then a rain of heads began to fall. Identical heads. "I know them all! Every one of those heads is known to me! And I must destroy them all!" That cry again. That voice. A shadow drew near. Hands grasped him. He whistled, bit, clawed. Louder, he heard the cry. His name. He decided then to deal the final blow, and, digging his claws into the substance that was, however, impalpable, he heaved obscenely, rubbing himself against the shadow, which was immediately subdued. And his dream ended with two convulsive moments of deliverance. Duplessis was well and truly awake now, and he began to wash himself.

Béatrice remembered him well. "The old soldier?" Mercedes dragged on her cigarette, squinting because of the smoke. "Soldiers, that's all we had yesterday, Betty!" "I know who, anyway. The one with the dyed hair. Is that the one?" "That's the one." "I'm surprised he squawked. He didn't do anything!" "That's just it!" Mercedes held her cigarette straight between her teeth and managed to speak almost without moving her lips. "If he *had* done

14

anything, he wouldn't've squawked!" "If he'd asked for something, he'd've got it!" "Maybe he didn't want to ask, Betty. Maybe he wanted you to take the initiative..." "Don't start using those fancy words. Talk simple." "Sometimes, when they don't do anything, it's up to you to take care of things." "I get fed up when they don't do anything." "It doesn't matter if you're fed up or not." Mercedes' bed was deep. Warm. Béatrice approached her employer, whose outstretched arm made a cosy shelter. "That's a hell of a nice nightie, Mercedes." "I worked for it. I took the initiative." "I can't get over these soldiers. I get sick just thinking they're going over to the Old Country to get killed. I feel as if they're already dead." "Don't think about it." "And besides, they're so full of themselves, thinking they're going to save France. And England too. I ask you! Both of them at once. Before this war, if they ever saw a Frenchman from France, they'd laugh at the way he talked and call him a fairy; and if they saw an Englishman, they'd say all kinds of stupid things about him because Englishmen are scummy and...kind of weird. And now, out of the blue, off they go to get themselves killed, cut into bits, lose part of their arms and legs, because France and England are in danger..." "France has been occupied for two years." "It deserves it!" "You say the craziest things." "Mercedes, you've tried to explain what's going on a hundred times, but I still don't get it. What can I do? Maybe I'm dumb, but I can't help it. I just don't see why our men have to go across the Atlantic to defend two countries they've hated all their lives." Mercedes smiled. "They don't all want to go." "There's one hell of a mob that's gone all the same." "If you don't want to understand, Betty, don't. But don't spit on the soldiers, they're how you make your living." They'd come here even if they weren't soldiers." "If they weren't soldiers, they couldn't afford you." "What were you doing before the war anyway, before there was soldiers?" "There's always been soldiers, Betty, and there always will be. Before the war, I was doing the same thing I'm doing now, but it was assembly-line fucking." "And just what does that mean?" Mercedes turned towards Béatrice. She took her cigarette from her mouth, butted it in an ashtray placed between her thighs, coughed and took a deep breath. "You like it here, Betty?" "No." "You hate it?" "No." Béatrice stood up, then sat on the edge of the bed and looked out the window, through the lace curtains. On the other side of the street, Marie-Sylvia's cat was meowing, its nose pressed against the restaurant door. "Duplessis wants to get in the restaurant and Marie-Sylvia's just standing there looking at him. She's standing behind that door doing nothing. She's nuts." Mercedes stood up too. "Ever notice how they yell at each other sometimes?" Mercedes got up. In two strides, she was in the bathroom. "You know, sometimes you'd think it was a serious fight." Mercedes looked at herself in the bathroom mirror. "Take a bath with me?" "Okay!" "Heat up some water in the kettle. . . . Go in the kitchen and. . ." "I know what to do, Mercedes. I was taking baths before I met you!" Béatrice smiled. "A nice hot bath. Come on, move!" "So what'd you say?" "To who?" "The soldier with the dyed hair." Mercedes stuck her head in the doorway. "I didn't *say* anything. I just did what you should've done."

When Duplessis was eating, everything in the restaurant came to a standstill. No matter what she was doing, Marie-Sylvia would leave the store and come and sit next to the plate of liver that Duplessis, indifferent to his mistress's presence, was devouring with his eyes shut,

16

tucked inside a round and perfect happiness where there was room only for him: chew, chew, chew and swallow these soft things, dark, that smelled strong and tasted even stronger, that restored his energy by leaving a trace of blood in his mouth, as though he'd killed a bird, another cat, or even the old woman watching him. Yes, as though he were devouring that woman before whom he had to grovel, rubbing himself against her and sticking his tail up so that she'd feed him. If Marie-Sylvia was unfortunate enough to make some gesture suggesting she was going to caress him or just encourage him, he would suddenly straighten up and spit at her, his claws out. Hatred would make his fur bristle like an electric charge. "I'm eating! Afterwards, we'll see if I'm in the mood to squirm around in your apron and pretend I'm enjoying it! We'll see!" He stuck his face back in his dish as though nothing had happened. "Ah! There's some left.... Oh oh! Not much though..." Marie-Sylvia would wait for him to finish, then unfailingly ask: "Did Mummy's nice big pussycat have a yummy lunch?" Duplessis would give her a contemptuous look which she interpreted as gratitude. Then she'd pick up the empty dish while the cat went out of the kitchen, heading for his box of clean sand. Conscientiously, she would wash the wooden dish. "Cats are clean, so we have to be clean with them too." Then she would return to her customers, who'd been left high and dry, or to her empty store. As she walked past Duplessis's box in the corridor, she heard the sand fly and she smiled. "Health." But that morning, as Duplessis was devouring a larger quantity of liver than usual, clicking his tongue and struggling a little with the pieces that were too big, Marie-Sylvia didn't admire his slender form, his striped fur, his long ears and striped muzzle. She gave him hell.

17

Mercedes had met Béatrice on the number 52 streetcar that left the little terminus at the corner of Mont-Royal and Fullum, then went down to Atwater and Sainte-Catherine, going by way of Saint-Laurent. It was the longest ride in town and the housewives from Plateau Mont-Royal took great advantage of it. They would set off in a group on Friday or Saturday, noisy, laughing, tearing open bags of penny candy or chewing enormous wads of gum. As long as the streetcar was going down Mont-Royal, they were in their element, giving each other slaps on the back if they choked, calling out to other women they knew; sometimes they'd even ask the driver how come he wasn't in the army. But when the streetcar turned down Saint-Laurent, heading south, suddenly they'd calm down and sink back into the straw seats: all of them, without exception, owed money to the Jews on Saint-Laurent, especially to the merchants who sold furniture and clothes; and for them, the long street separating rue Mont-Royal from rue Sainte-Catherine was a very sensitive one to cross. "Hope Sam doesn't see me! I'm two months behind!" When the streetcar passed certain stores, certain heads would turn away abruptly or dive into shopping bags. "You're awful quiet all of a sudden, Madame Jodoin. You scared of Sam Katz? How about that — there he is right now!" The woman would turn or bend down, pretending to tie her shoelaces. The other women burst out laughing. "You always bite on that one, Madame Jodoin. And we do it just about every week!" But usually, when they were really too far behind in their payments, they sat there silent, musing. They didn't even dare to look outside; they told themselves it was harder to recognize a face seen in profile than straight on. Some, but really just a few, even took out their rosaries. They'd scarcely pretend to hold their noses when an old Jewish woman got on the streetcar, laden down

18

with bags of groceries with carrot stems or leeks sticking out of them. "She's gonna make herself a dandelion salad!" they would snicker. "What do you think stinks so bad, the garlic she ate yesterday or the clothes she's going to wash next month?" They pursed their lips. "I hear they keep their transfers for toilet paper!" Madame Jodoin, the biggest giggler of the lot, was moaning like a cat in heat, on the verge of laughter. But as soon as they turned the corner of Saint-Laurent and Sainte-Catherine and headed west, they were more jubilant, filling the streetcar with loud shouts and heartfelt laughter. "You nearly killed me, you nut!" "You were as red as a banana—I mean, a poppy, Madame Jodoin!" "All of a sudden, the Jew understands French!" "No, she doesn't, she doesn't want to sell us anything!" The old Jewish woman, aware they were talking about her, would look down at her bag of groceries. All along Sainte-Catherine going west, noses were pressed to the windows in winter, arms rested on the windowsills in summer. "Tell us who's playing at the Gaiety, Madame Chose, you're on the right side?" "Woodhouse! My Lord, here's where I get off!" "Oh, stay with us till Eaton's, Madame Lemieux!" "Not on your life, they're a pack of thieves!" "So what? You never buy anything." "If all the women that never buy anything never went to Eaton's, there wouldn't be anybody there at all and they'd have to close down, the goddamn thieves!" "As far as that's concerned. . ." "Come to Woodhouse with me, Madame Guérin." "No, it's as dull as dishwater. I like a thief that's fun better than an honest man that put me to sleep!" The last women got off at Eaton's, at the corner of University. Never had anyone in their group gone any farther than Eaton's. West of the big store was the great unknown: English, money, Simpson's, Ogilvy's, la rue Peel, la rue Guy—till after Atwater, they started feeling at home again, because of the Saint-Henri district nearby and the smell of the port. But no one had ever gone to Saint-Henri and no one from Saint-Henri had ever come to Plateau Mont-Royal. They met halfway, in the aisles at Eaton's, and they'd fraternize over a chocolate sundae or an ice-cream soda. The women from Saint-Henri spoke with pride of Place Georges-Etienne Cartier, while those from Plateau Mont-Royal talked about boulevard Saint-Joseph. Be that as it may, one Saturday morning, very early, Mercedes was returning home after an active but disappointing night with a dentist from Sherbrooke Street and Béatrice was coming back from spending the night at a girlfriend's. Mercedes had already noticed the plump young woman, a salesclerk in a yardgoods store, who looked like an orphan and lived in the same building as she did, at the corner of Fabre and Gilford. She always said hello when they met on the stairs or the landing, but she never looked her in the eyes. "She's judging me." Unlike the other tenants, though, who went so far as to pound on her door and yell insults, little Béatrice was always very reserved. And said hello. Always. She'd even refused to sign a certain petition. . . . So, Mercedes came up to Béatrice on the number 52 streetcar. "You got circles under your eyes. Didn't you sleep last night?" "Just because you don't sleep, doesn't mean other people don't!" Mercedes laughed. "Not working today?" "Yes, I'm just on my way." "To sell your yardgoods and your fly buttons?" "Yes. And what of it?" "That's what you want to do for the rest of your life?" "I can see what's coming, you're going to stick your big nose. . ." "You'd rather sell buttons?" "Don't know. I've never tried what you do." Mercedes took her lipstick from her handbag. A twenty-dollar bill fell to her lap. "Lots of work available in my line these days, you know. . ." Béatrice looked at the money. "You know, the soldiers. . ." "Aren't you going to pick it up?" "What? Oh, that." She crumpled the bill nonchalantly.

"How much do you make a week?" Béatrice turned away. She looked outside, as though she hadn't heard Mercedes's question. The driver had just got off the streetcar, taking a long iron rod to fiddle with the rails so the car could turn along rue Mont-Royal and go east. "What's your name?" "Béatrice." Mercedes was still putting on her lipstick. "Mine's Mercedes. Mercedes Benz." Béatrice looked at her surreptitiously. "That's not your real name! Nobody's got a name like that!" Mercedes finally stuffed the twenty-dollar bill back into her bag. "No, my real name's too blah." Béatrice watched the driver get back inside the streetcar. He noticed that she was staring and he gave her a wink of complicity. Under a shower of sparks, the streetcar slowly turned right. Béatrice smiled, her head leaning against the window. "I'd call myself Betty. Betty Bird." "Why Bird?" "Because of my father. Because of you too. My father, he used to call twenty-dollar bills birds. Maybe because whenever he saw one, it was always far away, like a bird in a tree, or up in the sky — always far away." The two women smiled at one another. "Betty Bird's a swell name. Catchy." "Yes. I been thinking about it for a long time." Mercedes yawned. The shadows under her eyes grew larger. "You should come over one of these days and have a good talk about things..." "To tell you the truth, I'd just as soon come over right away..." "You don't waste any time, do you?" "I'm sick of fly buttons!" "When could you start?" For the first time, Béatrice looked Mercedes straight in the eye, looked into the depths of her soul. "You know as well as I do, I've been ready for ages. What else do you want me to do?" And Mercedes had been afraid. As she rubbed Betty's back in the tub, she thought about it all again and a broad smile lit up her face. "What's the joke?" "I'm thinking about how scared I was of you at the start. The

21

way you just let things happen to you." "And now, you aren't scared any more?" "Sometimes, yes; sometimes, no." "Anyway, that was all a long time ago . . ." "Not that long, Betty. Just a year." "It's a long time all the same." Betty grabbed the sponge which was dripping soap suds. "Come on, turn around and I'll do your back."

Edouard and Thérèse had got up at the same time. Their rooms faced each other, so they'd found themselves nose to nose when they opened their doors. "You're up early, mon oncle Edouard. And today's Saturday!" "When you gotta go, little girl, it doesn't matter what day it is." They both ran to the bathroom at the very back of the house, past the dining room and the kitchen. Thérèse got there first, but yielded her place to her mother's brother. Marcel, Thérèse's brother, who was so small, despite his four years, that people thought he was barely two and a half or three, heard them running and when Thérèse and Edouard passed him, he lisped a shy good morning, but the two runners didn't hear him. Marcel slept in the dining room, in a bed disguised as a sofa in the daytime. It was far too big for him and he hated it. Marcel witnessed all the comings and goings in the house — and God knows, there were lots. When his uncle Gabriel, who worked nights, came home around two in the morning, Marcel would wave at him. But Gabriel, preoccupied, tired, head drooping, rarely looked in the baby's direction. He would hurry into his own bedroom which opened off the dining room, where the fat pregnant woman, his wife, was waiting for him. When Albertine, Marcel and Thérèse's mother, got up at night to make some tea to calm her nerves, Marcel would slip out of bed and follow her into the kitchen. She would take him in her arms as she waited for the water to boil—and Marcel inevitably would fall asleep, his head resting against his mother's plump shoulder. Albertine would rock her youngest child as she stared at the tea kettle. Sometimes, she fell asleep on her feet, leaning against the stove, waking with a start just as Marcel was about to fall, or the water began to boil over on the coal stove making an unpleasant sputtering sound. And when old Victoire, the mother of Edouard, Gabriel and Albertine, got up every night to go to the bathroom, Marcel would huddle in a corner of his bed and close his eyes. Marcel was afraid of Victoire. Not that she was mean or nasty. But a strange sickness in her left leg made her limp, made her suffer dreadfully and made her irritable. And so, she was often impatient with her grandchildren. Victoire passed Marcel's bed like a shadow and slipped through the kitchen, then into the back room where she began to produce sounds that would have made Richard or Philippe, the sons of Gabriel and the fat woman, laugh, but which literally terrified the little boy. When she was finished, she would let out a sort of long moan and vigorously pull the chain. The sucking sound of the water flushing drove Marcel almost crazy with fear, because he knew it meant the old woman was about to limp past his bed again. Would she jump into his bed, jump on him with both feet as his cousin Philippe, four years his elder and already a smooth talker and storyteller, had promised? Would she beat him, kill him, eat him up? But Victoire walked past without giving him a thought. Marcel went back to sleep, trembling. "You been in there a long time, mon oncle. Let me make peepee, then you can go back." Edouard came grumbling out of the bathroom. Immediately, Marcel shot across the dining room and kitchen and threw himself into the arms of his uncle, who tossed him up to the ceiling, as the child shouted and laughed. "What do you want for breakfast, Marcel? Eggs? Two dozen? And bacon? Two pounds? And toast? Two whole loaves of bread? Coffee? Two coffeepots?" Thérèse shouted from the bathroom. "You're going to wake up the whole house!" "Shut up and piss!" "You know very well he doesn't eat any of that stuff anyway..." "If he doesn't eat any of that stuff, it's because you don't give it to him! I'm sick and tired of seeing him eat pablum..." "He doesn't eat it because it doesn't agree with him." "That's your mother's bright idea, Thérèse, that it doesn't agree with him..." Thérèse came out of the bathroom, tying her pajama cord. "You can go in now." "Will you start the coffee in the meanwhile, my pretty little chickie?" Edouard rushed into the bathroom as Thérèse bent over her little brother. "Did you make peepee?" "No." "Do you have to go?" "Yeth." Thérèse picked Marcel up and took him to the edge of the kitchen sink. "Go on, or it'll be too late..." Pink with pleasure, Marcel took out his little penis and bent his head over the sink. "Do you always look at yourself like that when you make peepee?" "Yeth." "Why?" "'Cause I like to." "Dirty!" "Diddy? Why, diddy?" "You'll find out soon enough!" Thérèse was eleven. The same age as Richard, the elder son of the fat woman and Gabriel. Thérèse and Richard had been born two days apart: Thérèse on October 31, and Richard, two days later, on November 2. Thérèse was a clown, merry, always making faces, like a Hallowe'en party, while Richard was serious, sad, pale and tedious as the Mass for the dead. But they were inseparable, Thérèse, having fun as naturally as breathing, Richard, being glum no matter what he did. "You're going to wake up my father with your fooling around and we'll get hell again!" Richard was standing in the kitchen doorway, tall for his age, his ears sticking out, his eyes puffy. "Your father

24

usually gets up on Saturday, Coco, so we can make as much noise as we want." "But you don't have to start at eight o'clock in the morning!" "I see, now you're starting, eh?" Thérèse put her brother down, went over to her cousin and kissed him on the neck. Richard wiped the kiss away with his hand. "Breakfast ready?" Thérèse gave him a withering look. "No, I've only had time to make noise!" Edouard came out of the bathroom just then. "Thérèse, go and dress your brother. And Richard, go somewhere else and sulk. I'm making the breakfast this morning!" The kitchen was vacated in two seconds flat and Edouard got down to work. He took one of the fat woman's aprons (he himself was rather corpulent, thank you), tied it neatly at the back, then opened the door of the icebox.

Richard shared a double room at the front of the house with Victoire, his grandmother, and his uncle Edouard. He slept in a folding bed under the archway. Every night, he went to a dark corner and pulled out the iron bed which was folded in two, with blankets and sheets hanging out of it, and began to struggle with two hooks that were too tight and refused to budge. Of course, the hooks would let go all at once, the bed would unfold and the slack, worn-out springs would clatter and twang. And every morning, Richard had to fold up the bed again, sweating bullets, and puffing and wheezing. The hooks would refuse to go into their spaces, the feet wouldn't fold, the thin mattress was suddenly too thick — and as his grandmother, who didn't even seem to be enjoying herself, looked on placidly, the boy, dishevelled, red and out of breath, would finally close up his bed. As he pushed the heap of iron into its corner, Richard would curse the fate that had condemned him to leave his parents' room and end up here, in this hole, that reeked of his grandmother's medicines and his uncle Edouard's cologne — Yardley Lotus. That morning, while his grandmother was still asleep, her mouth wide open, as if she were uttering a final cry of despair, Richard didn't tackle his bed. For lack of anything better to do, he turned his head towards the old woman. He could see her face between two bars of the brass bed. In the five years he'd been sleeping in the same room with her, Richard had spent an incalculable number of hours watching his grandmother die. In fact, every time he examined her in her sleep, grumbling, scarcely breathing, mouth open to reveal bare white gums as sharp as knives, Richard expected to see her expire. She was an exhausted flickering candle, a dismantled gasping clock, a motor at the end of the road, a dog grown too old, a servant who had finished serving and was dying of boredom, a useless old woman, a beaten human being, his grandmother. If she wanted to do anything in the house, her daughter-in-law, the fat woman, or her daughter, Albertine, very attentively would anticipate her intentions: "You just rest . . . you've done enough work in your life . . . sit down, Momma, your leg . . ." The old woman would lay down the dishcloth or the wooden spoon, swallowing so she wouldn't explode. Richard had often seen his grandmother weep with rage, leaning against the window in her room that looked out on the outside staircase. He'd even heard her curse the two women, cast impotent spells on them; he'd seen her stick out her tongue and pretend to be kicking them. From morning to night, she wandered from her bedroom to the dining room, from the dining room to her bedroom, a superfluous object of attention in this house where everyone and everything had assigned tasks or at least some use — except for her. She would have liked to take out the garbage, make supper, wash the fat woman, soak the curtains in the bathtub, wallop Philippe or Thérèse or Richard or Marcel, but wallop someone; instead, though, she invariably ended up in front of the radio, her ear pressed against Donalda's confidences or fat Georgiana's mercurial moods. In the very middle of a snore, Victoire opened her glassy eyes and her hand removed a white lock from her forehead. Richard immediately looked away. "What time is it?" Richard didn't answer. "What time is it? I know you aren't asleep, Coco. You're all dressed!" "Eight o'clock, Mémère. A little after." Victoire cleared her throat, took a small handkerchief from under her pillow and spat. Copiously. Richard shut his eyes. Victoire sat up with some difficulty and looked at her grandson. "Will you stop spying on me, for Heaven's sake!" Richard quickly turned his head towards his grandmother. "No." Long silence. Victoire, who was very short-sighted, couldn't see her grandson. But she could feel him looking at her. She could always feel him looking at her. It was the same look that had just drawn her from her sleep. "Someday when you're asleep, Mémère's going to get up and come and wring your little neck. Like a chicken." "No. You love me too much." The woman smiled. "You think so?" "Yes." In turn, Richard smiled. "I like it better when you're awake." "Me too!"

Dragging Marcel behind her, Thérèse burst into the other double room, the one that included the bedroom of her mother, Albertine, and the living room where she and her cousin Philippe had been sleeping for several years. Thérèse and Philippe shared the same sofa in a cavalcade of laughing, slapping, jumping, tickling and ill-concealed modesty. Misunderstood modesty, too. Philippe was only eight, but already he knew where to fumble and how to avoid slaps by assuming an innocent or a guileless attitude. Thérèse and Philippe's sofa was a constant source of amused murmuring, an oasis of gaiety in the midst of the desert of extinguished passions and unappeased desires that inhabited the four corners of the house. Albertine slept at the back of the double room, in a sort of boat, black in colour and black in mien, that her husband, Paul, now off at war, thank God, had brought from the wilds of his native Laurentians as a wedding present twelve years earlier. Albertine had always hated that rancid-smelling box where the worst experiences of her life had caught her by surprise when she was scarcely more than an adolescent, when she was ignorant and pure beyond common measure. She had been, and was still, subjected to this bed as to some inevitable catastrophe that might occur long after it has been announced and then go on to mark and direct an entire lifetime. The whole existence of this rather fat but very beautiful woman was contained between the painted planks, on the worn-out mattress, in the thin, frayed linen sheets: disillusion at the small amount of pleasure — when she had been promised paradise — could be read there just beneath the surface. Albertine had just awakened when her children rushed past the door like a whirlwind. Immediately, she sat up in bed, her head bristling with rag curlers, arms bare, in a pale pink cotton nightdress. "How come you're tearing the house apart so early in the morning? Isn't the baby dressed yet? Did he eat? Did he wet the bed again?" Thérèse looked at her mother with a broad smile, as Marcel hid behind her. She spoke softly, as though she were awakening her mother after a very peaceful night. "Bonjour, Momma. How are you this morning? Sleep alright?" Visibly disconcerted, Albertine stared at her daughter, taken aback, her arm still raised accusingly, but not so sure of herself now. "Bon, okay. I get it." She threw back the covers and swung her legs out of the bed. "Bring in the baby." Thérèse picked up her brother and brought him to their mother. Amazed to see her suddenly so gentle, Marcel looked at her as though he'd never seen her before: he was torn between a desire to cry, brought on by Albertine's anger, and a need to snuggle in her arms, because he loved her beyond reason —even beyond his fear. Sensing the baby's hesitation, Albertine decided to smile. Marcel opened his eyes wide, eyes that were wild with happiness, and began to laugh uncontrollably, so that his stomach quivered and his shoulders shook. "There's one you don't even have to tickle!" Albertine tossed Marcel onto his back on the bed. "Good thing I've got you!" Thérèse, who couldn't explain the mixture of delight and jealousy that stirred inside her, moved away from the enormous bed from which Marcel's laughter burst out in bubbles of joy. Thérèse and Albertine had had a serious conversation the night before. Or rather, Thérèse had tried to talk with her mother the night before. Wild with fear, but with her mind made up, she had come right out and asked her mother to stop shouting all the time when Marcel was around. The only answer the little girl received was a slap behind the ear, but all the same, she sensed that she'd made her point. And here was the proof. Seeing her mother smile and play with Marcel when she woke up, stroking the soles of his feet and nibbling at him, was a rare and brand new experience, too new, perhaps, for Thérèse to be able to relish it completely. And she knew very well that, in any case, her brother would be the only one to benefit from it. Hadn't she done it all for him? So as not to see him shift from laughter to tears whenever Albertine's frustrations exploded in rude words and hysterical cries? Her mother hadn't frightened her for a long time now and her abrupt changes of mood left Thérèse indifferent; no, not completely—her mother's changes of mood were beginning to awaken in her a brand new feeling that she didn't understand yet, but which filled her with a doleful joy that was ill-defined, almost unhealthy: contempt. She couldn't name this feeling, but she knew instinctively that she must bury it deep inside her, behind barricaded doors, in that place where you are alone, always alone, to savour the cold dish that leaves a sickly sweet taste in the mouth. Thérèse sat on the edge of the sofa. Philippe was pretending to be asleep. Thérèse lifted the covers, lay down beside her cousin and huddled against the little boy's plump, soft body. She pressed her mouth against her cousin's ear: "If you sleep so much, your little thing won't get stiff!" Philippe laughed so loud everyone in the house was startled.

"The bay isn't an open bay. It doesn't open onto the ocean. No. . . it's an enclosed bay. When you look straight ahead, you don't see the open sea. The two arms of the bay close in. . . they practically touch. If you want to get there by boat, you have to go in between those two closed arms. It's the calmest bay in the world because the waves from the open sea don't come to the beach. The waves are still. Always. And in behind you, there's the mountains. So high, the clouds get stuck on them and never come out to the bay. It never rains on the bay in the winter because the mountains hold back the clouds. It's never ever rained in the winter." Arms folded over her enormous bosom, head against the back of the chair that she hadn't left for almost two months now, the fat woman spoke in a soft, even voice, without intonation. The intonation was in her eyes. Her eyes saw the bay, the waves, the rocks, sensed the clouds clinging to the mountains, like angel's hair on the branches of a Christmas tree. When the vision was too beautiful, the fat woman's eyes filled with tears and she let them fall to her chin, to her neck. "I could sit in the water, just on the edge of the shore and feel myself sinking into the sand. Because when you sit in the sand on the edge of the water, the waves hollow out a hole underneath you. I'd put on a housedress with every colour of the rainbow in it and people would point to me and say: 'See how happy that fat woman is!' I'd lie on my back at the edge of the water and the waves would come and spread their foam around my head. The whole month of January. The whole month of February. The whole month of March. We wouldn't hear a word about the war and we wouldn't know who'd died or disappeared or been maimed for life. You'd read *Notre-Dame de Paris* or *Eugénie Grandet* out loud, and when the waves weren't filling my ears, I'd listen. . . . I'd stay there, pinned down by the sun, and fondled by the ocean. And I could have as many babies as I wanted!" Lulled by the sound of his wife's voice, Gabriel had been asleep for several minutes. He began to snore, gently, as though not to disturb the fat woman. She looked at him for a few seconds, then went on with her story, as though he were still awake. "At noon, you'd go and pick pineapples and coconuts. We'd eat under the palm trees, laughing and kissing. All the children I'd had would be at our feet, all the time, and we'd love it!" The bedroom door opened and Albertine, carrying a basin, burst in. "Sleep well?" "Not a wink." "Do you have to. . .?" "Of course." Albertine slipped the basin between the fat woman's legs. "It gets more and more complicated. Seems like you're getting fatter and fatter." "I *am* getting fatter, it's normal. . . . I've got another two months." "If you hadn't decided to have a baby at your age...." "Now, don't start that again, Bartine!" Marcel had followed his mother into the bedroom, but he didn't dare come up to the armchair. "Allô, Marcel.... I heard you crying last night. Did you have a bad dream?" The little boy scampered off like a frightened squirrel. "The coffee smells good." "I'll bring you some in a while, but I don't know how good it'll be. Edouard's making it!" The fat woman smiled. "Edouard! Edouard, doing us the honour of lifting a finger in the house? Now I've heard everything!" Albertine took the basin from between the fat woman's legs. "I'll come and change you after breakfast. You must be sweltering in here..." The fat woman frowned. "You're so nice this morning, Bartine." "I'll explain everything..." Albertine walked away from the armchair. "Wake up my husband. He has to eat." Albertine bent over her brother and gave him a gentle push. Gabriel opened his eyes. Albertine withdrew without a word, closing the door behind her. "Sorry. I fell asleep while you were talking. I had a hard day yesterday..." "Doesn't matter. Anyway, I think I dream more for myself than for you." "No. I like listening to you. It's as if we were there." "Go and eat." Gabriel got up and kissed his wife on her forehead. Her forehead was damp with sweat. "Want to try and get up this morning?" "You know very well I'm not supposed to." When the door had closed behind her husband, the fat woman turned to the window of their bedroom. She could see the shed at the end of the wooden gallery, part of the third floor of the house and a scrap of blue sky the size of a handkerchief. The rebellion she'd kept inside her for so long, that she'd managed to subdue at the bottom of her belly—a wild animal that refused to be tamed, which she had nourished with dreams and lies—suddenly awoke in her throat and the fat woman opened her mouth to scream. But a single word came out, like an admission of defeat or an accusation: "Acapulco!"

Three times a day, they set up the big table in the dining room: the morning meal took place almost in silence, with only Albertine's shouts sometimes flying through the house like butcher knives, but no one listened. Their noses stayed in their plates and Victoire's head, dishevelled by sleep, continued to nod. The noon meal, more animated, was the particular domain of the children home from school or from their noisy city children's games, a quick bowl of soup, a quick sandwich and it was over. As for the evening meal, it was something between a total free-for-all and "The Garden of Earthly Delights" by Hieronymus Bosch, each family going into it kicking and screaming—"Ham again?" "Blah, there's no salt in the soup!" "Poo, the soup's too salty!"—highly indignant because the others didn't know how to behave. Victoire was always enthroned in the same place, in the very middle of the table, "on the crack," as Albertine said, the ends being reserved for the two fathers of the household: Gabriel and Paul. Since Paul had gone off to the war, his wife, Albertine, had taken over his place in such an imperious way that Richard started calling her "mon oncle Albertine." The children were scattered around the table according to their rank in their respective families: Richard and Thérèse, the two oldest, sat on either side of their grandmother, "to keep her from drowning in the gravy," and Marcel and Philippe sat with their mothers on the other side. As for Edouard, his official place was across from his mother, but he enjoyed changing often, passing from Albertine's camp to the fat woman's, and sometimes even taking Paul's place — to the great dismay of his sister who would shout at him: "When you've got a wife and kids, you'll have the right to sit at the end! In the meantime, you can share the crack with Momma!" Ever since the fat woman had been sentenced to her bedroom, Edouard, perhaps as a joke on Albertine, who took herself for her husband, had sat in his sister-in-law's place, where he enjoyed imitating her politely, exaggerating the way she sighed, a woman who was too fat, and her way of threatening the children in a gentle, even voice. Slowly, he would say, without even looking at the child he was addressing: "Richard, you've got ears like a monkey now, but if you don't stop fidgeting, I'll do something about it and you'll look more like a jackass!" The imitation was so perfect the whole household burst out laughing, even the fat woman who had asked that the door to her room be kept open and who heard everything from the depths of her prison. But when he went so far as to call Gabriel "my husband," gently placing his hand on his brother's shoulder as his sister-in-law always did, Albertine would knit her brows and cast a reproving glance at her mother, who, to provoke her even more, would say to Edouard: "Encore! Encore! Sounds just like her, by God!" When the evening meal was over, when Hieronymus Bosch really took hold of the children and they started hurling glasses of water and pieces of bread back and forth, when the real foolishness started, the adults would get really fed up and inevitably there would be a scene. Every night. On slack days, Marcel would get a cuff on the head and everyone would be disappointed; on good days, anything could happen. Once, for example, Edouard, pissed to the gills, threw what was left of his steak in his mother's face, rendering her speechless for a good three days, but that was before the war when "steak grew plentifully in the garden of the cows," as Gabriel said (now when you found

34

a piece of boiled beef in your soup, you thought you were dreaming); once, too, Paul had taken Marcel in his arms because he was crying so loud, then sat him down in the spaghetti bowl, in the midst of congealed noodles and cold pork chops; but that, too, had been before the war; it had even happened — and this was the most heroic deed in the history of the three families — it even happened that Victoire got up, limped around the table and poured a cup of scalding tea over the Brylcreemed head of Edouard, her beloved son, the last born, the pride and joy of her accursed soul. Why? No one ever knew. Was it after one of their numerous rows from which they always emerged humiliated and happy? Was it because of something one of them hadn't said that, according to a prearranged plan, should have been said? Or was it just the end of a too peaceful meal when no one had paid any attention to the old woman so that she'd felt excluded and abandoned? The fact is that her scalded son had dared to answer back and Victoire found herself on the floor, skirt above her waist, one eye changing colour and size from one second to the next. They still talked about it. And they'd go on talking about it until the end of time. It was the most precious jewel in the crown of their daily crises — and when they referred to it, they almost fell to their knees. From laughing. That morning, then, Edouard had worked like a truly accomplished and happy mistress of the household, singing at the top of his lungs, "Heureux comme un roi," in a perfect imitation of Robert L'Herbier, his mother's idol, and therefore, his rival, a sworn enemy, his favourite whipping boy, his nightmare, his death. When Victoire talked about Robert L'Herbier, Edouard would puff up like a red balloon, and when the balloon burst, the poor singer would be spattered with shit, white secretions and gastric acid. But, for once, Edouard hadn't changed the words, he hadn't sung, "Happy as a Queen," swaying his hips and raising his arms to the ceiling like some bloated Mistinguett coming down a too-steep staircase on too-high heels. His mother didn't abuse him this time; she was content to listen to her idol's voice blossom from the mouth of her god. Simply because Edouard was working, Albertine found herself with time on her hands. She'd done her best to stick her nose in the kitchen, but her brother made as if he were going to unbutton his fly and Albertine vanished like a charm. What she called her brother wasn't exactly charming, but in any case, Edouard preferred Albertine's absence, with the sound of her voice in the background, to his sister's presence, with her voice in the foreground, because Albertine was never silent. Sometimes, Edouard would say: "You can hear Albertine talking even when she's gone shopping at the other end of town" or: "Albertine? She was vaccinated with a gramophone needle. They hired her to record his master's voice too, but the dog got scared!" For a long half-hour, the feverish atmosphere in the house kept mounting: for once, all the children were sitting on Marcel's sofa in the dining room, silent, craning their necks towards the kitchen, anxious. Albertine had made the beds, shaking the mattresses a little harder than usual. And Victoire hadn't turned on the radio to listen to "the news from overseas." Richard murmured in Thérèse's ear: "If you ask me, it'll be so awful we'll all get sick!" Richard clearly didn't like his uncle. Didn't he act as a buffer between his grandmother and Edouard when the latter came home late (which happened rather often), drunk and smelling of cheap liquor? And even cheaper perfume! Richard maintained that his uncle drank perfume because liquor wasn't strong enough for him. Thérèse watched him for two brief seconds, then shrugged. "Even if it's awful, at least it'll be a change!" But it was a complete surprise. Never in living memory had they eaten so well in time of war. In spite of rationing, the shortage of sugar, "the shortage of everything," as Victoire said, Edouard had managed to create a breakfast that not only had some taste, but also looked like something: the oranges were cut in quarters, the toast was nicely toasted, the eggs (all the eggs for the week!) were perfect, and the coffee...sublime. Everything was so good that morning, no one slept during the meal. And the silence that settled into the dining room was appreciative. Only Edouard allowed himself a few asides. For example, he walked around the table carrying the coffeepot, declaring in an affected French accent: "I'm the Star Fairy and all my supplies come from Father Christmas!" Victoire looked at him lovingly; his sister shot daggers at him, the children gazed at him flabbergasted. He made such an effort that at one point Gabriel, his brother, asked him slyly: "You sure the army turned you down because you got flat feet? If you ask me, those flat feet stir up a hell of a wind!" Edouard stopped smack in the middle of the doorway and answered without turning around: "Gabriel, are you sure you didn't get your wife pregnant just to stay out of the army?" The incident was closed. Once more, the two brothers had shown their true colours and the rest of the house pretended not to hear. Edouard opened the ice-box in search of a fresh quart of milk, muttering to himself: "I'd rather have flat feet than a brain on the skids!" He took out a quart of milk and came back to the table: "I'm the Star Fairy and Father Christmas supplies all my eggs, cream, bread, sugar and meat. But don't ask me what I do for him or you won't keep your breakfast down!"

Edouard tiptoed into the fat woman's bedroom. She was dozing, or rather, she was pretending to doze as she didn't want Richard or Philippe to come and see her before she was washed. Quietly, Edouard picked up the tray with the remains of his sister-in-law's breakfast. "Are you asleep?" She turned her smiling face to him, somewhat relieved. "Ah, it's you." Putting on his French accent again, Edouard murmured conspiratorially: "Did you think it was the drrreadful Alberrrtine?" The fat woman laughed. She pointed to the tray. "That was good." "Thank you." Edouard looked around. Aside from the fat woman's armchair, the bedroom was furnished with only a bed and a chest of drawers, but they were so large that they took over the room and made it look small, even though it was the biggest bedroom in the house. The chest of drawers in particular, a sort of brown dinosaur with quantities of drawers and massive, crooked feet, surmounted by an oval mirror that distorted everything, seemed to want to pounce on anyone who entered the room. This piece of furniture fascinated the children, who had been told that they had been found in various drawers the day that they were born: at the very top were the twin drawers of Thérèse and Richard, bigger than the others and blacker too; then came those of Philippe and Marcel, wedged into the interlacings of carved wood; and finally, a little lower still, the one for the baby to come. It was tiny, a glove-drawer, in fact, plain, somewhat lost. Marcel would often be seen gazing at this secret drawer. He didn't dare to touch it and if anyone asked what he was doing there, he said: "I'm waiting for the mail!" The fat woman pulled down her nightgown, which had a tendency to creep up. "Sit down a minute, let's talk." "I haven't really got time. . . . Albertine's waiting for me to do the dishes. . . . I wanted to cook, so I have to finish the job." "But you aren't usually so scared of her." "I'm not

38

scared, but she's acting so nice this morning, I don't want to do anything to get on her nerves. I have to enjoy it while it lasts!" All the same, Edouard sat on the edge of the iron bed, the tray on his knees. "You must be sick and tired, eh?" "And how! I'm telling you, if I'd known. . . . I say that, but it isn't true. . . . I want this baby so badly! Anyway, it'll have to be good-looking — and smart!" Edouard smiled. "That, I don't doubt. We'll spoil it and show it how to live, eh?" "But the two things don't go together." She looked at the little scrap of blue sky. "You came in at four in the morning again. . ." "You heard me? I'm sorry, I tried not to make any noise." "I wasn't asleep. And I'm not scolding you. That isn't what bothers me. . . . You know, I don't want to preach, Edouard, you're old enough to live your own life. . ." "But, there's a 'but' coming. . ." This time, she looked him straight in the eye. "I always think of Richard sleeping in between you and your mother. . . . Those fights you have just about every night are bad for him. . . . He hears things he shouldn't hear and maybe it upsets him. . . . You know, he's really. . ." Richard's voice, which hadn't changed yet, but in which you could already hear the severity and intolerance that would become the two poles of his existence, rang through the bedroom, startling the two adults. "Don't worry, Momma, I haven't bothered listening to them for ages. . . . Anyway, they always say the same things!" Richard had already disappeared, frustrated at finding his mother, whom he venerated like a saint, in conversation with his uncle whom he despised. Edouard and the fat woman were silent for several moments. A huge fly buzzed around the cup of coffee in which the fat woman had put too much sugar. Edouard shooed it away. "That's what they call getting caught with your pants down, eh?" "He's always sticking his nose into everything. I don't know what to do with him. . . . It's as if he could smell

39

when something's going on—and he's always there when you don't need him. . . . There's a good reason why he's got such big ears!" She pursed her lips. "I just mentioned his ears again. It's a real sickness that I've got. I have to stop, it doesn't make sense. That child's so complicated, I can't help thinking about the only thing about him that's simple!" She took refuge again in the view from her window. "Ask Albertine to come and see me—after the dishes." Edouard got up and walked towards the door, his head down. "Edouard!" He stopped in his tracks, one foot already outside the room. "What's wrong?" She gestured to him to come back and sit down again. "I'm not done yet." He came back to the bed, but remained standing. She took a deep breath before she spoke. "Sometime. . . . Sometime, when you haven't got anything to do. . .come and tell me what you do when you go out! Come and tell me about your nights on the town. You're the only one that goes out and sees people. . . . I don't really know how to tell you. . . . I feel all mixed up. . . . You know what I mean. I'm stuck in here and you're always gadding around. . . . You know how much I like people. . . . Come and tell me about the shows you see and the people you meet and what you do. . .if you want, I mean. You don't have to." Edouard took one of her hands. "You don't have to say any more. I understand." The fat woman was so moved that she could say no more. "You should have asked me before. I never thought you'd be interested. Albertine and my mother shut me up whenever I start to talk about it. . ." Just before he went out, Edouard said, without turning around: "But I'll tell you everything, and I mean *every* thing! I won't keep anything back. And if you're shocked, it'll be your own fault!" He crossed the dining room, smiling. The fat woman closed her eyes. She was off to Mexico again.

"Big Ears seems to be in a bad mood!" After their mother, Florence, made this observation, Rose, Violette and Mauve put down their coffee cups and cakes and burst out laughing. Rose (or Violette or Mauve) even dropped her little silver spoon onto her dress, catching it just before it fell to the balcony floor. "You sound just like his mother, Momma!" Florence stared at her daughter (Rose or...) before replying: "God forbid! His mother was brought up in the wilds of Saskatchewan by Cree Indians who'd never seen a mountain in their life and thought the world was somewhere in the hollow of the Great Manitou's hand. For a long time the fat woman's own mother even thought the Saskatchewan River was the Great Manitou's lifeline and that's no joke!" "I think that's beautiful." "And I think it's ignorant, my girl! Maybe I sometimes use the same expressions as that woman, but don't tell me I talk like her!" "But she's the one we're knitting for..." "We haven't got any choice, it's part of...our arrangements!" Richard, unaware of the presence of the four knitting women, was sitting on the second last step of the outside staircase that went up to his house on the second floor. He folded his arms and bent over, like someone with a stomach ache. All through the meal, he'd been thinking of the happy moment when he would finally be allowed to go and kiss his mother before he was sent outdoors ("Go out and play, children, it's Saturday and it's a lovely day! Richard, Thérèse, take the little ones to Parc Lafontaine, it'll do them good!") for the rest of the day. Ever since he'd seen his mother become fatter, almost as he watched, looking less and less like the soft, enveloping woman who had delighted his tender childhood, and more and more like a mound of soft fat with no personality or character, Richard, for the first time in his life, felt the need to talk to her, perhaps to tell her that he loved her, in spite of her sickness, in spite of what he heard about her, in spite of what he heard about her condition at night, when everyone was going to bed and the fat woman would burst out sobbing as she accused each and every one of them of hating her, of passing judgment on her, of blaming her. But not once in the three months his mother had been glued to her armchair, had he had the courage to really talk to her. Every morning, he would say the usual generalities in the language used only with the chronically ill, a language from which certain expressions and, in particular, any feelings are excluded, as he'o been told to do. For he had been told to be impersonal with his mother: "Your mother's very sick so don't bug her with your kisses and your sweet talk. It'll wear her out. So, just say good morning and make sure you don't say anything about your trouble at school or her trouble here." What was left for an eleven-year-old boy to say to his sick mother? At times, he felt that the fat woman would have liked to chat with him, laugh, and perhaps even cry as she held him in her arms, but Albertine or Victoire would always turn up with his school-bag and give him a push to hurry him on his way. Today was Saturday, though, there was no school and Richard had something important to say to his mother. About his uncle Edouard. About what Edouard had said during the night. And about what Edouard had done. He was sure Victoire had seen and heard everything, but could he talk about such things with a grandmother who was half-lame and half a witch and who was increasingly suspected of harbouring infectious weaknesses for her son? His uncle had told him things he didn't know, confessed offences he didn't understand, and asked absolution for sins that seemed to be complete fabrications invented to disturb

the child's mind. But wasn't it just drunken raving in the
early hours of the morning to exorcise ghosts grown too
big for him? That's what he wanted to ask his mother: to
confirm that none of what Edouard said really existed and
that he could forget everything, as he usually did. Instead, he had found the drunk "cured," fresh as a daisy,
amnesiac as far as his blunders were concerned — as usual
(but had Edouard really forgotten last night, hadn't he
put on his show at breakfast to try and make Richard
smile and perhaps even, yes, why not, forgive him?) and
on top of everything else, deep in conversation with his
mother, to whom Richard wished he could shout: "Plug
your ears, Momma. He's starting again!" But all he said
was that he wasn't listening to anything; that he knew
nothing. As he did every time a scene was being set in the
house, or actually blowing up, Richard took refuge outside. Outside was the only place where one of the
members of the three families who wasn't in the mood to
take part in the festival of shouts and blows, could find
shelter. To keep from crying, the little boy squeezed his
stomach with his folded arms and pressed his lips together, imprisoning them with his teeth. Seeing that he
hadn't moved for a good five minutes, Rose, Violette and
Mauve got up, walked down the two steps and over to the
staircase between the two houses. Rose (or Violette or
Mauve) said: "Momma, I think somebody's really unhappy!" Florence put down her cup, which clattered
against her saucer: "You know very well we can't do
anything for them. Now come back and work. He doesn't
even know you're there."

43

Thérèse crossed la rue Mont-Royal, heading south, dragging Marcel by the hand, and she thought about the great day of freedom waiting for them—for her, her brother and her cousins—at Parc Lafontaine. Her mother had told her: "Now be sure you don't come back before supper. I have to wash your aunt's room and I have to wash her too, so I don't want you kids underfoot!" Thérèse had thrown together some baloney sandwiches and stolen a big bottle of Coke from the icebox. Richard, of course, turned his nose up at the sandwiches. "I heard baloney's made out of garbage. Some people even found rat hair in it!" "Not in baloney, creep, in hotdogs! Anyway, that's dopey talk. If you don't like it, you can eat your toenails!" As for Philippe, he was delighted. As long as he had bread to eat, he didn't care what was on it. He would often remove the filling from a sandwich and eat only the two slices of buttered bread. A few paces behind Thérèse, Philippe and Richard were arguing over who would carry the food—or rather, who wouldn't. For the moment, Philippe claimed his arms were tired and he was crying, so his brother would have to carry the bag. "If you don't take it this minute, I'll drop it and the Coke'll bust and the sandwiches'll get wet and it'll all be your fault!" "I couldn't care less. I hate sandwiches and I can't stand Coke! Go ahead, drop it. Thérèse'll get you, you'll see!" Richard couldn't intimidate his brother because he knew very well how much Philippe hated violence, but he still threatened him with a thrashing by Thérèse. Philippe, though, knew his cousin too well to be afraid of her. He just had to make his eyes all soft or put on his sweetest smile and Thérèse's vague desires for a squabble would disappear completely and be replaced by a sort of uncontrolled admiration which he couldn't explain, but which he took great advantage of. So, he just made a face at his brother as he pretended to drop the bag of provisions.

Richard hollered. Thérèse turned around. Immediately, Philippe assumed a guilty expression. "I tripped!" Thérèse shrugged and lit into Richard. "You're always yelling for nothing! Lord in Heaven, is your head screwed on right?" She turned away and continued on her way, walking a little faster. They came to the corner of la rue Marie-Anne and Thérèse could already smell the manure from the stable behind the grocery store at the corner of Fabre and Rachel. "The smell comes all the way down here today." She laughed. "The neighbours'll be complaining again, for sure!" "I smell horsey-poop!" Every time he walked past the grocery store, Marcel took advantage of the occasion to say this sentence he'd been thinking of ever since he left the house, because it was the only time he was allowed to use the word "poop." He would savour the word for several minutes before saying it, and then for several minutes after, as it was too short for him to savour while he said it. Sometimes, before he went to sleep in the dark dining room, he would repeat it several times, trying to recapture the delightful sensation in the bottom of his mouth: "Poop, poop, poop, poop, poop . . ." But taken out of context, it was a word with no taste at all, a meaningless sound, and Marcel fell asleep without enjoying it. Here, though, surrounded by the very odour of "horsey," and supported by big greasy splotches or trails of yellowish dried paste that were barely concealed by layers of straw, the word "poop" regained all the importance of something secret, forbidden, unnamable — all qualities that made it fascinating; and Marcel, excited, repeated tirelessly: "I smell horsey poop! I smell horsey poop!" until he was silenced by a clip on the ear or a threatening frown. This time, though, his disappointment was great: the smell was there, persistent and pervasive, but the horses and manure had disappeared after the Saturday morning cleaning — the horses, out delivering orders; the manure, rotting at the bottom of the drains, where it still smelled, but invisibly. Marcel couldn't get over it. "There's no horsey and no poop, but you can smell it anyway!" He looked everywhere; he even wanted to go over the fence to see for himself if the "horseys" were playing a trick on him, hiding in a shed or behind the barrels of pickles, but Thérèse held him back with a firm hand. "If you get too close to the horses, they'll eat you!" As Marcel had once seen a horse eat an apple and been so frightened that he dreamed about it for a whole week, he was content to climb up on the fence and shout: "Horsey! Horsey! Where'd you put your poop?" At that moment, a Rachel streetcar crossed la rue Fabre, shedding a shower of sparks on the pavement, changing the course of Marcel's thoughts, so he exclaimed with no transition: "It's raining fire!" as he clapped his hands. Richard, though he was eleven years old, was still afraid of the streetcar's sparks and he stood there, frozen, under the amused look of his brother, who took advantage of the moment to call him a scaredy-cat. Thérèse, Marcel and Philippe ran across la rue Rachel and rushed into Parc Lafontaine, howling with delight. Richard remained behind, leaning against a grocery store window. His heart was beating like a watch. "He's right, I am a scaredy-cat." His brother's voice came to him, dimmed by the sound of another streetcar coming in the opposite direction: "Stop bawling, fathead, then you can come and play with us."

Mercedes had told her: "Be sure you're back by two, it's Saturday!" Béatrice kissed her forehead and left. "You're a doll, Mercedes. I'll work harder tonight." On her way down the inside staircase, she ran into the first clients of the day: three tipsy soldiers, besotted by cheap booze, who obviously hadn't slept all night. They must have dragged their tails from club to club, from one illegal gambling joint to the next, shamelessly spending the meagre pay they got as second-class soldiers, and shouting: "We're gonna conquer the world!" or: "We'll get them Germans! We'll show them Anglais!" as they raised their arms to Heaven in a sign of victory, unaware that their flies were unbuttoned or their pants were stained with vomit. At ten a.m., then, they were heading for Mercedes' place, half asleep, sapped by desire that the dancers at the Casino Bellevue, the girls in the clubs, hadn't been able to appease, caught between their need to sleep and their need to come. They were clean-shaven, red-eyed, cold-handed and mirthful for a few seconds, stiff-necked and irascible for the rest of the time. "Hey, cutey-pants, where you going all dolled up?" Béatrice made her way through their arms, which wanted to give her a feel, and their legs, which wanted to hold her back, squealing like a squeamish teenager. But they weren't mistaken. "This a whorehouse or not, goddammit?" Béatrice handed out a few slaps; she even bit an ear and managed to get past them. "She don't work here, that's for sure! She'd ruin the customers!" The soldiers laughed till their guts ached and Béatrice thought: "That's it. Now the neighbours'll complain again! We'll have to move out, and fast, if this keeps on!" She left the soldiers to their delights and hurried past the janitor's apartment, its door always ajar, even at night, even in winter. By chance, he wasn't in, and for once, Béatrice didn't hear his sarcasm and coarse laughter. She slipped out into the first grand day of spring with a light heart, her head held high, her chest straight, a winning smile on her lips. For a few moments, she stood on the doorstep, deeply breathing in the aromas of spring that were settling into the big city:

the lilacs, early for once, because of the exceptional mildness; the lily-of-the-valley that for several days now had been invading the yards where winter's last ravages could still be distinguished; and even the cold, still present behind the mild air that, in May, would turn to perfume before it disappeared for good. The three poplar trees beside the street were overloaded with plump glossy buds, but so far, not a single leaf had succeeded in breaking out of its prison. The rain that had fallen the night before had washed the streets clean and there was a smell of water in the air. Taking short steps, Béatrice crossed the street, swinging her purse. She opened the door of Marie-Sylvia's restaurant, humming one of those hymns for the month of May that we learn in school and that, for the rest of our lives, become symbols of spring, of renewal, of grace, in fact, even if we lose our faith or forget everything else about our childhood. Marie-Sylvia was serving a fat man in his thirties, whom Béatrice often saw rocking on the balcony of the second house on the left, on the other side of the lane, the overpopulated house where you frequently heard shouting and squabbling, or howls of joy, which Mercedes called "the haunted house," because of the old squinty-eyed grandmother who looked at everyone with the evil expression of a frustrated witch. "Like a witch locked up in a bottle! And let me tell you, I don't want to be around when they take out the cork!" Béatrice leaned on the candy counter, jauntily exclaiming, "Hi, Marie!" The fat man turned towards her and asked her straight out: "And how's your little business going, Mam'zelle Betty?" Not a hint of aggression in his voice, no criticism or even any irony: he'd asked as you'd ask a butcher how his business was going, or a shoemaker if his customers were wearing out their shoes. Accustomed to being laughed at and insulted, Béatrice just stood there, unable to reply. She stared at the fat man, but she

48

couldn't move a muscle. The fat man picked up his change and winked at Marie-Sylvia. "She knows how to use everything but her head!" The man said goodbye to both women and walked out of the store without a sound, as though he were skating across the hardwood floor. Marie-Sylvia frowned, without speaking to Béatrice. She'd often been heard to say: "If they weren't such good customers, I'd have locked my door to those chippies a long time ago!" She still spoke to Betty without looking at her, as if the mere sight of her would be a sin. "One or two this morning, Betty?" "Five, this morning, Marie. I'm going to see my aunt!" "But it isn't Sunday." "I know, but I got the morning off." Marie-Sylvia's frown deepened. She didn't like Béatrice to allude to her profession, not even remotely. She removed five "surprise packages" from a metal stand and placed them in front of Béatrice. The girl took a nickel from her change purse and sent it clattering across the scratched glass. Marie-Sylvia's "surprise packages" were a veritable institution on la rue Fabre. Everyone bought them, more out of habit than desire as a matter of fact. Once a month, Marie-Sylvia would dig around in the bottom of her candy boxes, pile up the vestiges thus obtained—pieces of licorice too hard or too short to be sold, pieces of suckers in every colour, crumbs of sugar from red-and-white candycanes, pale chocolate dust—and fill dozens of little brown bags with them, adding a "surprise," some useless trinket or a whole undamaged candy, which she then sold for a penny each. In fact, people bought the surprise packages more to get rid of their small change than to savour their contents. Some adults even tossed them on the sidewalk without opening them. The children, on the other hand, had a real passion for the stale candy that tasted of the bottom of a cardboard box, or even, sometimes, of dust. Was it the word "surprise" that

49

piqued their curiosity or just the unhealthy taste for sugar often developed by poor children? Marie-Sylvia couldn't have said, but whatever the case, she was interested in getting rid of her scraps, and, at the same time, showing a reasonable profit at the end of the month. All the money that she made from these left-overs was put in a jar beside the cash register: she used it to buy food for Duplessis who was, thus, fed by the whole street. "Your aunt still living on boulevard Saint-Joseph?" "Well, yes. You know she can't move now that she can't get around any more!" "Tell her hello from me . . ." "Sure." "Bonjour, là." "Bonjour." After Béatrice had left, Marie-Sylvia watched her until she'd crossed la rue Gilford. "It's a crying shame. Such a pretty girl."


   The three of them were fast asleep in the big double bed, limp, snoring, snorting, sleeping off the cheap alcohol which, for them, distilled bad dreams. The shortest was resting his head against the shoulder of the one with the mustache, abandoned, confident, happy; the third, with the thick head of a congenital lout, took up half the bed, convinced of his physical superiority, wrapped in the unconditional right bestowed by the best-developed muscles, in a world that has for its horizon only a general's stripes or war medals. He was the one, in fact, who had said to Mercedes: "We'll start with a little snooze — and you, you wait for us! Afterwards, we'll swing into action. And make sure you're good and ready, *tabarnac*, because we're real sewing machines!" Mercedes sat by the window which she had just opened and looked outside or, rather, her head was turned that way, but her eyes saw nothing. She was concentrating on her memories of spring in the country, where nature's face changes abruptly from one day to the next, with no warning, changing from the motionless white of clean snow to the seething, luxuriant black of the earth at work. She saw again the crows flying over the village graveyard in the middle of April, croaking their eternal question: "Pourquoi? Pourquoi? Pourquoi?" and her mother who always answered: "Good grief, because winter's over!" She saw herself again, an ungrateful child whose pigtails were always grubby, running out of school onto the hard-packed dirt road, uttering the cries of an animal set free. It smelled of spring and you could almost hear the sap rising in the trees, letting itself be sucked by buds about to burst. The dirt on the road was damp, and her footsteps made a sucking sound that her mother called "April kisses." And she saw the house, all lopsided, never painted, flaking, where her mother bravely raised her eight children, between the two markers that contained the limits of her life: morning prayers and evening prayers. She was religious to excess, more submissive to the curé than to her husband, trusting the Catholic religion so much that she had managed to erase any trace of personal character or clear features from herself. She was *la mère* as the Church understood her and she carried her naïveté to the point of boasting: "I've never done anything against the Church or against the good Lord. And I know for a fact my Guardian Angel dusts off my place in Heaven every morning!" Mercedes had always dreamed of destroying this execrable naïveté, but her mother retained it to the very end. She died saying: "I see the good Lord! I see the Blessed Virgin! And I see my Guardian Angel with his duster!" Mercedes had laughed. Fifty years of misery: eight births, each more painful than the last — to end up like that! With no happy old age either. No rest. The woman had never rested. Ever.

Mercedes smiled sadly. "She's likely dusting right now. But not for me!" The fat thickheaded soldier let out a belch and a fart simultaneously, ridding himself of all his alcoholic gasses at once. Mercedes closed her eyes. "I never thought I'd envy that woman some day!" The fat thickheaded one abruptly turned over. Mercedes got up, approached the bed, bent down, picked up the three pairs of pants that the soldiers had dropped on the floor and methodically began exploring their pockets.

"If I get soap in your eyes, you tell me, eh? Don't be shy." "Don't worry, go ahead and rub. It feels good!" Albertine had tied a tablecloth around her sister-in-law's neck and put a basin of warm water on her vast bosom, saying: "I couldn't make the water too hot, I was afraid I'd scald you." When the fat woman could no longer bend over, washing her hair became very difficult, and Albertine had a tendency these past few days to turn a deaf ear when her sister-in-law told her: "Dammit, Bartine, I itch! I've never had dirty hair in my life and I don't intend to start at the age of forty-two!" But this morning, a mysteriously transformed Albertine (Victoire looked at her, her eyes screwed up: "She's got something up her sleeve, I've never seen her act so nice!") filled with goodwill that was rather awkward because it was so new, swept into the room. "Time for a good housecleaning! If the baby's born into a mess like this, he'll be scared silly! So, get ready. I'm going to wash you. Head to foot! Especially the head! I've never seen such a haystack!" Her sister-in-law slipped in timidly: "It's your fault, you know. I don't know how many times I've asked you!" Albertine abruptly stopped plumping up a pillow. "That's right, call me a slut." Then she went on, as if nothing had happened. The fat woman smiled. Albertine had found a book from the Nelson collection under her brother's bed. "*Bug-Jargal.* Lord Almighty, now he's talking Chinese!" She was about to suggest putting the small cream-coloured book on the bedside table, but stopped short when she saw the author's name. "Victor Hugo!" She looked at her sister-in-law, panicstricken. "That book's on the Index!" The fat woman sighed. "I couldn't get to sleep last night. I asked Gabriel to read to me. It's a good book, you know." "You didn't answer me! That book's on the Index!" "You know, we're just finishing it and I wonder what it is in that book that could put it on the Index." "Victor Hugo's on the Index, that's all! The works. We aren't allowed to read him, you know very well! Committing a mortal sin like that in your condition, that takes gall!" "But it's so beautiful, Bartine, if you only knew!" "What's so beautiful about it?" "It happens far away." Albertine rubbed the fat woman's scalp vigorously and long streams of suds fell onto the white tablecloth. "Ahh, that feels good. Don't stop!" Blithely, Albertine released all the hostility she'd been holding in since morning: the firm flesh of her arms and her double chin bounced in every direction while her sister-in-law moaned softly with pleasure. "You and my brother, I think you're playing with fire sometimes, reading those books! It's no good, reading too much. They told us that often enough!" "Bartine, if you don't mind, just be quiet! If you read a little more, maybe you'd understand a little more about life. . ." Albertine cut her off so vigorously that the fat woman almost dropped the basin. "I'd rather be ignorant and in a state of grace than know about everything and be damned!" Edouard, who was reading a newspaper in the dining room, burst out laughing. "That's going to get around, little sister. That's going to get around!" Crimson with rage, Albertine plunged her arms into the basin and poured a generous quantity of water over her sister-in-law, who began to laugh as well. "Tell the whole world, if you want, Edouard. I'm not ashamed! When you're boiling like a stew in the big kettle down there and I'm fanning myself with ostrich feathers up in Heaven while I listen to a concert, you'll be sorry about an awful lot of things!" "Albertine, don't drown me. I'm not in a state of grace!"


Given the proximity of Doctor Sanregret's office, Tante Ti-Lou's apartment always smelled of medicine, so people expected to find there syringes and flasks, glass cupboards full of jars with vaguely disgusting things inside them, and even the inevitable waiting room, perpetually crammed with all the misfortunes, all the diseases, all the deformations dragged around by a people kept in ignorance and poverty: the little bumps at the base of the neck, detected in childhood and left to develop, that turn out to be tumors; the pimples that appear and disappear at regular intervals, syphilis almost too far gone to be cured; bleeding hemorrhoids too long neglected, the beginnings of cancer. Doctor Sanregret often went across to see Ti-Lou, bringing her sedatives (only one landing separated them and they shared the same entrance), and he sometimes stayed for hours, telling the old woman how he had to chew out his patients, who almost always waited too long before they came to see him, and then howled as they demanded, yes, *demanded* a miracle! Ti-Lou listened patiently to the doctor (it was the price that she had to pay for her sedatives), half-closing her eyes and gently agreeing with him. Then, the old family doctor would limp away, bent over by fatigue, and at last Tante Ti-Lou could open her box, open her flasks, take the caps off her bottles, trembling, grab a glass half-filled with water and pour into it six, seven, eight drops of a syrupy yellowish liquid: peace, exhilaration, apathy, insouciance — but most of all, insouciance. Béatrice came into the living room where her aunt was waiting, carrying a tray piled with slices of buttered bread (Ti-Lou had real butter, so rare in wartime, but Ti-Lou had connections!), a few slices of ham, a pot of coffee, cups and — the greatest luxury of all — a bit of fudge Ti-Lou had kept just for her. "Must of taken all your rationing cards to buy that, ma tante! Gee — butter, cream, ham!" Ti-Lou replied with the vaguely American accent she'd first assumed when she was working in Ottawa at the turn of the century and held onto ever since: "Since when does Ti-Lou, the she-wolf of Ottawa, need rationing cards, I'd like to know! They're presents, Béatrice. How many times do I have to tell you, you'll never meet the man who'll shower you with cream and butter and ham when the war's on if you stay at the back of a rooming house on la rue Fabre or go on selling fly buttons on la rue Mont-Royal!" Béatrice put the tray on a pouffe in front of her aunt's armchair, holding back a smile. She still hadn't admitted to Ti-Lou that the days of fly buttons and yardgoods were over now and that she, little Béatrice, "auntie's little baby," as Ti-Lou called her, had taken the great leap that turned a "potential whore" into a "powerful whore," still in the words of the Ottawa wanton. Béatrice thought: "There's no butter or cream or ham yet, but it sure beats spending Saturday night deciding between a French show at the Passe-Temps or a chocolate sundae chez Larivière et Leblanc!" The former she-wolf of Ottawa picked up her crutches, which were leaning against the piano, and got out of her chair, hopping on her one leg. "We'll eat beside the window. I'm sick and tired of being in the dark." Béatrice picked up the tray again and took it to the little table by the window. A bus went along boulevard Saint-Joseph just then and Ti-Lou sighed. "Soon as you decide you want to sit by the window, a bus comes and spits gas in your face!" "We can shut it." "No, jeez, it's too nice out. The weather's so warm!" On the other side of boulevard Saint-Joseph stood the Ecole Bruchési, nondescript and brown, which Béatrice remembered attending in the early thirties. The children in the parish went there for their first two years of school; in the third year, the girls went to the Ecole des Saints-Anges, across from the church, which Béatrice had left barely five years ago; and the boys were transferred to Saint-Stanislas, on la rue Gilford. "Whenever you come here, you look at that school.... You liked school, didn't you?" "When I was really young, yes.... Afterwards..." Béatrice bit into a piece of bread and chewed on it for a long time, staring at the Ecole Bruchési. Suddenly, Ti-Lou seemed impatient, as if she'd been waiting for something that hadn't happened. After a few seconds, Béatrice brought her gaze back to her aunt. "How about you, ma tante, did you go to school in Ottawa?" And voilà, the word was spoken. Ti-Lou smiled a little stiffly. "Not on your life! I was born right here in Montreal! Ottawa came a lot later!" Béatrice leaned back in her chair. She stopped chewing. There was a tacit agreement between Béatrice and Ti-Lou: when the older woman wanted to talk about Ottawa, she would send someone, usually a little boy from the neighbourhood, to invite Béatrice for lunch the next day. Then, as they ate, Béatrice would ask her aunt a question about Ottawa. It was simple, it worked and both women were happy: Ti-Lou to tell of her incredible life filled with revelling, roaming and scandalous adventures; and Béatrice to listen, her heart pounding and her imagination in full flight. Sometimes, hours passed before Ti-Lou felt any fatigue, which was manifested by imaginary shooting pains in the leg she no longer had. She would straighten up in her armchair then, and say to her niece: "You're tired. That's enough for today." And Béatrice would say nothing, but kiss her aunt on both cheeks and leave. In the house on la rue Fabre, her first clients would find her remote, cold: it was because Béatrice was still out on the Rideau River in a rowboat, some time in the summer of 1910, with a cabinet minister or a foreign cardinal visiting Canada, her dress wrinkled by repeated and insistent caresses, her mouth tasting of a tobacco-singed mustache. Béatrice closed her eyes beneath her parasol and craned her neck so the wind could brush against her cheeks. But then she awoke suddenly, thirty years later, underneath a potbellied lieutenant on the verge of apoplexy, who was shouting in her ear: "Move your ass, do something! I feel like I'm in a plate of spaghetti!" Ti-Lou wiped the corners of her mouth with her cotton napkin on which you could still see, embroidered in blue silk, a wolf. "When I went to Ottawa, I was around your age — seventeen, to be more precise. That was in 1898. Ottawa was practically a village back then: one church, one tavern, one floozy." She laughed at her bon mot, poured herself a cup of coffee and gazed out the window for a moment. "Don't worry, there was more than one church. But there was just one whore: me! When I got there, it was the middle of winter and the wolves were prowling the town. . . . Somebody even saw one on a street in Hull. He'd hidden under a gallery and they had to shoot him in the head. When I got to the Château Laurier with my little suitcase and the black dress of a brand-new little orphan, and my virtue ready to be sold to the first degenerate that showed up, the women in Ottawa sized me up right away and all hell broke loose in Parliament. The first night, yes, the first night, in my room at Château Laurier, 2732, I'll never

57

forget it: three cabinet ministers came to offer me their hearts, their lives, their families and their fortunes. They got down on their knees on the Turkish rug, waving their arms like in the theatre and making their voices tremble like in the House. Obviously, the only thing they wanted was to rape a poor little seventeen year old who wouldn't go and complain to her father afterwards. But they didn't know who they were dealing with! That night, my girl, I lost my innocence three times! But they paid for it — all three of them! I had them by the chequebooks and the balls! Yes, that's called blackmail — and so what!" She seemed to be replying to some reflection, to some accusation even, but Béatrice said nothing. "That's how I got them and that's how I hung onto them. And I'm proud of it. I'm the only woman that ever laid down the law in Ottawa! For twenty years, I ruled over Ottawa like la reine Victoria over her empire — except I wasn't treated like any grandmother! When I moved from the Château Laurier to the house on la rue Roberts that six cabinet ministers got together to buy me, the women in town followed the carts carrying my baggage, waving placards that accused me of bringing Hell into Parliament! That was my triumph! I climbed up on the first cart and I howled at the moon like a she-wolf in heat! Ti-Lou was moving into her new burrow and taking possession of her new turf. As soon as I got to my new house, I started cleaning out my clientele. I was sick and tired of those provincial ministers on visits to Ottawa, who nearly always smelled of the stable, the barnyard, or beer. I wasn't provincial meat, I was federal! If I'd wanted to make money off the Beaucerons, I'd have set myself up in Quebec City! Okay, the little ministers from the backwoods of the province of Quebec were often more generous, but they weren't nearly as refined as the tall Anglais, so clean and polite, that got off the train from Toronto. I skimmed my clientele and just kept the ones that floated to the top. And that's how, for twenty years, I ruled over the biggest fortunes and the loveliest vices in Canada! I went through three Prime Ministers, two Solicitor-Generals, a few dozen bishops, cardinals, and seven ordinary curés when I was feeling generous. . . . The ones that didn't come to see me, it was either because they were fairies or too old. I gave dinner parties for fifty where I was the only woman and nobody was bored! When the great Sarah Bernhardt came to Ottawa, I was the one they introduced to her because they knew we'd understand each other! What I didn't know, back then, was that one day I'd lose a leg too. . ." Ti-Lou was silent. When reality and dream came together in the midst of her speech, the vision of her amputated leg intruded like a bite of the present, reminding her of Doctor Sanregret, the smell of medicine and his patients coughing on the other side of the wall. Ti-Lou suddenly stopped talking and Béatrice knew she mustn't dwell on it. Silence settled over the double room like a lead cover. Béatrice waited for her aunt to indicate it was time for her to leave, but Ti-Lou was lost in the present, staring at the protuberance that her stump formed, beneath her long dress: the perfect horror, round and smooth as an egg; the end product of her life. After several minutes, Béatrice took it upon herself to move a little, to remind her aunt she was there. Soon, it would be two o'clock and she had promised Mercedes that she'd be back early. Without coming out of her torpor, Ti-Lou slowly uttered the words that broke the spell: "You're tired. That's enough for today."

Suddenly, Duplessis woke up: "I'm hungry!" He stretched, yawned and jumped up onto Marie-Sylvia's lap. She began to make him purr by foraging about in his striped fur. Less to make his old mistress happy than to encourage her to feed him again, in spite of all he'd eaten a few hours earlier, Duplessis started his motor and rubbed against Marie-Sylvia's chest, which she took for a sign of affection. He even went so far as to stretch out on his back on the woman's lap, offering his belly and his fleas to her expert caresses, caresses that verged on the violent and that weren't unpleasant in the least, as it happened. "Let's enjoy it while we may. . ." But as soon as Marie-Sylvia opened her mouth to speak, calling him her "pussy love," her "little baby tabby cat," and her "little devil that stays out all night," the spell was broken: Duplessis' motor jammed and "pussy love" sat motionless for several seconds in the hollow of his mistress' skirt, like the corpse of a cat that had died in a ridiculous position. Duplessis took advantage of the respite to wonder whether to go outside after eating or go back to sleep on the ledge at the bottom of the stove. "We'll see. For the time being, we'll eat." He jumped nimbly to the floor and headed for his empty bowl, meowing imperiously. "Enough of this nonsense, bring on the meat!" "Poor little kitty cat's hungry? So soon? Mummy's going to make you a nice lunch." Marie-Sylvia dragged her bedroom slippers to the icebox, reached for a dish of beef liver and stopped in mid-action: "Good grief, Mummy forgot to buy your liver! You ate it all this morning, mon trésor!" Duplessis gave a start. "What? Did I hear you right? No more liver?" He looked at his mistress, eyes round, unblinking, evil. "You want some cereal and milk?" "Some what!" Duplessis shot off like an arrow and threw himself at the door. "Mummy can't go out and buy it right away, she has to close the store!" Fur bristling, back arched,

Duplessis clawed the bottom of the door. "Bon, okay, we'll go see Monsieur Soucy and ask him for some scraps..." Marie-Sylvia let the cat slip out the back door, walked through the store, grumbling, and ran smack into Madame Lemieux, the little woman just arrived from Saint-Eustache, pregnant to the eyeballs, poor thing, who'd come to buy lighter flints for her husband who was too lazy to get out of his rocking chair in the kitchen. "Madame Lemieux! I didn't hear you come in!" "And I've been standing here coughing like a lost soul for a good five minutes, like somebody with TB!" She craned her neck towards the back of the store. "Somebody out there?" "Just my cat..." "You mean, you talk to your cat? As if he was a real person? You call him 'mon trésor'? And 'my man'? You sure that's a cat in your kitchen, Marie-Sylvia? You sure it isn't a boyfriend, an admirer, a...?" Marie-Sylvia, sincerely offended, raised her hand in protest. In five seconds, she had turned as red as a beet and was trying to catch her breath. "My Lord, what's wrong with you, for the love of...? You'd think I'd just told you the Pope was dead! Get a grip on yourself, Marie. Pius the Twelfth is alive and well!" Madame Lemieux laughed quietly. She'd heard that Marie-Sylvia was very sensitive on the subject of men, and as a newcomer to the neighbourhood, she'd decided to stick her neck out and see if it was true. Marie-Sylvia finally got her breath back. "Maybe Pius the Twelfth is all right, but you've got a screw loose, that's for sure!" "Don't fly off the handle so..." "It's easy for you to say that! You'll leave here and tell the whole neighbourhood that I've got a kitchen full of men..." "Oh, come on now, Marie. I never said your kitchen was full of men..." Anyway, it just takes one to ruin a woman's reputation!" "It was my cat! My cat! Duplessis!" "Duplessis! The former Premier of the Province of Quebec in your kitchen! And you call him 'mon

61

trésor'! I knew he was a bachelor, but I didn't know he was a tomcat!" "You don't understand a thing! The name of my cat is Duplessis!" Madame Lemieux rested her elbows on the glass counter. "Marie-Sylvia, I'm pulling your leg. I know all that. Now, give me some Ronson flints for my husband." The latch moved and the women turned around to see who was coming in the door. Duplessis was stretched out on the top step, his left front paw swiping furiously at the metal door latch. "Look, there he is. There's Duplessis." "Did you show him how to do that?" "No, he learned all by himself." Madame Lemieux approached the door, holding her stomach. "I don't know if the real Duplessis could do that!"

When the children went to spend the day at Parc Lafontaine, the problem was staying together. The park was enormous, but as long as Thérèse, her brother and their cousins were satisfied with walking around the two lakes, visiting the tiny stinking, dirty zoo or running through bushes and embankments, everything was fine. Thérèse led the games, with Marcel clinging to her skirt, and Richard and Philippe blindly following the leader, laughing when Thérèse laughed, yelling when she was afraid, applauding when she won a game of tag; but when Marcel, already dirty, his pants soiled, shoelaces untied, hair dishevelled, stopped smack in the middle of a dirt path and said in his flute-like voice: "When do we play?" the situation got trickier. Richard and Philippe were sitting on the ground, pulling out blades of grass with which they hoped to make kazoos, while Thérèse tried to discourage her brother from going to the playground, which they had been circling but carefully avoiding since their arrival. For Marcel, getting his pants dirty and playing hide-and-seek as he walked through a park, no matter how beautiful it was, wasn't playing: he could get his pants dirty just as well, even better perhaps, playing in the lane behind his house, with friends his own age besides, who wouldn't complain about how he smelled, friends whose movements wouldn't present a constant challenge to his short legs. No, for him, playing meant swinging on the high swings, the ones that were built for the littlest children, where they imprisoned you inside four wooden slats that slid on chains, making a noise like a happy ghost; it was tearing open the sky with your feet as you shouted: "I'm kicking the sun in the belly!"; it was being the lightweight at one end of the seesaw, scared that you'd shoot into the trees, which wasn't completely impossible; it was climbing to the end of the moving ladder to save limpy-grandma from the fire, then, thinking better of it, and shouting to Thérèse: "No, we'll let her toast — and then we'll spread peanut butter on her and eat her!"; it was being afraid of the attendant, who was certainly a maniac ("What does that mean, maniac?" "Never mind, you'd be just dumb enough to go and find out!"); and most of all, ah yes! most of all, it was whirling on the whirligig until the park spun in every direction and Thérèse, in a frenzy, began screaming: "Now you've done it, he's green again! He'll throw up all over the place and I'll get hell and he'll stink all the way home! What did I ever do to God to deserve such a simple-minded brother?" For Marcel, "playing" meant going into the green area beside la rue Calixa-Lavallée, across from Le Plateau auditorium, where all the games were, the part of Parc Lafontaine that was also called "the park" (when you asked someone: "Are you going to the park?" you had to stress the word "park," so the other person would know if you were just inviting him for a pastoral stroll or to have fun in the midst of the parallel bars, swings and wooden slides), where, to enter, the group had to break up. In fact, only little boys under six and little girls under twelve were tolerated on the playground: the officials claimed it was unhealthy for boys and girls to play games together in which there might be a certain tendency for skirts to rise at the wind's slightest whim. That was the one and only reason. The City of Montreal had so decided — and all the children suffered as a result. If anyone found a little ten year old boy having fun with his sisters or his younger brothers, pushing them on the swings or holding the ladder that they were trying to climb, he'd be chased away like some hooligan, accused of looking up his sisters' skirts (they probably took their baths together at home), while the rest of the children were left without supervision, or almost, as all the park attendants were rather suspect old monsters who enjoyed replacing the big brothers at the bottom of ladders or behind the swings. Which meant that for Marcel to have any fun, Richard and Philippe had to go to their side, leaving him with Thérèse, who would thereby become guard and slave to his childish games. Thérèse adored her brother, but she hated spending a whole day listening to his somewhat incoherent prattling with its endless mixture of the most ordinary everyday acts and the poorly expressed fantasies of his overactive imagination. Thérèse was very down-to-earth by nature and her brother's fabulous adventures in a sandbox drove her crazy. And so, after their baloney sandwiches, when Richard and Philippe went to make peepee in the public toilets, Marcel looked up at his sister with pleading eyes and said: "I pwomise I won't fwow up if we go pway on the swings!" and Thérèse raised her arms to Heaven — but not before she'd stuck a piece of gum in her mouth. "Go play in the dirt for a while. Dig holes." "Police says no." "We won't tell them."

Marcel, too easily persuaded, sat on his little bottom and began to dig a hole under a picnic table. "It's too hard and I haven't got a sovel!" "That's right, you haven't been bugging me for a while. . ." Thérèse sat beside her brother in the grass. "It's only noon and you're so dirty you look like you've spent two weeks in a pigsty!" "Do I look like a piggy?" "You look like a piggy and you smell like a piggy, but we love you anyway." Marcel burst out in a loud laugh, and a squirrel that had approached the table, as bold as brass, jumped. "But we love you even more when you're clean. . .two minutes before you get into bed." Thérèse lay on her back. She could see the sun playing through the branches of still-bare trees, not yet awakened from a too harsh winter. "Soon there'll be leaves." "When?" "Soon." "Tomorrow?" "Soon." "When, soon?" "Marcel, you ask the dumbest questions! Yes, tomorrow! Tomorrow, there'll be great big leaves on the trees!" "If I don't go to sleep tonight, can I see them grow?" Thérèse hesitated briefly. "No, it'll be too dark." Marcel got up and came and plunked himself beside his sister, blocking the sun. "Can I sit on your tummy?" "No you can't, Marcel. I'll throw up my lunch." Marcel fell onto his sister's stomach all the same and she bent double with pain. "Dammit, Marcel, can't you sit still for two minutes! I told you not to sit on me and you just flung yourself on me like a sack of potatoes. It's dangerous. You could've killed me! Sometimes you're such a pain, I can't believe it!" After being swatted on the rear and clipped behind the ears, Marcel, of course, began to howl, sitting on the ground with arms dangling. Rather than console him, Thérèse, impatient now and rubbing her stomach, walked away from her brother and stepped onto a path. She leaned against a tree and watched her cousins coming back from the toilet — Philippe, ahead, running; Richard, walking behind. When Philippe came up to her, he pointed to Marcel. "I got a feeling your brother wants to play on the swings! You can hear him all the way to Sherbrooke Street!" "Let him holler, it'll do him good!" "Did you hit him?" "No, I chewed him out, but he was asking for it!" Philippe ran to Marcel and picked him up. "How'd you like to go for a swing?" Marcel was crying so hard that he couldn't reply. He merely nodded. "All right, we'll go and swing!" Thérèse was still under the tree, rubbing her stomach. "That's right, promise him the moon. You aren't the ones that'll be stuck with him for the rest of the day afterwards!" At that very moment, Richard came up beside Thérèse, holding a dandelion that he timidly offered her: "It isn't much, but it's better than nothing. It's all I could find. The other flowers aren't out yet." Thérèse turned around. "Well, wait for them! I hate dandelions! They stink!" Thérèse ran over to Philippe and pulled Marcel from his arms. "That's my little brother!" Marcel, terrified, suddenly stopped crying. "See! He stops crying when I take him!" A nasty little smile appeared at the corner of Philippe's mouth. "Maybe he stopped crying, but he's pissing now!" In fact, upset by the quarrel with Thérèse, Marcel had forgotten to let her know he had to go—and now, he was going as she held him, his expression blank but serious. Philippe caught his cousin in mid-flight, just as Thérèse was throwing him to the ground. She'd turned so white it was scary, and, as happened every time her anger got the better of her, she stood in the middle of the road, stiff, silent, trembling a little, as though she weren't really there, but withdrawn into herself, concentrating on her rage. Richard took her in his arms and held her tight. "Don't have a fit, Thérèse. Don't have a fit, it isn't worth it!" Thérèse's fits were almost as famous as her mother's: there was something terrifying about them, final, complete, that left witnesses horrified and stunned. The fights between mother and daughter were often devastating. The women would throw themselves at each other's faces, literally beating one another, Thérèse answering her mother's slaps with punches, her cries with howls, her reproaches with curses. Beside Albertine, Thérèse was tiny, but even so, you could sense that the woman was afraid of her daughter. No one tried to separate them any more, they knew it was useless; the battle had to be consummated, consumed, until Albertine and Thérèse threw themselves into one another's arms and cried out their love. Richard gently rocked Thérèse and Philippe did the same with Marcel, who looked all around, recording everything to feed his nocturnal terror. And as her mother wasn't there to give Thérèse the cue, she slowly calmed down, relaxing in the arms of her cousin, who was blushing, moved. "It doesn't matter, Thérèse, he just peed a little. It didn't even get on your dress. Go wash off your arm and it'll be all gone."

Claire Lemieux took her leave of Marie-Sylvia and Duplessis on the doorstep of the restaurant. She lived down the street a little, on the third floor of one of the most miserable houses in the neighbourhood (it was called "the dump") in an apartment that consisted of three rooms joined together—living room, bedroom and kitchen —that were hot in summer, cold in winter, with her husband, Hector, a sort of slow and whitish whale, housepainter by trade, who hadn't worked for years—not, in fact, since Claire, slender, gay and lively, had found a job selling shoes for Giroux et Deslauriers at the corner of Mont-Royal and Fabre. The job was why Hector and Claire had recently moved to la rue Fabre: the young woman had been working for Giroux et Deslauriers for a little over three years now, and she had to travel from Saint-Eustache to Montreal twice a day, half an hour by train from Saint-Eustache to Windsor Station and an hour by streetcar from the station to the store. . . . And yet, she'd done everything she could to find work in her home town not too far from her whale of a husband. But she quickly realized that working would be bad for their reputation in the village, where everybody knew one another, spied on one another and was out to get one another (a husband who stays home and a wife who works —just think of it!). Already, they'd started calling Hector, "Lemieux-la-sans-coeur". . . . Heartless, he was, as Claire knew very well, but she preferred to laugh at it and break her back to support the two of them, instead of scratching the sore and starving to death with him. Claire Lemieux spoiled her cetacean; she watched him getting fatter and she took strange pleasure from the fact. Hector's sexual appetites (so tedious and limited) subsided as the layers of fat accumulated on his already soft skeleton and Claire got some peace. No longer was she subjected to his pitiful assaults, and when she wanted to make love, she made the first moves—and the others. She never thought, however, of cheating Hector. Not that she particularly loved him, but that wasn't playing the game. It wasn't done, and besides, she wasn't all that crazy about the other men she knew. Her boss thought of nothing but money (he did look up his customers' skirts when they were trying on shoes, but Claire imagined herself in their place and laughed. "A man that looks and doesn't touch isn't any more fun than one that touches and doesn't look to see where!"), the two salesmen who worked with her lived together (discreetly, but the phonebook never lies), and the men she saw on the street were all too old or too young. The war had kidnapped all the males who were in even remotely good health, tied them up, disguised them, indoctrinated them, shipped them off to the other side of the Big Water and sent them back home in pieces or unhinged; it had left the women only their priests, who certainly took advantage of the fact, their little boys, who were too young to offer their flesh, their fathers, who told them about the atrocities of the other war to spur them on — and sometimes, their husbands, if they were disabled or prolific, for fathers of large families weren't required to go to war unless they wanted to get away from their families or if they were too poor to support them (the war smiled down from all the posters: "Give me your husband, I'll give you eighty bucks a month!"). And so, Claire Lemieux had been very surprised a few months earlier, just before they left Saint-Eustache, when suddenly her husband came to her in the middle of the night and murmured: "I want us to make a little ba-beee!" Claire understood immediately and burst out laughing: "Don't worry, you dirty bugger, they won't want you for their army, you're so fat and slow, you'd lose the war for them!" But Hector insisted (for once) probably out of fear that he'd be called up and Claire thought: "Go on, fatso, make me a baby. The time's right.... But after he's born, you'll have to move your ass to support us!" Claire was now seven months pregnant (the little one was due at the end of June) and Hector still didn't seem aware that very soon his wife would have to quit her job to take care of their child. He ate more and more as he listened to the funny programs on the radio. Sometimes, he made the effort to go for a walk along la rue Mont-Royal. "Getting the kinks out of my legs." But soon he'd be back, out of breath and red, with one hand on his heart. He had trouble climbing the two flights of winding stairs and he'd reach the third landing on his knees sometimes, his respiratory tract whistling like organ pipes, his ears buzzing and his eyes bloodshot. Claire thought that he was laying it on a bit thick and found this funny. "Hector, you're touched in the head! You get too much exercise! It's no good for your health. Here, come and lay down." "Fuck off!" But he'd lie down all the same—and the shooting pains in his left arm would start again. Claire would leave for work or go on eating, humming away, which had the happy effect of driving Hector wild. "Here I am, just about dead, and you're singing!" "I hope you won't hear me after you're dead!" Claire was really very happy to be pregnant. She'd decided to go back to Saint-Eustache, to her mother, as soon as the child was born, dragging her heap of soft fat behind her. She'd tell her mother: "Poppa left you a little money, so take us in—all three of us—and I'll go back to work when I'm feeling better." She didn't mind Hector being the way he was; she hardly ever thought of him as a human being anyway, but rather a cat or a dog. And perhaps that's why she would have liked it if Marie-Sylvia had, not a Duplessis with fur, but a real Hector in the back of her shop. But the baby kicked her, bringing her back to herself. She stopped smack in the middle of the sidewalk. "Well, you, so there you are. . . . Haven't heard from you for a while. . . . I was starting to think you'd gone for a walk 'to get the kinks out,' like your Pa." She rubbed her stomach gently, trying to find the places where she could feel the feet move. "Hey, that's fun! My little Claude! Or Claudette! If I knew which kind you were, I wouldn't have to say everything twice!" Hector was out on the balcony, waving desperately at her. "All right, all right, pinhead. You'll get your flints!"


Victoire and Edouard were eating alone together, because Albertine had announced that she wasn't hungry after drinking the last two eggs beaten up with some milk and Gabriel had fallen asleep in his bed after two pages of *Bug-Jargal*. Victoire had always had a man's appetite and eaten with a man's gestures. She cut slices of bread as thick as your hand and spread them with a layer of butter that would have turned the strongest liver yellow. Even now, at seventy-five, she ate everything: pork, head cheese, cucumber sandwiches with a glass of milk, tourtière, cakes. If she was told to be careful, she would answer, mouth full: "Leave me be, I spend my nights alone!" Only Richard and Edouard knew about the long nights when Victoire, livid and ghostly, painfully got out of bed and paced back and forth in the small room, muttering: "Come and get me, God! Come and get me or I'll go find you and give you a piece of my mind that'll last till the end of time!" Sometimes Edouard would get up and offer to help his mother, but she would send him back to bed with a single sentence: "If you didn't smell so much of booze, maybe I could breathe!" or: "Sleep in peace, I'm paying for your sins!" When Richard timidly asked his grandmother if she needed anything, she was less mean but just as firm: "If I've managed to stay on my feet this long, I can do it a little longer!" Meekly, Richard would go back to bed, but rarely would he fall asleep again. If Victoire heard him sigh, she said: "Go to sleep. Pretend I'm a flock of sheep jumping over a fence!" Richard smiled, and Victoire, in pain beside him, would make a grimace that might just as well have been a smile. And when the great liberating belch finally came (Victoire's theory was: "A belch is the breath of life."), the old woman would sit up in bed and hurl invective at the cucumber that wasn't going down as it should, or the roast pork she'd devoured before bed, as Albertine and the fat woman looked on with alarm, sipping very weak tea cut with milk. Victoire took a bite of her ketchup-butter-brown sugar sandwich, grunting with satisfaction, and Edouard looked away. She chewed noisily, not realizing the tip of her nose was adorned with a dab of ketchup. "Wipe your face, Momma, for the love of God, you look like you've got a nosebleed!" "You'd like that, eh?" She drew her sleeve across the tip of her nose. "You never tried that mixture, eh? Never wanted to. And it's good! Real good! The ketchup and the brown sugar really go great together..." "Momma, cut it out, you're turning my stomach! You've been telling me the same thing for thirty-five years now!" "And it still turns your stomach, right? You're more of a sissy than I thought. It's been a long time since you could get to me! For thirty-five years I've been looking at you, too, but I don't lose *my* appetite!" She burst out laughing, without swallowing her food, choked briefly, pounded the table, coughed, burped and wiped her eyes with the same sleeve she'd used to wipe off the ketchup. "Blow me over, I'm still good for a laugh!" Edouard could hear the fat woman laughing too, in the next room. "That's right, both of you, gang up on me!" The fat woman blew her nose. "We aren't laughing at you, Edouard. It's a joke!" Edouard got up from the table abruptly, knocking over his plate. His mother took another bite of her sandwich. "It's good, you know, you ought to try it... Ketchup and..." "Ow, if you don't mind! Shut up, okay! We've had our share of fights, but I've never hit you with a plate. But, it's never too late!" Edouard went into the kitchen and practically hurled his dishes into the sink. Victoire swallowed her bread and ketchup. "Whew! I'm saved! The sink got it all!" Edouard passed her again on the way to his bedroom, but Victoire stopped him: "Don't run away. I've got something to ask you." "If it's money, I'm fresh out." "I know that, I'm the one that gave you some yesterday! Now, sit down and let's gab." "Finished your bloody sandwich?" "No—and

72

you're going to watch me finish it and you're going to put up with it too. I'm your mother and you got no business telling me what to eat and when to eat it!" "You know I'm going to end up choking you one of these days!" "That's just what I was telling Bartine the other day. I said, 'Edouard's going to end up choking me!' I can't wait! For once in his life, he'll make up his mind to do something! Now, sit down and listen." Edouard sat down and began nervously crumbling a slice of bread. He knew very well that when his mother asked for something, there was no possible way to escape. She'd stop at nothing to get what she wanted. Once, she'd hidden the only three pairs of trousers that Gabriel possessed to keep him from courting a girl that she didn't want as a daughter-in-law; she'd pretended to die because Albertine refused to turn the radio to the station she wanted to listen to; she'd shouted "Fire!" from the front balcony because it was too warm in her bedroom, and Gabriel, who was in charge of the heat, refused to stop feeding the coal furnace in the middle of January; one day (but that was something which she'd never admit, she was truly ashamed of it), she'd even stolen an ice-cream cone from Marcel, who wouldn't give her a lick of it. Edouard looked at her, amazed, almost relieved. "It's been a while since I went down those damn stairs, and if I don't do it today, I'm going to rip them up. So, I've made up my mind. I'm going to go for a walk on la rue Mont-Royal, to show off my fat son and that ugly straw hat you gave me for Easter! A granny's hat if I ever saw one! Now, make yourself handsome and I'll do my best!" She crammed the last piece of bread in her mouth and aimed a broad smile at her son.

After leaving Ti-Lou's, Betty lingered a few minutes on the steps of the Ecole Bruchési, although she'd promised Mercedes that she'd come back to the apartment early. Leaning on the cement rail beside the small staircase that went up to the main door, she looked towards the four big windows on the left of the second storey, where she'd spent the most beautiful year of her life, her second year of school, beneath the protective wing and within the deep folds of the nun's robe of Soeur Marie-de-Fatima, who people said was crazy, but whom Béatrice revered, devoting to her all the love of a little girl who is brought up by a negligent mother and a father whose dreams were too grand for him, who spoke of nothing but money and escape ("Birds, give me birds and I'll build you a city someplace else, someplace where it doesn't snow!"). They used to say ("They" were the other girls in her class; and the bigger ones, the ones at the Ecole des Saints-Anges, who often went past "la p'tite école" in groups of five or six, whispering, laughing, ignoring the smaller girls in grade one, but warning the ones in grade two about the crazy woman, the lunatic, creepy Soeur "Fatimette," who would end up one of these days with her cornet in some insane asylum, behind bars) that Soeur Marie-de-Fatima was crazy because, sometimes, right in the middle of a class (especially arithmetic), she would stop, run over to the window and fly away, murmuring: "You've put me in jail!" or: "I know my body has to stay here, but at least open a door for my soul!" She stood on tiptoe for long moments, watching the sky, and Béatrice, though she was only seven and knew nothing of what might trouble the soul, sensed that Soeur Marie-de-Fatima had gone flying over the surrounding roofs, so that she wouldn't explode. The girls took advantage of the teacher's crisis, of course, to raise hell: pulling pigtails, making faces, calling each other fatheads or pounding their feet on the floor as they chanted: "CRAZY, cra-cra-crazy, CRAZY!", but Béatrice remained glued to her place, concentrating on the caged bird slowly dying beneath the jibes and laughter of the insensitive, spiteful children. When Soeur Marie-de-Fatima returned to the class, breathless, her wings folded, with patches of sky reflected in her eyes, everything in the classroom was topsy-turvy: there were bits of chalk all over, some of the girls were down on all fours, while others were standing on their seats—but she said nothing. She went back to her blackboard and resumed the lesson exactly where she'd left off, as though nothing had happened. And her gaze always fell on Béatrice, frozen there, who seemed to be asking her: "Was it nice, ma soeur?" And the nun would answer: "If you only knew!" Béatrice got up and walked along the wrought iron fence to the third window. She pressed her face against the iron and felt the metal between her thighs. It was from this window that Soeur Marie-de-Fatima had flown away for the last time. Béatrice had seen her. She had seen the bird take flight. That day—it was at the beginning of May, like today—Béatrice was having trouble writing the word "ange," which she kept spelling "anje," and she had asked the nun to come and help her. "Ma soeur, I don't understand why you write it with a 'g.' It looks prettier with a 'j!'" Soeur Marie-de-Fatima bent over her and wrote the word in her "beautiful" nun's handwriting, the perfectly formed letters with no personality, moulded forever by religious and community rules: rules of chastity, poverty and obedience. To thank her, Béatrice buried her head in the folds of the nun's robe. She'd started doing this at the beginning of the school year and Soeur Marie-de-Fatima let her. Sometimes, she would even place her hand lightly on the little girl's unruly head, listening to her sigh and moan like a child being consoled. They never spoke to one another, but an impassioned affection had sprung up between them, an affection that united them through their expressions, dazzling them by what they didn't have to say, by what they understood perfectly well: Soeur Marie-de-Fatima found in Béatrice's eyes the courage to continue her Calvary; while, in the nun's eyes, the little girl found the desire to learn how to fly. Suddenly, the nun began to tremble. Béatrice withdrew her head from the folds of her robe. The nun was looking down at her notebook. In an awkward gesture of affection, Béatrice had upset her inkwell. It spilled onto a sheet of paper, drowning the word "ange" in a sea of total blackness. Soeur Marie-de-Fatima cried out, pushed Béatrice away from her, and ran to the third window, which she opened so vigorously that two of the panes shattered. And Béatrice, hands and face black with the angel's blood, watched the bird spread its vast raven's wings and, with a cry of horror, awkwardly try to fly. Leaning against the fence, Béatrice heard once again the angel's fall, the dull thud of bones breaking beneath layers and layers of heavy fabric, a sound that followed her throughout her childhood. Sometimes, she heard it again when someone (Mercedes or a client) opened a window to breathe, or drive out the odours of love poorly experienced and poorly executed. Béatrice walked away from the red brick building, unworthy witness to this first great love, stained with blood and ink, crossed rue de Lanaudière, and walked past l'Eglise Saint-Stanislas, without even glancing up.


Violette took the needles out of the bootie she'd just finished. She turned the small soft fuzzy ball in her hands for a few seconds, then, making a face, began to unravel it, pulling on the end of the green yarn. Florence, her mother, stopped her by putting her hand on the bootie. "Don't unravel it, it's fine." Violette shrugged. "It's smaller than the other one. Look, the one that I just finished is bigger.... Only a cripple could wear this one!" Rose and Mauve looked at their sister, astonished at her words. Mauve even frowned and spoke very quietly. "You know very well, nobody's going to wear these booties..." Rose took the bootie from Violette's hands. "I'm going to do it again. You start another one." Florence ran her hand gently across her daughter's forehead, smoothed back her hair and tucked it behind her ears. "Your head aching?" "No, I just forgot. As usual." Violette picked up her knitting needles again, selected a ball of green wool and silently resumed her work. Florence waited until Rose had finished re-doing the yellow part before she spoke. "Never undo what's been done, Violette." "I know, Momma, I was daydreaming." "If you're tired, go inside and rest a while..." "I know, Momma, but I'm not that tired." Florence spread her hands on her knees. "Never look back. We're here so that everything will keep moving ahead. What's knitted is knitted—even if it isn't knitted right." "Yes, Momma." Rose, Violette and Mauve looked at their mother briefly, and then, at the same moment, as though by signal, they all looked down at their work. "Is today the first time?" Florence asked in a troubled, almost trembling voice. "Yes, Momma. Don't worry. I didn't undo anything." Florence closed her eyes and began to rock again. The familiar creaking of their mother's chair dissipated the uneasiness the sisters had started to feel. And their needles began to click more regularly. Only Violette was still a little behind in the rhythmic movement of elbows and hands, just as a false note or a poorly executed measure remains in the mind for a long time after order has been restored in an orchestra. Then, Violette broke the silence with a forbidden question that rang out on the balcony like the crack of a whip, startling her sisters: "Momma, how long have we been here?" Florence didn't move, but her eyes filled with fear, or rather, with uncertainty, as though Violette had uttered a word so unthinkable, formulated a statement so absurd, that no reply came to mind, leaving her head empty, herself a victim of concern. Violette pursed her lips and lowered her head. "Momma, I want to know. I feel as if I'm forgetting everything when I knit my baby booties — and it scares me." Florence still did not move. "Momma, I can't remember yesterday. I mean, it's as if there was just one yesterday in my head! As if we came here yesterday and it was our first day in this part of town . . ." Violette spoke faster and faster. "Momma, I feel as if I got here yesterday, but, just now, all of a sudden, I remember that we saw Gabriel and Edouard and Albertine being born and . . ." Abruptly, she turned towards her mother, dropping the ball of green wool which rolled off the balcony, leaving an end dangling. "Momma, I even remember when Victoire was born! It's the first time it's ever happened, but I remember! We were living in the country then, next door to her mother's place, just like we're living next door to them now. . . . Momma. . . . Momma. . . . I remember when Victoire's mother was born!" She shouted this last confession, suddenly jumping to her feet, trembling, her hands clasped over her heart, her eyes filled with tears. Then, Florence stood up and took her in her arms. "Go inside and rest . . ." "Momma, answer me!" Florence gently drew her daughter towards the glass door. "All right, we're going to talk. Then everything will be like it was before. You'll just remember what's important . . ." She opened the door and turned to Rose and Mauve, who had gone quite pale as they went on with their knitting. "If you feel tired, come inside too." When the door slammed slightly as it closed, Rose looked up at her sister: "Do you remember all that?" Mauve looked at her surreptitiously, her hands never still. "Yes. We've always been here, Rose. And we always will be. Don't stop. That's what we're here for."

When his second bowl of liver was finished, licked and washed, Duplessis asked for the door without even going by his sandbox. In vain did Marie-Sylvia plead with him, cajole him, threaten him ("Three days! You were away for three days and now you want to take off again! I haven't even had time to see you! You spent the whole morning sleeping! Stay till tonight at least. . . . I'll stroke you and make you purr. . . . I won't move, you can sleep in my lap. . ."), but it was all for naught. Duplessis clawed the bottom of the door, meowing as though it were the middle of July, when the moon is red with desire and passions explode at the ends of alleys. White with rage, Marie-Sylvia opened the door, screaming: "Okay, go out! But don't bother coming back! Ever! I never want to see you again! And don't come meowing at my window tonight. It won't do you any good. You're staying outside!" But Duplessis was already far away. He jumped over the Ouimets' fence on the other side of the lane, and now he was hiding in the dandelions, his eye on a bird perched on a low branch of the lilac tree (the only one in the neighbourhood), excited at the prospect of an orderly hunt crowned by the usual apotheosis: the victim writhing in the executioner's paws, its wing broken or its neck smashed, with a heart that would suddenly stop beating as incisors searched through blood-soaked feathers for a tender spot in which to sink triumphantly. But the bird (a common sparrow, if the truth be told, hard to catch and a wretched trophy) guessed at Duplessis' presence among the yellow flowers and flew off without asking any questions, not even fascinated by the cat's eyes that tried all at once to be engaging, beguiling, authoritarian, dominating. Duplessis immediately lost interest in the lilac tree (Why linger over failures?) and inched his way beneath the Ouimets' gallery to do his business. At that very moment, a mouse slipped through the nascent blades of grass, and, heart pounding, reached the alley. Duplessis, occupied with a more important task, pretended not to see the mouse. He heard the Ouimets' door open above him. Then, he heard heavy footsteps that made the floor of the gallery creak. He carefully buried his excrement, then cautiously approached the four front steps. Stretching out, he saw the feet of a woman shod in moccasins that were worn but clean. A woman, long, lean, with a protruding belly, walked jerkily across the yard, then emerged into the alley without closing the wooden gate behind her. Duplessis followed her. He knew that odour very well: the woman liked cats and Duplessis was her favourite. (She called him "the lecherous premier" and when she ran her hands through his fur, it had the pleasant effect of exciting Duplessis quite deliciously.) He moved ahead of her with little leaps and sat in front of her, looking her straight in the eye. The woman stopped and smiled. "Don't bother making goo-goo eyes at me, dirty old Duplessis. I haven't got anything for you today." She walked around the cat, who ran between her feet, purring. "I haven't got time, Duplessis. I'm on my way to work!" They came to the corner of the lane and la rue Fabre, in front of Marie-Sylvia's restaurant. "Your mother's probably looking for you — again!" The woman bent down, picked up the cat, opened the restaurant door and literally threw the animal into the middle of the room, shouting: "Marie, here's your goddamn cat! He looks hungry!" The woman closed the door before Duplessis had time to react. He began cursing like the Devil himself. Marie-Sylvia got out of her armchair. "You're back, mon trésor! Come up on mummy's lap!" A few moments later, Marie-Sylvia, her hand bleeding, opened the restaurant door, and all the way to la rue Mont-Royal, you could hear: "Out! Get out, you stinking rotten animal! I don't care if somebody picks you up and gasses you! I don't want to hear another word about you!" Duplessis shot across la rue Fabre. Immediately, a smell struck him and he remembered why he'd wanted to go out in the first place. Somewhere on the second floor of the second house, a little bit of a man with whom he'd had frequent conversations, who seemed to understand him, and whom he, Duplessis, understood very well indeed, lived with a bunch of lunatics, each one more hysterical than the other, and it was that little bit of a man whom Duplessis suddenly wanted to see. It was the very special smell of that house (for Duplessis, all houses and all humans were smells, but there was something remarkable, something stubborn and tenacious given off by the occupants of that apartment, which he never entered, but one of whose inhabitants was dear to him, so that, very often, Duplessis came and slept on the doorstep, his nose against the crack at the bottom of the door, happily revelling in the magical, soothing, regenerative emanations given off by this little bit of a man he could talk to, who listened to him calmly, and who, O miracle! answered in his own roaming cat's language) that reminded Duplessis he hadn't seen Marcel for three or four days and that the little boy must miss him. He crossed the lane, went past Doctor Laporte's house, which gave off a disgusting smell of cleanliness that was maintained by disinfectants that were too powerful and perfumes that clung once they'd been applied. Duplessis intended to climb up the steps without lingering, to slip his muzzle into the slit at the bottom of the door that served as a mailbox, and then to meow until Marcel opened the door, ecstatic, undeniably adorned with the smell of dried pee, lisping in cat-talk what he was thinking in human; but then something attracted his attention just at the bottom of the steps, in front of the house next door, where two ageless women were knitting: a ball of green yarn (a ball of yarn, O bliss!) sat imposingly in the middle of the pavement, promising all sorts of acrobatics, mad races and exciting games for a cat whose only toy was Marie-Sylvia, who was fat, unwieldy and often very difficult to move. Duplessis literally threw himself onto the yarn and began to struggle with it, pretending it was the bird that he'd missed a while ago, or the mouse at which he'd turned his nose up, or any other animal that's hard to catch but which he'd finally got the better of, and now was delighting in tearing it up, biting it, and almost suffocating himself with the wool as he imprisoned his claws in the rebellious strands. In the very heat of the battle, when Duplessis, at the summit of his joy, shouted to the ball of wool: "No use putting up a fight, you silly bitch, you know the end is nigh! Give up! Give up and I won't harm you!" Florence came out of the house and sat in her rocking chair. Immediately, as though he'd been stunned, Duplessis calmed down, crumpled to the cement, and looked at the woman, his eyes twice as big as usual. "She fell asleep. Everything will be okay in an hour. Keep working." Rose looked over her left shoulder and said very softly: "Momma, why's Marie-Sylvia's cat playing with Violette's yarn...?" Her mother cut her off in a firm but neutral voice. "Cats can see us. Cats and sometimes crazy people." Duplessis sat on his rear, began to clean his muzzle with his paw, then stared at Florence again. He blinked. "You bet I can see you!"

When Madame Ouimet arrived at Ti-Lou's (she had the key and never rang the bell, as Ti-Lou hated dragging herself and her crutches down the hallway: "I know when people come to the door, they see me with my three legs and it's humiliating."), she was still sitting by the window where Béatrice had left her. Her eyes were closed and her head bowed, so Madame Ouimet thought she was asleep. The young woman took a thousand precautions as she cleared the little table, careful not to knock the plates together, wrapping the silver spoons in one of the two cloth napkins, centering the delicate, fragile cups in their saucers to avoid any inopportune vibration. She was about to leave the room, bearing the lunch tray, when Ti-Lou said abruptly: "That you, Rose?" The other woman started and nearly dropped the tray: "Hey, you scared me!" Ti-Lou hadn't moved, her head was still down, her eyes closed. "I could've sworn you were asleep." "I've told you a million times, I never sleep in the daytime." "I know, but I thought just this once..." "Never, understand? I never sleep in the daytime! It's hard enough getting to sleep at night!" Rose Ouimet headed for the kitchen, thinking: "Never sleeps during the day! I'd like to know what she does when she spends the whole afternoon in her bed with her eyes shut, not moving a hair. Meditate?" Rose pushed open the kitchen door, grumbling. "I hate it when people treat me like a nitwit!" She put the tray on the table and opened the icebox to pour the rest of the milk from the silver pitcher into the nearly empty bottle. Immediately, she shouted: "You're out of ice! When does

83

the iceman come?" The reply seemed to come from very far away, as though the living room was on the other side of boulevard Saint-Joseph, on the grounds of the Ecole Bruchési. "Around four this afternoon. What time is it now?" Rose Ouimet picked up a card printed in large letters: "50 lbs., s.v.p." and slipped it onto the nail that her own mother had driven into the wall above the top windowpane in the kitchen many years before. Rose Ouimet had been cleaning Ti-Lou's apartment for only three years, replacing her mother, Rita Guérin, who was too sick now to "do houses," as she put it. "After two. And you're out of milk!" Ti-Lou and Rose Ouimet weren't crazy about each other, but Rose was a good worker and Ti-Lou paid well, so they put up with each other, but shared no warmth or contact, which made the crippled woman very sad for she had been very fond of Rita Guérin's smiling face and the songs from the Lower St. Lawrence that she would sing all day long, for a few hours driving away the old wanton's intolerable present and replacing it with an imaginary past, a past filled with the good smells of the country and homemade bread. But Rose Ouimet, too serious for her years for Ti-Lou's liking, didn't sing like her mother, and sometimes the she-wolf of Ottawa thought she could even see the mark of unhappiness — of unhappiness too great, of suffering too intense for her lean, dry body — cross Rose's expression, tracing purple shadows around her eyes when, as often happened, the young woman stopped suddenly in the middle of her work and stared into space, frowning, her mouth hard, as if she were contemplating some vision of horror, and silently, inevitably, giving in to it. Ti-Lou had pleaded with Rita Guérin to come back to work, even offering to double her salary, but Rose's mother resisted, shouting into the telephone like a woman still unaccustomed to those electric contraptions: "Why should I kill myself for a few extra bucks a week? I want to enjoy the little bit of time I've got left!" (Rita Guérin was barely forty-five and Ti-Lou had raised her eyes to Heaven as she pounded the wall with her fist.) "I'm sick of cleaning up after other people, I'm taking a rest! I'll send you my girl, Rose. She's a sourpuss, but she's a good worker." Rose Ouimet was, in fact, very efficient, but her presence depressed Ti-Lou, who often wanted to take her by the shoulders and shake her, shouting: "You're only twenty-two, for Chrissake, wipe that martyr's look off your face! Don't frown like that and don't scrunch up your eyes! You'll look like a prune before you're thirty! If your life's such a pain in the ass, then change it!" But when you walk on three legs, two of them made of wood, it's not easy to take anyone by the shoulders and try to shake them awake; it's a matter of balance. Ti-Lou preferred to take a stronger dose of Doctor Sanregret's drops and sink into that blessed lethargy, so dangerous but so gratifying, that she called her "divine coma," rather than watch the dismal Rose Ouimet's unhappiness slinking about the apartment, hugging the walls, hiding in the corners, ready to leap on its victim at any moment, paralyzing her in the middle of the hallway, broom in hand, or surprising her on hands and knees in the bathroom, her head in the washbasin. There was nothing about Ti-Lou's past that Rose Ouimet didn't know — and the old she-wolf sometimes wondered if that wasn't the real reason for her coolness. Rose Ouimet knew everything about Ti-Lou because her mother had repeated everything the Ottawa wanton had told her, so she didn't want to listen to her employer talk about her past. When Ti-Lou — for want of anything better to do, or simply because she wanted to do it — had tried during the first year to tell Rose about her unbelievable life, the young woman always managed to avoid the issue by muttering: "That's not what I'm here

85

for" or: "I haven't got time for that" or: "If you want somebody to keep you company, I'll send my sister, Gabrielle. She can talk a blue streak. But I'm here to scrub and I'm scrubbing!" Ti-Lou quickly understood that Rose, though so young, blamed her for her past, whereas her mother enjoyed it and was even a little jealous of it, sometimes declaring between two swipes of the mop: "You were in Ottawa in 1900 and I was in Montreal in 1920. You were having fun in a hole everybody else thought was a dump and I was bored to tears in a place everybody raved about," then resuming her song with no further explanation. Ti-Lou had several portraits of men in carved frames, pretentious and ugly, that Rose Ouimet was loath to touch. Just once, she asked her employer: "You knew all these men?" and made a face at Ti-Lou's affirmative reply. And Ti-Lou asked her: "You don't like men?" to which Rose responded: "Only floozies like men. The rest of us put up with them." Rose Ouimet ran her hand over her rounded belly. "Goddamn balloon!" She was expecting her first child joylessly — cold, remote, resigned. She came out of the kitchen, held her stomach as she crossed the house, and burst into the living room, asking: "Where do I start? The house or you?"

Béatrice climbed very slowly up the first of the two inside staircases that led to Mercedes' apartment. She stopped every four or five steps, leaned on the wall or the bannister and sighed. "It's such a beautiful day!" She stopped at the top of the first staircase and sat on the doorstep of her own room, where she hardly spent any time at all now, but kept "just in case all hell breaks loose." It was her refuge, the only place in the world where she could be alone. Sometimes, Béatrice, tired of the awkward caresses of sloshed and inexperienced soldiers, would go down to her room, shut the door and cry silently in her bed or sitting by the window that looked out on the alley. Sometimes she even missed her former life: the fly buttons, the yardgoods, the tortoise shell barrettes; no responsibilities and innocent nights when she did nothing but sleep; her pay at the end of the week, cheap but steady, in a brown envelope that you didn't open right away, if you had any money left from the previous week, to see how long you could tough it out; the Passe-Temps movie house on Saturday night: three films, four and a half hours in a stifling hall, formerly a bowling alley, long, with many of the dirty seats broken and the strong smell of unwashed workers and overly perfumed women; the long hollow hours of Sunday afternoon when you'd tell yourself: "I wish tomorrow would hurry up! Anything except these goddamn Sundays!" But these little fits never lasted long. Béatrice knew Mercedes was waiting for her, counting on her, and that the work had to be done. When Béatrice came back to her friend's apartment with its red and yellow lights, the shadows under her eyes were slightly larger than usual and the soldiers liked that. Arms seized her, lips crushed her and Béatrice quickly forgot about movies and hollow Sunday afternoons. Béatrice decided to change her clothes before going up to Mercedes. As she entered her room, she immediately noticed a piece of white paper folded in four that someone had slipped under her door. She bent down and picked it up. "Hope it isn't somebody from home come for a visit.... That's all I need!" A somewhat sybilline phrase that Béatrice didn't understand immediately had been hastily scribbled on the paper: "Meet me at Parc Lafontaine." No signature.

"Now, that's dumb — leaving a message without signing it! But maybe the name wouldn't mean anything to me. Maybe it's a client that wants to do it in the bushes!" Béatrice smiled. "I wouldn't mind. Just once. Out in the open. But likely the ground's still wet." She changed quickly, slipping into the dress that she usually kept for special occasions, for Mass or going out on a Saturday night — but she hadn't gone out on Saturday night for ages; Saturday was a "heavy" night — the yellow cotton dress that made her look so young and emphasized her smooth brown skin, the dress that made Mercedes say: "Usually, I look like your mother, but when you wear that, I look like your mother's mother. No matter what I do to try and look younger, I've still got a good twelve years headstart on you!" Béatrice whistled as she brushed her hair. "I'll tell Mercedes we ought to take the afternoon off, then we'll go to Parc Lafontaine, but I won't mention the message. Then, we'll see what happens." Satisfied with what she saw in the small round mirror above the basin, Béatrice smiled a broad smile at her reflection. "I look just like a calendar girl!" She took a few dance steps as she headed for the door. "I'd like to go out some night!" She picked up the note folded in four and slipped it in her purse. She climbed up the second set of stairs, humming, "Ramona, you stink of feet, tobacco too," joyous, heart pounding. "Hey, a message. My very first one!" At Mercedes' apartment, she stopped short and a dreadful foreboding seized her heart: the door was ajar, something unthinkable for Mercedes, who shouted twenty times a day: "Did you shut the door? And lock it? You can't be too careful with some of the jokers we get here!" and the smell of vomit extended onto the landing. Without thinking, Béatrice pushed the door open, sure that she'd find Mercedes awash in her own blood or beaten to death, lying in her own excrement — but the big bedroom was deserted. It was, however, in incredible disarray: everything had been smashed, knocked over, searched, broken, trampled on. The mattress, slashed open, was on the floor. The dresser drawers had been pulled out, thrown against the walls and had landed on the floor, and the bathroom door had been pulled off its hinges. Béatrice ran through the tiny apartment shouting: "Mercedes! Mercedes!" like a madwoman, tripping over objects strewn on the floor, bumping into furniture that had been moved around. Someone had vomited a little inside the bathtub and a lot right next to it. "Bunch of pigs! Filthy pigs!" She saw again the three soldiers who had tried to stop her on the stairs that morning and felt anger rising up her spine. "If only I could get my hands on them! I don't know what I'd do, but it'd hurt like hell!" She felt somewhat reassured when she realized with certainty that Mercedes wasn't in the apartment. She went back into the bedroom, sat on the bedsprings, and let her sobs come gushing out as she pounded the foot of the bed with her fists, stamped her feet and cried: "Goddamn bunch of filth!" twenty or thirty times, though it didn't make her feel any better. She had barely started to calm down when she saw the shadow of Monsieur Soucy, the concierge, outlined in the doorway, his arms laden with packages that the fat man hadn't even thought of putting down when he heard Béatrice shouting as he entered the building. "What's going on? You can hear you hollering out on the street! What happened? Did you get beat up? And where's your friend? I knew it'd happen! I knew it! I can't set foot outside for two hours without a ceiling falling on somebody's head or some idiot forgetting to turn off the tap! I'm calling the police!" Monsieur Soucy disappeared before Béatrice had time to react. The words struck her like a whip and she straightened up, as if she'd been slapped. Police! She picked up her purse, which she had dropped near the door, and ran out of the apartment. She ran down the stairs, past Monsieur Soucy, who shouted: "And where do you think you're going, Mademoiselle Béatrice? The police'll be wanting to talk to you!" Béatrice left the building without slowing down, then headed down la rue Fabre towards Parc Lafontaine. "Mercedes left that message. She beat it to Parc Lafontaine! Mercedes is waiting for me!" Rose, Mauve and Florence, their mother, watched her pass without batting an eyelash. Florence, however, said: "That girl's going to run into trouble!" But Florence was mistaken. Béatrice wasn't heading for trouble. Béatrice was on her way to twenty years of glory, splendour and power.

Philippe had discovered a subterfuge that guaranteed he could enter the playground openly and publicly, without a word from the attendant, though it was a ploy that required Thérèse and Marcel to play roles — and Philippe was a little worried about his boy-cousin (his girl-cousin was, in his words, "a born actress" and would eventually be able to make anyone believe that she was a "forty-year-old mother who still looks young" or a "four-month-old baby advanced for its age"). As for Richard, his older brother...Philippe had a way of totally excluding his brother from his games, and even from his life when he didn't need him, to drop him whenever he was no longer useful, and this confused Richard, left him speechless, arms dangling and mouth gaping, wounded, dismayed, and generally, in a position that was delicate, if not impossible. At school, when they wanted to beat him up in the yard because he'd just done something mean, Philippe would run to his brother, who was peaceful and weak, bring him back to the heat of the battle and forget him there, without even recalling, later, either the battle or, even more important, his own misdeeds. If he needed money, he came and cried into Richard's shirt, but once his brother gave him part or even all of his assets, Philippe would disappear without a word of thanks and come back a few minutes later carrying an ice cream or a paper cone of french fries, not looking at his brother, "forgetting" to offer him a lick or a piece of greasy potato. Philippe hovered around Richard like a parasite as long as his brother could be of some use to him, but disappeared without fail as soon as Richard needed him. And so, when Philippe's plan was adopted (Thérèse and Marcel understood nothing, but were ready to put up with anything if it meant they could play on the swings), Richard found himself alone at the end of the path where the four children had taken refuge after going to clean up Marcel and his mess. He asked timidly: "What about me?" but neither Thérèse nor Philippe picked up on his question, only Marcel, who bent over his sister to ask: "Coco coming too?" To which Thérèse replied stoically: "Coco's a stick-in-the-mud. He doesn't want to play on the slides or the sandboxes with us. He's going to the municipal library to read, eh Coco?" while Philippe looked elsewhere. Richard immediately got up, murmuring submissively: "I get it," which seemed to relieve his brother and his cousin. He walked away without another word, not turning around, his shoulders slumped, but not too much: he'd wait till he was all alone before giving in to his hatred for his weakness, to his contempt for his lack of courage, kicking out at trees and weeping with rage. "I know, I'm a scaredy-cat!" As soon as Richard had disappeared behind the huge building that housed both "Les Amis de l'Art" and the public toilets (a building that Richard and Philippe's father, Gabriel, called, as a matter of fact, "Les Toilettes de l'Art"), Philippe let out a great guffaw that embarrassed Thérèse a little. "Watch out, Philippe, maybe he can hear you!" "That's okay, it'll teach him to stick to us like a leech!" Marcel looked up at his cousin: "What's that?" "What's what?" "What you just said." "A leech?" Philippe looked pleadingly at Thérèse, but she just shrugged. "You ask too many questions, Marcel. People will think you're ignorant." Thérèse got to her feet and picked up her brother in her arms. "If you pee your pants again, Thérèse is going to leave you all alone in the middle of the park!" Marcel flung his arms around his sister's neck and squeezed very hard. Thérèse could feel Marcel's heart beating against her breast. "And the dusteroos'll eat you up. The bogeyman'll get you!" Marcel released his embrace and looked at his sister, incredulous: "There's no dusteroos here. There isn't any bed!" Thérèse put her brother down. "You know, Marcel, there are house dusteroos, but there are park dusteroos too!" (Dusteroos were the piles of dust that accumulated under beds when Albertine or the fat woman were too busy to mop every day. And dusteroos proved very convenient when you wanted to frighten children at night and keep them in their beds: "If you set foot out of bed, the dusteroos will bite you!" Thérèse had been afraid of dusteroos; Richard had been afraid of dusteroos; but Marcel was literally terrified of them. As for Philippe, at eight, he still wasn't exactly sure if they existed or not and if he boasted about them, claiming he'd never believed in them, that he'd always just pretended to believe in them to please his parents who went to so much trouble to terrify him, it was because one evening, out of bravado, he got off the sofa he shared with Thérèse to go and check and he saw — he was sure of it and when he thought of it, he could feel the hair stand up on the back of his neck — he saw something move (in the dark, everything moves) and he stood there, glued to the spot, deathly pale with fear, short of breath, liquid shit trickling between his legs.). Thérèse hoped to find a clump of moss at the bottom of a tree to back up what she'd said and force her brother to be quiet for the rest of the afternoon. She'd tell him: "Look, park dusteroos aren't grey. They're green. That's worse!" As she walked away from the bench, Thérèse put her hand on her cousin's neck. "At least Richard would've known what a leech is!" Then the three children went towards the playground, sure in advance of their victory. Thérèse had told Marcel: "When we get near the games, don't say a word. Let us take care of everything. Otherwise, we'll leave you behind and you can go to the library with Coco!" Marcel swore that he wouldn't say a word no matter what happened. As soon as they'd crossed the heavy chain-link fence that surrounded the playground to "protect" the children, as it was claimed, Philippe, out of the blue, without even saying: "Watch out, here I go," almost in the middle of a sentence, went into contortions, crossing his eyes, sticking out his tongue, limping so grotesquely that he looked like a marionette with tangled strings, which made Thérèse say: "Don't go too far, Philippe. You'll scare them and that'll be worse!" Marcel asked fearfully: "Is Fwip sick? Do we have to take him home?" Thérèse crouched beside him. "No, Marcel. Flip isn't sick. It's just a game. . . . You'll see, they'll let him come in with us and we'll have lots and lots of fun. . . . Now, you be quiet." She stood up and turned to her cousin. "Limp a little, Philippe, but just a bit. . . . And make one arm crooked, just one. . . . Good, that's right. . . . Don't hold your head so crooked. This isn't a horror show!" Philippe moderated his efforts in an attempt to look somewhat spastic (he had in mind a classmate with muscular dystrophy whom he always made fun of and whom he exasperated with his sarcasm and his imitations) and the trio bravely approached the first set of swings: Philippe hobbling beside Thérèse, who was holding back her laughter, and Marcel, watching him, dumbfounded. Thérèse took a handkerchief from the pocket of her dress and concealed her giggles behind it. When she'd finished pretending to blow her nose, she realized that Marcel, carried away by Philippe's game, had begun to contort himself as well, mimicking his cousin's every gesture and expression with obvious delight. Just then, she noticed the park attendant approaching them, looking concerned, and she chose that moment to shout at her little brother: "Marcel, will you stop making fun of your big brother? It isn't nice! I've told you a hundred times!" She took Marcel by the arm and began to shake him, hoping to make him cry so that he wouldn't say anything silly. But Marcel shouted in his shrill voice: "I was just playing!" When the attendant came abreast of them, he let out a "What's going on here?" in a voice that said a great deal about the narrowness of his intelligence and his general lack of subtlety. But when Thérèse looked up at him, she was struck by his good looks and stood there, somewhat taken aback. The playground attendant wasn't the doddering, grimy old man she'd been expecting, but a young man in his early twenties with fine features and eyes that were splendid if not intelligent. Instead of answering him saucily as she'd been prepared to do, she began to stammer, looking down, blushing, getting her words mixed up, all of which had the ultimate effect of making more credible the unlikely story she and Philippe had concocted: their mother, tired of looking after her disabled son, asking her daughter, so reasonable and responsible, despite her youth, to take the child and their younger brother to the park so she could get a few hours' rest. . . . As Thérèse told her story, Philippe, who was watching the attendant from the corner of his eye, saw the man's hesitation melt, to be replaced by a heavy-handed pity that he thought was funny and couldn't wait to imitate. But Marcel, though he'd sworn to keep quiet, nearly spoiled everything. When Thérèse had finished her explanations and finally looked up at the guard, who she thought was definitely very handsome, the little boy said quite candidly and very loud, probably to make himself more interesting: "He isn't my brother. He's my cousin!" For a moment, everything seemed to hang in the air. Philippe would gladly have stepped on his cousin right then and there, but he was imprisoned in his personality, and as for Thérèse, she was too exhausted by her idiotic story and too excited by the attendant's beautiful eyes to come up with a somewhat believable answer in a hurry. Eventually, it was the attendant himself, in his great naïveté, who got them out of the trap by saying reproachfully to Marcel: "It's not nice to be ashamed of your big brother! Jeez! If I had a brother like that, I'd take care of him!" Marcel hid in his sister's skirts, for he thought the gentleman was, quite frankly, a jerk. The attendant gave Thérèse a smile that nearly made her faint. "You have a good time with your brothers, girly.... And if you need me, just shout. My name's Monsieur Bleau...Gérard Bleau." He rumpled Philippe's hair in a gesture of friendly protectiveness, then walked away. As soon as his back was turned, Philippe stopped his act. "I'm worn out!" In his great candour, then, Marcel once again uttered a remark that his sister, and particularly his cousin, found profoundly depressing, raising a problem neither of them had thought about: "Will Fwip have to act like a dumdum all day long? How can he play if he's all cwooked?"

95

"How do I look?" Victoire, dressed to kill, painted, ridiculous, stood before the fat woman, a mauve straw hat stuck crookedly on the side of her head, her skinny body draped in a brown crepe dress that hung unevenly around her twisted legs, her face invisible beneath a garish layer of makeup borrowed from Albertine. The fat woman had always been frank with her mother-in-law and the older woman appreciated it, often saying of her daughter-in-law: "Maybe she's silly, but she's okay. Not like my daughter, Albertine. She's so scared of me, she'd sooner die than tell me she dropped a plate." Which was false, in fact, as Albertine regularly broke pieces of crockery that belonged to her mother, on purpose, just to get her goat, and every time, she howled: "One less cup! Your estate's going straight to hell, Momma!" or: "I hope you aren't too stuck on that ugly goddamn Chinese plate because if you are you better get ready to bawl your eyes out!" The fat woman was a little taken aback. She had never seen her mother-in-law so badly put together and she wondered how she could tell her. The total frankness that she usually practised would require her to say something like: "Go and hide, you'll scare people!" or: "I think you ought to start all over—from scratch...", toning down her remarks with a smile of complicity or a great burst of laughter. But the fat woman knew that Victoire had decided to go out, come what may, and it would have been cruel and useless to delay her pleasure, so she merely spoke of the hat which, in any case, her mother-in-law detested. "You're right. It's an ugly hat. When Edouard gave it to you at Easter, I couldn't figure out why you hated it so much, but now..." Victoire came a little closer to her daughter-in-law's armchair, bent over her and said with obvious insincerity: "Listen, I know just what you mean. But I'm going out with Edouard, so I haven't got any choice—I've got to wear it!" She'd lowered her voice, but she was whispering so loud (when she went to confession, everyone could hear her and the priests were forced to tell her: "Talk in your normal voice, you won't make so much noise!") that she awakened Gabriel, who was sleeping in the bed beside his wife's chair. As he opened his eyes, the sight of his mother made him retch — and his wife smile. "Calvaire, Momma, what're you doing all decked out like that? It isn't Hallowe'en!" Victoire didn't flinch. She simply stared even more insistently at her daughter-in-law. "Do I really look that bad?" The fat woman shrugged. "Answer me!" "Well, you see. . . . Maybe it's a bit too much. Mauve and brown isn't the prettiest combination in the world. . ." Victoire straightened up and cut off her daughter-in-law, clicking her tongue in satisfaction. "Even better! I decided to put Edouard's nose out of joint and I think I'm off to a good start!" Finally, she turned to her son and said gently: "Go back to sleep, Gabriel. You're tired. Your mother and your brother are going for a walk on la rue Mont-Royal. It'll give everybody a good laugh and it'll help us pass the time! Go to sleep. You'll hear about it soon enough!" She turned and, with dignity, walked out of the bedroom. The fat woman smiled, shaking her head. Her husband looked at her. "Know what?" She took his hand and patted it. "Either your mother really wants to get even or she's decided to shift her big battle with Edouard onto new territory." Gabriel noticed the book on his wife's lap. "Now you're talking like *Bug-Jargal*! Pretty soon, nobody will understand a word you say!" He sat up in bed, leaned on the arm of his wife's chair and kissed her on the mouth. "Did he move today?" "And how! I've got the feeling he can't wait to come out!" "You pick a name yet?" "Yes. If it's a boy, Pierre; if it's a girl. . .Denise." "You sure — about Denise, I mean?" "Yes." Gabriel and his wife had lost a daughter, Denise, their eldest, two years before, and the night they'd decided to make another child, the fat woman said: "If it's a girl to take the place of the one we lost, we'll call her Denise, like the other one." They'd never talked about it again, but Gabriel hoped his wife would change her mind. The fat woman ran her hand through Gabriel's hair and over his damp forehead. "If you really don't want to, we'll try to find another name. But, well. . .I'd like it." Gabriel laid his head on his wife's vast bosom. They stayed like that for a long time: Gabriel, on his knees in the bed, head against his wife's breasts, as if he were asleep; the fat woman, stroking his hair, his neck, his face. "I love you, you know." It was hard for him to say those words, the fat woman knew that. Her husband, skilled tavern orator and life of the party, was astonishingly powerless and bereft when it came to speak to love. An almost pathological sense of propriety kept him from talking about "those things," as he called them, and when the time came to prove his love for his wife, a slap on the bottom or a wink of complicity had to be interpreted as passionate declarations, replacing the letters he'd never written, the flowers he could never afford and the words that almost always stuck in his throat. "You smell good." After a long caress, the fat woman murmured: "Go on, shut the door."

The kettle had been whistling for several minutes before Ti-Lou heard it. Rose Ouimet was on her hands and knees in Ti-Lou's clothes closet, a bucket of water beside her. You could hear her scrubbing and swearing. "This floor looks like it hasn't been washed since Adam was screwing Eve!" Rose had helped Ti-Lou into her bed, where now she reigned, surrounded by chocolates and pillows. "Rose, the water's ready for my bath..." Rose didn't hear—or pretended not to hear. The kettle continued to whistle. Ti-Lou took a big chocolate-covered cherry, her favourite, placed it on her tongue and burst it open against her palate. The juice flowed into her throat. Ti-Lou closed her eyes. She chewed slowly, swallowing just a bit at a time, keeping the pulp of the chocolate and the juice of the cherry imprisoned for as long as she could between her tongue and palate. When there was nothing left in her mouth, she didn't move, but savoured the aftertaste that tickled her taste buds. "Rose, if the water boils away, you'll have to put some more on because I have to take that bath!" Rose Ouimet sat up on her heels and ran her arms across her sweaty forehead. "What'd you do in this closet, for the love of.... It's all sticky!" "If I told you, you'd be shocked..." "Bon, okay. Enough of your jokes. I'll get your bath ready." She threw her scrub brush into the pail of water and walked out of the bedroom, muttering. Ti-Lou selected another chocolate, one with maple filling this time, and concentrated on the taste of maple that blended so well with the taste of the chocolate. In order to clean the closet floor, Rose had to take out Ti-Lou's improbable collection of left shoes that had been lying around for years. Once her pride and joy, ever since the removal of her right leg, they'd been the object of curses and loathing. When Ti-Lou was still powerful and wanton, she'd sing her own praises to anyone who cared to listen, because she owned one hundred and eight pairs of shoes (she actually had only fifty-four pairs, but the she-wolf of Ottawa always multiplied everything by two), and as many pairs of gloves (she was always seen, however, wearing the same gloves, long black silk ones, but perhaps they were all the same), and when a client, a little more skeptical than most, ever dared question her power and influence over Ottawa, Ti-Lou would spring from her bed, as if it were a font and she a demon, dash over to the wooden armoire that filled a corner of her bedroom, fling open the doors and say: "Look! A hundred and eight pairs! Do you know a single woman with a hundred and eight pairs of shoes that isn't powerful?" As the recalcitrant client, in any event, did not know anyone who was even interested in owning more than four or five pairs of shoes, he would apologize politely, amused at Ti-Lou's naïveté. . . . Some even went so far as to offer her a hundred-and-ninth pair, to which Ti-Lou inevitably replied: "You think I'm crazy? A hundred and eight's enough. More than that would be indulgent!" (She had learned the meaning of the word "indulgence" one night while entertaining certain personalities from France: an ambassador, two cultural attachés, and the inevitable tame bishop, Mgr. Brunet, who spent his time haunting the corridors of Parliament in search of "persons interested in meeting an Ottawa society lady, the most beautiful and the shapeliest. . ." (Ti-Lou suspected several cabinet ministers of hiring Mgr. Brunet to advertise her house and the ministers suspected her of the same thing, but the bishop was simply crazy about Ti-Lou and he would balk at nothing to find a reason for coming to see her), when she'd gone to her room to change three times (parading before her distinguished visitors first, in a fuchsia-coloured frock "to remind my guests that summer exists, even though it's the middle of February," she had said; then, in an emerald green dress of repulsive ugliness, a dress of which she was particularly fond; then, in order: in white, for "the purity of my soul" and in black, for "the purity of your intentions" — all in appallingly bad taste — painted like a clown, but much funnier, winking her eye and swaying her thigh, really, to excess) and Mgr. Brunet had come up to her in the middle of the night and whispered in her ear: "The way you show off your wardrobe comes perilously close to indulgence!" Ti-Lou took his remark as a compliment or, at most, a reproach; she liked the way it sounded, and the word "indulgence" had taken its place in her vocabulary.) Opening her eyes when the taste of chocolate and maple was exhausted, she saw the heap of left shoes (after her operation, she had thrown out all the right shoes, insisting on putting them in the garbage can herself, even though the new crutches complicated her comings and goings) that towered beside her bed and she began laughing bitterly. "Sometimes you think you've forgotten your problems at last, but your bitch of a life can always bring them back just by multiplying them all by a hundred and eight!" "You talking to yourself now?" Rose was standing in the doorway, holding the kettle. "I've always talked to myself because I've never met anybody interesting enough to have a real conversation with!" Astounded at the pretentiousness of her remark and, in particular, at its inaccuracy, she who had spent her life talking about herself in great detail, always overdoing it, omitting only the boring details — and even then, not always — Ti-Lou glanced down and nervously coughed. "Is it ready?" "Yes. Want me to carry you?" "I can get there on my own!" Rose Ouimet turned her back, hoping she would have the hardest possible time extricating herself from her bed. Ti-Lou seized her crutches, placed her left foot on the floor and, with a push, managed to stand up without too much effort. "While I'm in the tub, after you scrub my back, you can hide all those goddamn clodhoppers! Nobody ever teach you any refinement, you silly sow?" No reply. "Do you hear me?" She was now walking down the hallway. "If the bathroom wasn't so far away either! You hear what I said, Rose? Yes or no?" Rose Ouimet came out of the bathroom and for the first time, Ti-Lou noticed how badly her pregnancy was going. "That kid must know its mother doesn't feel so good." "Sure, I heard you. You yell loud enough! If you didn't have a hundred and eight pairs of shoes, the pile wouldn't be so big!" "I haven't got a hundred and eight. I've just got fifty-four!" "Then how come you always say you got a hundred and eight?" "I count them by pairs. Fifty-four pairs makes a hundred and eight!" "But you never say fifty-four pairs. You always say a hundred and eight!" "Yes, but I've just got one out of every pair! You never noticed I just got one leg, you sow?" "Well, that's just it. You threw out half your shoes, but instead of dividing in half, you multiply everything by two! A hundred and eight pairs makes two hundred and sixteen shoes, not fifty-four!" "Say, who's the boss around here, anyway?" Rose Ouimet opened her eyes very wide. "Just because you're the boss, don't mean you're right!" "Yes, it does — and quit pestering me!" A shooting pain at the tip of her stump startled her. She lost her balance, dropped one of the crutches and leaned against the wall. "What's wrong?" Ti-Lou had turned dreadfully pale. She was shaking like a leaf. "That hurt. Good God, that hurt!" "Whereabouts?" "I don't want that pain to start all over again!" Ti-Lou looked at Rose with pleading eyes. "If it starts again, it's the end!" "No, no. It isn't. It'll go away. . . . Here, lean on me and get in the tub." Ti-Lou slipped off her bathrobe. Rose Ouimet helped her get in the water. "Not too hot?" "No, no. It's fine. It feels good. . ." Rose Ouimet, her hand in a ratteen glove, began to scrub Ti-Lou's shoulders and neck with the soapy water, but then something attracted her attention: the end of Ti-Lou's right leg was floating on the surface and a black spot had blossomed behind the scar at the tip of the stump. "Funny, the end of your right leg's all black!" Ti-Lou howled as though her heart had been ripped out.

Usually the smell was so strong that most of the few visitors who ventured that far cut short their visit, plugging their noses and snickering, the parents sometimes embarrassed, the children always laughing themselves silly. As for Richard, he found a refuge in those musty smells that made him feel safe — and every time his frail body was assailed by some pain too hard to bear, he would run here, sometimes without stopping, and lean against the circular fence that kept the turtles — already half-dead from heat and malnutrition, dried out, wrinkled, sick, their shells soft and grey — from getting out. He never stopped to look at the two bears since the day he realized that the poor creatures had alopecia and that the disease was getting worse from week to week; he ignored the monkeys, whose obscene gestures made him blush, for they masturbated all day long to the great delight of the pimply-faced adolescents who came there solely to see them find their relief; sometimes he'd glance, but very quickly, at the single fox that howled in frustration as it ran back and forth in its cage during its season for love; but the turtles.... He could spend hours watching the hideous things trying to cool off in the tepid, stagnant water, their heads raised towards the sky in a gesture of supplication, their mouths open, toothless, motionless, as if they were players in a tragedy. It was their immobility that fascinated Richard the most, the tableau that the creatures presented: of unchanging misfortune, subdued yet permanent, frozen forever in time and space, denying the past, already masters of the future, moulded by defeat and wallowing in it. Richard would have liked to be one of these turtles. He was one of them when the anguish of his soul prevented his body from reacting: he had chosen the turtles' immobility rather than try to resist his own natural, morbid penchant and get on with living. He was a born victim and the turtles at Parc Lafontaine reflected his image of the world in which he was evolving — or rather, not evolving. But this superb day in early May, beautiful and mild as it was, was too early in the season for the animals and the little zoo was still closed. Richard walked among the deserted cages, seeking the stench of sick animals clinging to the branches of trees or the bars of their prisons, but winter had long since driven out all vestiges of misery, and the pleasant smell of spring reigned over all. The strong, insistent smell of animals rotting on their feet would not come again and make his soul secure until summer holidays began. Richard always wondered where they hid the animals in winter. He enjoyed imagining them closed up in a deep, damp cellar, underneath the park, with no air or water or food, so that their summer prison would seem like a reward. He crouched on the ground still saturated with water, beside the turtles' cage, and let his loathing surge out of him like a torrent swollen by the spring run-off, smashing everything in its way, carrying whole clumps of earth, logs that broke like matches on sharply pointed rocks, invading everywhere at once, submerging everything, even before anyone had time to react. Some day, he'd jump on his brother, Philippe, and tie him to a tree as the Indians used to tie up the white missionaries; he'd sit on the ground before Philippe and shower insults on him, bellowing and gesticulating, calling down the wrath of God, the only punishment worthy of him; then, he'd hit him on the face, the body, with his fists, enjoying the sight of his body turning blue, hearing his voice become, at last, pleading, pleading; then he'd skin him alive, one small piece at a time, putting out his prying eyes, tearing out his viper's tongue, stripping him bare, plucking off his

104

obscene monkey's limbs, and finally giving him the coup de grâce, strangling him with his own hands, as he screamed in his ear: "Die, dirty dog! Go to hell with the rest of your kind! And leave me alone once and for all!" A gentle warmth took hold of him as he dreamed, the happy vengeful destroyer of Evil, receptacle of Good, worthy of the most Deserving Saints and Bravest Soldiers, but he realized to his great shame that an erection had caught him by surprise in the midst of his elucubrations and a warm sticky liquid was wetting his underwear. His first ejaculation. And at last he understood that there could be something gratifying about the turtles' immobility.

Victoire hadn't set foot out of the house for more than two years. The last time, she remembered all too well, was at the very beginning of the war: Christmas, 1939, the famous night when Albertine's husband, Paul, announced that he'd just enlisted and might well have to leave for Europe any day. The news had somewhat dampened the réveillon at the house of Victoire's sister, Ozéa, who'd been living on rue des Erables near Marie-Anne for forty years, and who thought it was still a fashionable neighbourhood, even though she saw more and more families from Hochelaga moving into the neighbouring houses. (Ozéa often said to Victoire: "I can't figure out why you stay where you are? There's a million children on that street. A body can't rest for five minutes!" To which Victoire replied: "Lord on a muffin, Ozéa. You're as deaf as a stone! Just open your window and listen! There's as many kids on rue des Erables now as where we are!" Ozéa merely smiled. "You're jealous. You've always been jealous because you married a man without a pot to piss in and my Gaspar's got enough money for a whole collection!" Nevertheless, Ozéa's réveillon ended in a total hullabaloo, as Paul, who had decided to get royally pissed with the family one last time, started telling everybody exactly what he thought of them: he insulted his brother-in-law, Gabriel, calling him soft, heartless and afraid of his own shadow; he heaped insults on Edouard, whom he always called his sister-in-law manquée, even going so far as to slap his face and call him "mummy's pansy," which made Edouard laugh, but not Victoire; finally, in the small hours of the morning, he took his wife and mother-in-law aside to pin on them the blame for his ruined life, his domestic unhappiness, the beginning of his alcoholism, his early baldness, rotten teeth, weak muscles and even the holes in his socks and the sweat stains under his arms. All in a loud voice in front of the whole family and Ozéa, in particular, who pursed her lips and placed her hand over her heart. Ever since that night, Victoire had refused to go out, even to Mass. She never spoke to Paul again; in fact, he disappeared from circulation quite quickly, the nails in his soldier's boots ringing on the sidewalk and his beret planted firm; pleased, proud, imagining that he was finally going to make a success of his life. Nor had Victoire seen her sister, Ozéa, again, though the latter, in fact, hadn't tried to get in touch with her either. That Christmas night had been the ridiculous event, the grotesque break that sometimes separates members of a family forever. Victoire was ashamed of her son-in-law and her daughter, who had taken advantage of the situation to throw a hysterical fit that was quite ugly and went on far too long — and nothing could ever make up for this humiliation. She shut herself inside the house then and never went out again. Only Josaphat-le-Violon, Victoire's older brother, still paid regular visits, but for a long time the old woman was ill at ease even with him. "Maybe Josaphat doesn't remember, but I do!" On this glorious spring day, though, without really knowing why, Victoire suddenly felt the need to go out, to get a change of air, to fill her lungs and eyes with new life, new sap that would regenerate her and perhaps give her the courage to face the heatwaves that were fast approaching, that she hated so much. Victoire was a winter woman and she found summer depressing. But when she saw herself all dressed up and ready to go, she felt a moment's hesitation. She held Edouard's arm and was about to put her foot on the top step, when she stopped suddenly, stiffened and leaned on the bannister. Did she really feel like parading along la rue Mont-Royal on the arm of this big baby she adored, but whom she knew was ridiculous and even laughable? "Are you sick?" Edouard leaped on the word "sick," one of the words that his mother used so often, which seemed to hold her entire life together, hoping she'd decide at the last minute not to carry out her plan. But Edouard made the great mistake of letting his hope show and his mother smiled. "Me, sick? Since when? No, no. I just felt a bit dizzy. Get a good grip on me now, then we'll be in business." She took her son's arm again. "Let's go!" Rose, Mauve and Florence, their mother, heard the brief exchange between Edouard and Victoire and Mauve, surprised, murmured: "Momma, Victoire's going out..." Rose got up, walked down the steps, terrifying Duplessis who was still playing with the ball of green yarn. She planted herself against the fence and looked up at Victoire and Edouard who were slowly coming down the stairs. Mauve walked over and stood beside her. "My, she's aged..." Florence stood there motionless, hands placed sedately on her knees. "Momma, come look. She's having a hard time getting down the stairs!" "I know she is, I don't have to look." At each step, Victoire sighed. At the eighth step, she said: "Whew, halfway there!" She stopped to get her breath. "What'll it be like on the way back?" She noticed Duplessis who, ignoring Rose and Mauve, had thrown himself on the ball of yarn. "Look, there's Marie-Sylvia's goddamn cat playing with thin air! I'm telling you, that cat's out of its mind!" She began to go "Ssst! Ssst!" to frighten the cat, but Duplessis decided that he didn't hear her. "Momma, you're going to fall!" "I am not! I've walked down a set of stairs before, for heaven's sake!" "But not when you were trying to scare a cat! Do one thing at a time! You can scare the cat when you get to the bottom!" Victoire and Edouard began walking down the stairs again, slowly, one step at a time. "Rose, Mauve, come and sit down." Florence hadn't looked up. Rose and Mauve obeyed reluctantly. They sat on their straight-back chairs without taking their eyes off Victoire. At the bottom of the stairs, Victoire straightened her dreadful hat a little. "We're over the worst of it. I always thought those stairs were too steep!" She took a few steps, still cling-ing to Edouard's arm, then stopped short at Florence's front steps, feeling as if she were being watched. Florence had just looked up at her. Rose and Mauve saw that their mother's expression had become infinitely tender. There was even a vague smile on her lips. Victoire turned her head abruptly towards the house where the women were knitting. "What's going on now, Momma?" Victoire drop-ped Edouard's arm and, taking short steps, approached the fence that Rose and Mauve had just left. "Leave the cat alone. He'll go away by himself. . ." Without knowing it, though perhaps deep down she could sense it, Victoire was looking straight into Florence's eyes. Rose and Mauve held their breath. Victoire placed her purse on one of the fence pickets. "Funny, eh, Edouard? That house has always been empty. It was empty when we moved here forty years ago and it's still empty today." She was looking now at the door, the windows, the front steps. "And it's always clean." She removed one glove and ran her hand over a section of the fence. "Fresh paint, just like every year." She looked up at Florence again. "Funny, wherever I've been, wherever I've lived, there's always been an empty house next door. When I was little, in Duhamel, the house next door was abandoned and my father wouldn't let us go in. It was abandoned, but it was always as clean as a doorknob that's been rubbed with Brasso. As if somebody was taking care of it. In the winter, there were double windows and in the summer there were screens. In the fall, it smelled of red ketchup and in the spring it smelled of fresh paint. But we never saw a soul. Ever. Just like here." At that very moment, the door opened behind Florence, and Violette came out on the steps. From the window in the living room where she was lying, she had seen Victoire stop in front of their house. "Momma, she's looking at you! She sees you!" "No, Violette. She isn't crazy enough—not yet." When Victoire saw the door open, she gave a sudden start. She stepped back a few paces. "That door opened all by itself! Isn't it locked?" Edouard took her arm. "These old houses.... Everything opens by itself.... Must've been kids playing inside..." "Go shut the door, Edouard!" "Momma, it's after three and we still haven't gone anywhere!" "Go shut that door!" Edouard opened the gate and walked onto the little cement path that went across the lawn. He climbed up the three front steps, past Florence, who hadn't moved, beside Violette, who'd moved over a few paces, and slammed the door. "Okay, fine. Now, let's go." When Victoire and Edouard had walked away, Florence burst out laughing as her three daughters looked on in horror. "I hope the door isn't locked!"

Albertine paced back and forth past the closed door of the bedroom that belonged to Gabriel and the fat woman. "At their age—I ask you! And her nearly eight months gone! Sometimes I wonder if I'm living with a bunch of perverts. . . ." Now that she was alone, she could give in to her usual bad mood, as her promise to Thérèse not to act up didn't concern her personally. . . . "I promised I'd try and be nice with the rest of them, so I wouldn't scare Marcel, but I didn't promise anything about myself!" When Thérèse and Marcel left for Parc Lafontaine shortly before noon, Albertine, feeling somewhat relieved of her promise, almost began to curse and scream. She felt words, blazing with anger, rise in her throat, ready to come out in bursts of bile, splattering everyone, gluing her mother to the wall, sprinkling her brother Edouard with contempt; but she held back, telling herself it might be better to try and end the day the way she'd started it, that, since morning, it hadn't been all that hard, really, to be kind and gentle on the outside, though her insides were knotting and unknotting, according to her anger; that she was serving an apprenticeship now, and, who knows, by working on her new personality, she might even make herself believe, in the end, that life wasn't so bad, that a smile always wipes out the irritations, rages and squalls that wear everybody out, especially those who are subjected to them. "Take a deep breath, count to ten and smile. . ." But she'd nearly blown up a little earlier when she was washing her sister-in-law's hair and she had to control herself to keep from leaving the other woman stranded, head full of soapsuds and neck dripping wet, as she shouted: "Before you were like this, goddammit, you used to be able to wash yourself! And after that kid's born,

110

you can wash yourself again! If you want a baby at the age when most women are grandmothers, it's your tough luck!" There again, she'd managed to control herself—but at what a price! When she left her sister-in-law's room, her work done, the soapy basin slipping in her arms, she felt the first warning: the iron ring that squeezed her forehead, her temples, the nape of her neck, at the onset of one of the horrible migraines that usually came after a battle with her daughter or some dumb trick by her son. She went to empty the basin in the kitchen sink. "I can't get a headache. If I get a headache, I'll smash everything in the house!" And when she saw her mother on Edouard's arm—all dolled up like a scarecrow on its way to Mass—stop on the doorstep, turn around and say: "I know you're bending over backwards to act decent today, Albertine, but let me tell you, it doesn't suit you! You look like a cow that's chewing a cud full of bile!" A wave of pain struck at her brain and she raised her arm towards the old woman, to plead with her or strangle her, she didn't know which. The pain stayed there, hooked behind her left eye, pounding wildly at the same rhythm as her blood. And now, the door that was closed between the solitude which she'd never been able to relieve—badly married as she was, badly fucked, quickly disgusted by a selfish, awkward husband—and her brother's happiness which she couldn't help finding grotesque, that door, which closed on their childish guilty laughter, insulted her, like stinging abuse. She walked back and forth past the room, coughing, blowing her nose, knocking over dining room chairs as noisily as she could, unable to admit that she envied Gabriel and the fat woman. Her head hurt dreadfully, and from time to time, she stopped in the middle of the hallway or in the kitchen doorway, as if she'd been struck dumb, eyes filled with tears, shoulders shaken by sobs until, unable to hold out any longer, she

111

threw herself against the closed door and began pounding with her right arm as hard as she could, screaming in a voice filled with despair: "You don't have the right to enjoy it! You don't have the right! Not under my eyes! Not as long as I'm here! Do your dirty business all night long if you want, but let me have my days in peace!" The door opened and Albertine fell into her brother's arms. The fat woman was looking out the window. Her arms hung down on either side of the armchair. *Bug-Jargal* had fallen to the floor.

(This was how Ti-Lou enjoyed describing the facts: "I've always been very hard on my body. Work and suffering never scared me, and the good Lord's my witness, I've worked like an ox and suffered like a saint! In my house in Ottawa, I didn't take any days off, no sir. It was seven days a week, fifty-two weeks a year—and that was that! It was some lease I signed at that house!... But praise be to Heaven, I was healthy as hell, with a constitution like a horse, so whenever I had some little ache or pain, I'd knock it out with a twenty-sixer of rye or gin, and then, bye-bye! I sprained my back three times, broke an arm, had disgusting headaches and more shameful diseases than I can keep track of—but it never kept me from my work! If you want to reign, you've got to forget yourself, because if you think about yourself too much, other people take advantage, and then they take your place! When you're at the top, you can't afford aches and pains! So even when it was all I could do to stand on my feet, and even when I couldn't stand on my feet at all, I acted as if everything was okay. I'd smile and strut my stuff and I'd go on sending those men to seventh heaven, even though they didn't deserve the bargain basement! Once, I remember, my back was sprained, I was bent double, I could hardly move, but even so, I entertained the Prime Minister himself, sitting up in bed with pillows all around me — and I stayed like that all the time that he was there — and he never knew I wasn't well! What do you think about that? Ti-Lou charged a lot, but you sure as hell got your money's worth! My house was all painted white and I paid for the paint myself. . . . When I retired in 1930 and moved here, because Ottawa's no city to retire in (it's too frigging dull), but mostly because people there knew me too well and there was a danger my old age might be ruined by jealous women or a new generation of cabinet ministers that knew too much . . . when I moved to Montreal, I said to myself, "Ah! Le boulevard Saint-Joseph, doctors, dentists, retired folks like me. I'm gonna be just fine. Nice and peaceful . . . not too far from la rue Mont-Royal and the stores, but not too close either. . . . The church across the street (I still had a few dresses to show off that weren't full of worm holes), the little school too, the kids yelling during recess, Heaven on earth!" So, I moved in here twelve years ago, after a party that lasted for thirty years, with my head full of memories, my bank account full of postdated cheques, and the table in the salon full of ads from travel agents and shipping lines: Ah, Cunard! That word made me dream all my life! Ships, islands, the ocean, Buenos Aires, Montevideo, Vera Cruz, Miami, Rio de Janeiro! Around the world in a floating palace, with Ti-Lou, the floating she-wolf, finally getting her turn! I'd earned it and I was going to pay for it myself! But then, three weeks before I left, I started limping like a cripple: there were pains shooting down my right leg that hurt like a son of a bitch and I had a hell of a time getting to sleep. . . . I sent for Doctor Sanregret next door (he just had to come across the

corridor) because I wasn't in any mood to hang around for hours with his bunch of down-and-outs coughing and spitting, so ashamed that they never looked at each other.... And damned, if I didn't have diabetes! No more sugar! Forbidden! Me, cut off sugar? No more chocolates? No more Honeymoons? I told that doctor he didn't know me very well and then I booted him out. And I stayed here with my pain. For the first time in my life, I couldn't do something because I was sick: I didn't take that trip because my leg hurt too much. But I was pigheaded and I didn't cut out sugar. Even today....
And, I stayed the same for years. When it hurt too much, I asked Dr. Sanregret to prescribe some of those drops, but then, I needed more and more, because the pain got worse and worse — but so what? I put up with it and didn't breathe a word to a soul. I'd noticed the little toe on my right foot was turning black, but I thought I'd hit my foot against something or other.... Then, one fine day, I was taking my bath — I remember like it was yesterday — and my toe was as black as coal. The rest of my foot was starting to go black too.... I told myself, I'd better get the doctor over here. Still, I got back in the tub though and started washing my right foot...and there I was, holding my little toe! I had the washcloth and I could see my little toe right in the middle of it; it looked just like an old dried-up raisin...and it didn't even hurt!" When Ti-Lou came to this part of her account, she always stopped for a few seconds to give her listener time to take in the full horror of what she was saying; then, when she was quite certain of the effect, she'd add candidly: "Want to see it? I've still got it..." Of course, no one had ever wanted to see her blackened right toe and no one ever knew if the she-wolf of Ottawa really possessed that little lump of coal.... Nevertheless, Ti-Lou went on: "Three days later, I woke up with my right leg cut off. Me, Ti-Lou,

the she-wolf of Ottawa, terror of ministers' wives, queen of Parliament, there I was, over fifty, like a World War I veteran that stepped on a mine just before he got on the boat for Canada! I screamed and carried on for one whole year. . . . I felt as if I was just half of myself. You know what I mean? Those legs had put in some good years! Those legs had damned a hell of a lot of people; they'd enjoyed over thirty years of dancing and screwing! It's no joke, learning to walk again when you're fifty! Crutches . . . . I could go on about those goddamn crutches for weeks and I'd still have things to say about them! You stand at the mirror in a brand-new dress and you've got three legs, two of them made out of wood, that keep you from moving — it's the worst thing that could ever happen to a scarlet woman! And now. . .when my eyes get glassy, I tell myself that I'm okay, that I've forgotten everything, that Doctor Sanregret's drops still do the trick. . . . But when my eyes are dry, don't make any mistake: if I'm in a good mood, don't believe me; and if I'm in a bad mood, don't talk to me; and if I'm really pissed off, stay away!") When Rose Ouimet had dried Ti-Lou and put her to bed, the old woman was still crying. She kept repeating: "It's over. It's over, Rose. Everything's finished!" Rose had a lump in her throat that kept her from speaking. She wished she could console Ti-Lou or at least try to console her, but something told her it wouldn't do any good. The black line at the bottom of Ti-Lou's leg was the final sentence, the ultimate death sentence, signed by the demon himself — and nothing, neither words nor caresses, would make the slightest difference. Ti-Lou asked for her drops. Rose brought them from the living room. "You can go now. Never mind the cleaning. I'm in no mood to watch you lumbering around the house with your belly sticking out. Go lie down. You're tired." When Rose Ouimet left Ti-Lou's house, distraught, the grandfather clock at the end of the hallway was sounding three o'clock. "That's a hell of a price to pay—even for a scarlet woman!"

The memory of Marcel, and his smell of dried pee, caught Duplessis by surprise in the very midst of his massacre of the ball of green yarn. He disappeared from Florence's lawn so fast that the four women who were knitting (but who could, nevertheless, see everything) didn't even notice. Only Mauve, from the corner of her eye, thought she spotted a shadow dart between the wooden slats (she'd pulled her chair over to the left so that she could rest her head against the column that held up the second-floor balcony), but she'd just dropped a stitch and wasn't paying attention to the cat, concentrating on her work instead. Rather than follow the fences or the sidewalk, Duplessis decided to cross flower beds, lawns and fences to get to la rue Mont-Royal. It was longer, but more pleasant. It would have been even more marvellous at the height of summer because of Madame Rivest's flowers, which attracted bees and butterflies, treasured victims of Duplessis ("Butterflies are hard to catch, but they're so good! And bees, my dear! It's worth the risk of getting stung for the divine luxury of biting into those fat juicy bodies..."), or the Beausoleils' grass, which was never cut, offering the neighbourhood cats an ideal hunting ground and refuge, with natural hiding places and green tunnels, especially when the sun became intolerable. But Duplessis told himself there was something promising about the new grass, the crocus blossoms and the omnipresent dandelions that he found touching: the grass would grow fast and furious; the crocuses would disappear to make way for lily-of-the-valley; the

116

dandelions would turn to balls of white silk that he'd have fun demolishing with one swipe of his expert paw, spreading to the four winds flimsy ballerinas that would land on the earth, drifting wherever the breeze might carry them, frozen figures that were complicated, but oh so graceful. As soon as he realized that Marcel wasn't around (at this time of day the little boy would normally have been up to no good under the stairs or in the square of dirt beside the street, but no joyous cry rang out, no uncontrolled laughter), Duplessis decided to go and look for him in the only other place he could be: Parc Lafontaine. The previous summer, when the friendship between Duplessis and the little boy was being transformed into true passion, that illness blessed among all others, which left Duplessis throbbing at night, intoxicated with love and anxious to go to sleep, so that the next day and the moment when he'd see his friend would come more quickly, Marie-Sylvia's cat understood one vital point: when Marcel disappeared for a whole day, making him anxious and concerned, it meant he'd been literally carried away to Parc Lafontaine, where he'd be flung about in some nonsensical way on a piece of wood between two lengths of rope. Marcel would squeal then in a way that Duplessis was pleased to think was inspired by horror and the tiger cat, superbly brave and glowing with passion, would throw himself beneath the swing to deliver his friend. As soon as he saw the cat, Marcel would begin to laugh, shouting: "Plessis! Plessis!" and ask the others to stop pushing him. And Duplessis would jump onto Marcel's lap, purring hard and overwhelmed with caresses and kisses. Then, convinced he'd saved Marcel from mortal peril, at the very least, Duplessis would escort his friend home, meowing with joy. And so, Marie-Sylvia's cat walked unhindered across the L'Heureux' lawn, then the Amyots', and the depressing asphalt square of the

Guillemettes', who thought that they'd pulled off a good one by paving the front of their house, but were quickly disenchanted when the tar had started to melt and stick to the soles of their shoes in the middle of August, and then, at last, the huge square of freshly turned-over earth at the Rivests, known as "the gardeners," because, every year, they managed to grow things no one else even thought of planting (the fat woman often said: "The year that I saw pumpkins puffing up like balloons in their front yard, I thought, this time, they're going too far . . . but when they gave us each a big pumpkin at Hallowe'en, I thought, well, maybe they're crackpots, but it makes sense!"), but he stopped against the Jodoins' fence to listen to a conversation between Gabrielle Jodoin, so gay and beautiful that the other women on the street baptized her "the lark of la rue Fabre," and Victoire, who'd stopped in front of her house to the great dismay of her son, Edouard. "When are you due?" Gabrielle Jodoin rubbed her stomach, smiling. "End of June. Same as my sister, Rose." "My daughter-in-law, too." "That's right, she's got one on the way too . . ." "I wouldn't say 'on the way'. She looks like she's going to have twelve!" "I hear she isn't too well?" "She's all right, but she has to stay in bed all the time . . ." "She's got a lot of time on her hands." "Well, she's got lots to complain about as far as that's concerned, but she wanted that baby so badly!" "Me too, I wanted mine badly! It's my first, but it won't be the last! Mastaï thinks we ought to stop after three, but I want as many as I can have." "You won't be saying that a few years from now, Gaby." "Don't worry about me. I'm crazy about kids!" "Not like your sister, Rose . . ." "Oh, her . . ." Gabrielle Jodoin gestured hopelessly, then decided to laugh. "Know what she said yesterday? We were up to our elbows in dishwater — they'd come here for supper, her and that nut she's married to — and all of a sudden, she says to me: 'You're so crazy about being pregnant, I wish you could carry mine.' Now, I ask you, is she touched in the head? I had a good laugh, but all of a sudden I realized, she was dead serious..." "That sister of yours never should of got married." "Don't say that. We had a double wedding and when I see how bad things are going for them, I'm scared it'll happen to us too..." "Now, don't get yourself worked up about that, Gaby. Even if your Mastaï didn't invent the wheel, he's got a lot more on the ball than her Roland." Edouard sighed, exasperated. "Come on, you two. I got more to do than listen to you gabbing like a couple of women with nothing to say!" His mother didn't even look his way. "No? What've you got to do that's so important?" Gabrielle burst out laughing. Duplessis chose that moment to walk across the lawn. He went between the legs of Gabrielle, whom he rather liked, greeting her with a friendly meow. Victoire started. "That goddamn cat again! He's going to follow us all the way to Larivière et Leblanc, for Chrissakes!" Duplessis ran all the way to la rue Mont-Royal without stopping. He was afraid that Victoire and Edouard were on their way to Parc Lafontaine too and he didn't want Marcel to disappear into the arms of the fat man, who reeked of some unnatural perfume that always left his little friend smelling disgusting, like a somewhat stale cadaver or rotten flowers. "I have to get there first or they'll spoil my whole day!" He crossed la rue Mont-Royal without slowing down and almost caused an accident between a french fry wagon being pulled by a horse and a bashed-up old 1935 Ford: the horse nearly bolted in fright at the sight of a lump of tiger-striped fur darting past him like an arrow, but the french fry seller knew the horse well and the accident was neatly avoided. But scarcely had he reached the other side of la rue Mont-Royal, when Duplessis stopped short and felt his heart freeze: just at the corner of the lane, fifty feet away from him, stood his great enemy, the dread Godbout, a solitary, generally peaceful dog, who turned obstinate and even vicious whenever a cat, especially Duplessis, whom he particularly abhorred, tried to cross his territory, which extended from Mont-Royal to Rachel and along la rue Fabre from Papineau to de Lanaudière. Godbout had seen Duplessis and he was ready for him, cursing and grumbling, front paws well apart, mouth open to reveal absolutely terrifying teeth. So that he wouldn't lose face, Duplessis began to clean his muzzle with his front paws, as if he hadn't seen the dog. He could feel his heart pounding as if it were about to burst, but he'd never let it show. Godbout, however, was nobody's fool. He came up to the cat, barking like the entire population of demons in Hell. Duplessis let his paw dangle in mid-air, looked Godbout in the eye and said: "Go bark up another tree, dear heart, you're interrupting my ablutions!" Two and a half seconds later, the battle was on and blood started to flow.

"I'm so tired, I think I'll die here!" Philippe had taken refuge behind a tree, the only place on the playground where the attendant couldn't see him — or so he thought. He was sitting at the foot of the tree, exhausted by two hours of grimaces and contortions. He had managed to get in the playground, but the two hours he'd just spent had proven rather difficult: how do you have fun, in fact, when you must keep perpetuating a role, inventing a character who isn't you, one who is also trying to enjoy himself in his own way, particularly when that character is crippled and deformed? At first, Philippe found it amusing to try and imagine how a cripple would behave in the middle of the playground, but he quickly realized that it was no place for a cripple to have fun: the slides and ladders were too risky; he mustn't even think about the whirligig unless he sat on it and let someone else push him (but the great joy of the whirligig was precisely to make it spin by yourself, wasn't it?); the sandbox was full of dirty, squalling children — that left the swings, and even there, he had to play a role! Marcel joined his cousin at the foot of the tree, surprised to see him suddenly stop crossing his eyes and his arms and legs. "Flip stopped pwaying?" "Flip's worn out, goddamn it! Go play in your sandbox — and if the guard comes back, you tell me..." Marcel sat between his cousin's legs. "Marcel's tired too!" He leaned against Philippe's chest. "Sleepy-bye..." "That's right, go to sleep and they'll nab us!" Marcel contemplated the branches above them, covered with buds. "Leaves on the twees tomorrow. That's what Thérèse said." He shut his eyes and immediately fell asleep. How many times had Marcel come and fallen asleep against his cousin like this, abandoning himself utterly in his arms, at the table after supper, or later, while Philippe, Thérèse and Richard were doing their homework on the dining room table, when Marcel would climb up on his cousin's chair on the pretext of giving him a peck on the cheek, then linger in his arms, and finally, fall asleep, trusting and content? Thérèse, in fact, was a little jealous of Philippe and told him: "You're really a pain when you put him to sleep like that!" To which Philippe replied: "Good thing that there's somebody in this house to put him to sleep; there's more than enough to yell at him!" Marcel wriggled, wrapped his thin little arms around Philippe, sighed and smiled. "Looks like I'm stuck here for a while." Philippe decided to try and sleep as well. He leaned his head against the tree trunk and closed his eyes. He usually took a nap with Marcel on Saturday and Sunday afternoons, and sometimes even after school. It was his way of reassuring himself, of forgetting the grammar he couldn't make head nor tail of, the arithmetic he always managed to understand, but only after everybody else, the religion he couldn't care less about, the geography in which he inevitably got lost. Philippe was a mediocre student, he knew it. He'd even come to terms with it in a way: "I'm a dumbbell, but I don't care. When I'm old enough to quit school, I'll go and work with Poppa. . ." Unlike Richard, who did his homework maniacally every night, armed with pens of every colour, rulers to underline his headings, and always impeccable notebooks, Philippe was so untidy that he rarely finished his homework and, even then, only after a lot of slogging and sweating, generally in vain. When Richard came home from school, he was rested, calm, with the calm of those who are sure of themselves and convinced of their superiority; but Philippe was nervous, anxious, and Marcel's regular breathing, as he snuggled against his heart, provided him with the self-confidence that he missed so much, which he made up for with boasting, tricks, jokes and even blows. Unable to fall asleep in such an uncomfortable position, Philippe opened his eyes and looked at his cousin's small face. "If I didn't have you. . ." Thérèse's laughter came across the playground, tearing the afternoon in two. Thérèse laughed this way only when something very important was happening and her laughter was always the line of demarcation, the final point between two periods of time—the one before she started laughing and the one after. Philippe thought: something has just happened to prevent the day from ending the way it's begun, but he made no attempt to crane his neck and find out what the girl was doing. He knew he'd find out everything eventually. For the moment, he was interested in nothing but Marcel's breathing and his smile.

Mastaï Jodoin, carrying his empty lunchpail, was walking along la rue Fabre towards his house. He was humming "Les Goélans," a song he hated, but his wife had put it in his head that morning and he couldn't get rid of it. He'd driven his Saint-Denis streetcar all day long humming that song, which he interrupted with a loud "câlice" or "tabarnac" whenever a car cut him off on the right or a passenger took too long getting off. Mastaï Jodoin had a reputation as a peerless streetcar conductor, so he was allowed to rant and rail and curse in peace, even if the rules of the transportation company strictly forbade it. If a passenger complained about the lack of breeding of driver number 423 on the Saint-Denis line, the reply was always: "Maybe he swears like the devil, but he hasn't had a single accident in five years! Would you rather risk your life with a driver as meek as a lamb?" In fact, they'd tried hard to persuade Mastaï Jodoin not to blasphème in public; in the beginning, he'd even been punished in various ways: he'd been put to work on the Rachel line, the most boring line in town, he'd been made to work Sundays and holidays, he'd even been suspended for several days following some escapade, but all without success. As soon as he was at the controls, Mastaï would let fly some well-chosen oath, with a nice wink at his discomfited inspector, and sometimes, he'd even say: "You won't get me, hostie! I'm the one that's gonna get you!" Finally, he was asked to try to contain himself when a priest or a nun got on his streetcar. "I don't like curés and old-maid crows are a joke. Why should I hold back for them?" Nonetheless, whenever a pair of nuns showed up at his ticket box or some priest or brother greeted him with a

"Bonjour, mon brave," as they mounted the three metal steps, Mastaï Jodoin's language was transformed somewhat and a series of disguised blasphemies would ring through the streetcar. Mastaï would bellow a "tabar-name de cibolaque de câline de binne de boston de calcinusse de chrusantème" that would turn the nuns pale and the priests red. Sometimes, to amuse himself in the middle of an afternoon, when his humming vehicle transported only old ladies and ordinary housewives, he'd call out the stops in a somewhat unorthodox manner: "De Montigny, ciboire!" "Laurier, for shit's sake!" "Rachel, bordel!" Then, he'd burst out laughing as he saw the horror-stricken faces of his passengers. "Got you, eh, Madame? Falling asleep were you, câlice?" Often he'd be helping an old man or woman get on or off his street-car — from pure kindness, for the rules of his job didn't re-quire it — but as soon as he completed his noble gesture, he'd close the door and shout: "Vieux calvaire! Next time I'll kick you out on your ass, câlice!" to the great displeasure of the other passengers, who had, in fact, just exclaimed ecstatically over the young conductor's kind and thoughtful behaviour. Mastaï spied his wife, Gabrielle, waiting for him in the distance, leaning against the fence around their lawn and waving to him cheerfully. Gabrielle was outside waiting for her husband as she did every day in the summer. This was the first time this year and Gabrielle was excited. "It means that the nice weather's here to stay!" She'd come out a good half hour before her husband's arrival, so she'd have time to stroll around the yard and hum a tune to the baby sleeping in her belly. Her conversation with Victoire had been a pleasant diversion. And she'd watched Victoire walking away on Edouard's arm, nodding her head. From as far away as he could, Mastaï shouted: "How's my baby to-day?" As soon as he was abreast of her, she replied:

"Before, when you used to talk about your baby, I knew it was me. But now, I don't know..." Mastaï put both hands on his wife's belly. "Okay, I get it. From now on, I'll ask, 'How's my two babies?'" "And everybody'll think I'm expecting twins!" "That'd be too much!" They exchanged a long kiss right in the middle of the sidewalk, an absolutely amazing thing on this street, where all feelings were hidden as much as possible. On the other side of the street, from her balcony where she was sitting to get a little sun, Claire Lemieux watched Mastaï and Gabrielle Jodoin, a glimmer of envy in her eyes. Her big white whale of a husband was asleep on the living room sofa again. "It's bad enough that it's been ages since we've kissed like that, but I'm the one that comes home from a goddamn shitty job everyday!" She swallowed some more warm Coke. "I'm going to break out in pimples again..." She placed the bottle on the balcony floor. "But who cares? Nobody'll notice!" Mastaï wrapped his left arm around his wife's shoulders and with his right hand took two theatre tickets from his pocket. "Ma belle Gaby, tonight I'm taking you to see La Poune!" Gabrielle Jodoin squealed with delight and grabbed the tickets. "La Poune! I've been dying to see her for ages! We'll eat early so we can get there in time for the double bill before the show!" She hopped up and down, clapping her hands. "Ooh, I'm so glad! What's the funny show this week?" "'La Buvette du coin'—and they say it's a laugh a minute! I nearly took you to see 'La Dame de chez Maxim's' with Antoinette Giroux at the Monument National, but I was scared it'd be too serious...I wanted a laugh!" "Me too!" I want to have some fun!" Suddenly, she placed her hands on her rounded belly. "He's excited too, the little bugger. He's kicking me!"

Mercedes had spent the whole day wandering, first along la rue Mont-Royal where to pass the time she systematically visited every store on both sides of the street, between Papineau and de la Roche, then in Parc Lafontaine, where she hung around smoking cigarette after cigarette, a little disappointed because they hadn't yet taken out the green wooden benches that were piled up in a shed for the winter, but happy to smell once again the fragrance of spring rising from plots of grass and the sun drinking up all the dampness from the earth. Mercedes knew Béatrice wouldn't come to meet her before half-past two or even three o'clock, so she decided to go all the way around Parc Lafontaine, walking along Papineau, Sherbrooke, Parc Lafontaine and Rachel, lingering in front of the Hôpital Notre-Dame, where she was born, and the municipal library, where she'd never set foot, which she thought was open only during summer holidays, since children didn't have time to read in the winter. As for adults. . . . She hadn't known anyone who had time to read since she was a teenager. . . . It had taken her exactly an hour and a half to walk around the park, and at precisely half-past two she was back where she'd started, at the corner of Fabre and Rachel. She wondered if the three soldiers were awake, and if so, what they'd done. "I hope they don't remember a thing and think that they lost their money somewhere else! But I'd better not count on it . . ." It was the first time she'd robbed clients. Not that she hadn't wanted to before, but fear of reprisals always prevented her from going all the way. She'd known so many girls who came back on Sunday morning with a black eye or a bloody face, because they'd tried to fleece a client. "Goddamn men! You can do anything to them — spit in their face, humiliate them, kick them around like dirt — they like it, it excites them! But don't try and take a cent from them! They'll get their dignity back in one hell of a hurry and have you waiting on them hand and foot!" At Larivière et Leblanc, she'd lunched on a hotdog and a Coke, taken out the fifty-two dollars that she'd found in the soldiers' pockets and spread the money on the counter. The sight of this money (so much all at once and so easy to pick up!) had warmed her heart. "Béatrice and I could use some new shoes — new sheets too.... And we'll get it all free-for-nothing!" But her thoughts always returned to the three "subtle" soldiers. "I got a feeling the apartment's too hot for us tonight. We'll have to sleep in a hotel for once. Tomorrow, there won't be any danger." She was used to thinking no further than tomorrow. In the houses where she'd worked, Chez Suzy de Coteau-Rouge on rue Sanguinet, or at La Grosse Petit, everything was always settled within twenty-four hours: fights, money problems, even diseases. It would never have entered her mind that the soldiers' hatred could be so tenacious that they'd come back the next day to seek vengeance. For her, soldiers paraded and never came back. Since Béatrice still wasn't there, she crossed la rue Rachel and went into the corner grocery store to buy some more cigarettes. "The place smells of horse manure! When'll they get a truck like everybody else?" Armed with a brand-new package of Turrets, she went back to the park, lighting another cigarette with relief. On the little path that began at la rue Fabre and then veered off to the right until it eventually got lost in the park, a little boy was walking slowly, visibly upset. Mercedes recognized the eldest of her neighbour's children, a serious boy she'd often encountered, who always looked away when she approached. She walked towards him, glad of the diversion. When the boy saw her, he stood there, frozen, and Mercedes noticed a dark spot drying on his left leg. She guessed that it was sperm and she smiled. Richard blushed to his ears and turned around so that he could get away as fast as possible. "Hey, little boy, are you lost?" Richard stood still and answered without turning back. "I'm old enough to know where I'm going!" "You going home?" "Yes." "You all alone?" Mercedes had come abreast of him. Richard answered, still without looking at her. "My brother and my two cousins are playing in the girl's park. I think it's dumb, so I'm going home." She held out her cigarettes. "You smoke?" "No!" "Not even on the sly?" "I'm not interested in things like that!" "You do other things in secret though, eh?" Richard crossed his hands in front of his penis and blushed even more. "You don't have to go all red like that. It's normal. You're old enough. . ." Richard moved away from her, but in the wrong direction: he was walking deeper into the park. "Why won't you talk to me? I won't eat you!" For the first time, Richard faced her. When she noticed his big red ears, almost transparent, Mercedes nearly burst out laughing, but she restrained herself. "A woman that smokes cigarettes on the street could do just about anything!" "Ah, so that's it. . ." Mercedes was always forgetting that a woman who smoked on the street automatically had a bad reputation. Accustomed as she was to being banished, no matter where she was or what she was doing, she cared little about such details; sometimes, she even deliberately lit a cigarette in public, out of bravado, sending out clouds of smoke she'd more willingly blow in the faces of women than men. She threw her cigarette to the ground and stepped on it with her right foot. "Now I'm more respectable, eh?" Richard looked away again, but this time he didn't move. Mercedes put her hand on his shoulder. "Something's bugging you, right?" Richard lowered his head and began to sob. Mercedes sat down, right in the middle of the little path then, and drew Richard to her side. And for nearly two hours, she listened to the story of his life: what bothered him, how he hated his brother, his frustrated passion for his mother and the new sensual pleasure that he didn't understand but which felt so good. So, while Béatrice, nearly frantic, was looking for her, Mercedes, hidden by a clump of budding bushes on an out-of-the-way path, was hearing the confession of an over-sensitive little boy. With this child, she experienced again — but for the first time with joy — the role of confidante that the hundreds of men she had known had imposed on her, the still and silent person who was part of the five-dollar trick, a role often more difficult to play than the one of the fulfilled mistress which, in the end, required nothing more than technique, whereas the other, the substitute for the confessional, required a patience that was sometimes inhuman, so similar were the problems of her various clients in all their mildness, their pettiness and meanness. Richard's problems were serious and beautiful compared to those of the men who had forgotten long ago and too quickly that they'd once been children, who had replaced their questions about existence and their preoccupations with life — if they'd ever had any — with beer that made them heavy-eyed, and ill-digested lust, performed and paid for in five minutes. Richard told his story with gasps and lumps, never taking his eyes off Mercedes, submitting to her gaze and demanding absolution. And Mercedes listened to him and dispensed that absolution, relieving the boy's frail shoulders of their burden of guilt, encouraging his confidences, provoking them when they came reluctantly, and washing away with her smile all the horror of his confession.

Gabriel was sitting at a table, looking lovingly at four cold drafts. The fat woman had told him: "You can come home plastered, but not so plastered that you can't stand up. I don't care if it's Saturday, but the rest of the world doesn't have to know it too!" Gabriel had already disposed of four drafts as soon as he got to the tavern, hardly taking a breath between the glasses of beer, anxious as he was to feel the warmth that begins at the solar plexus and gradually radiates through your whole body, making your limbs heavy, relieving your head and chest of all their cares and tracing on your lips a blissful smile. "Waiter! Four more!" But now that there were four fresh cold beers in front of him, he didn't touch them. He was waiting for the right moment. He often said: "Four beers get the motor running, but the next four make me take off!" He'd wait till his motor was running, then, before he filled up again. He watched the drops of liquefied condensation slide down the glasses, tracing a path, clear transparent furrows that revealed the golden beer in all its splendour through the moisture that clung to the glasses. As he followed the course of the drops of water to the table, he thought of his sister, Albertine, and saw her blow her nose and wipe her eyes after her outburst that afternoon, daring to look at him and his wife only surreptitiously, apologizing in a hoarse voice that contained a hint of shame. For once, he hadn't been weak with her. He'd closed his bedroom door after telling her gently: "Now you go and let us finish what we started. Go in your room or out on the balcony and think about something else." When he came back to his wife, she murmured: "When can we be by ourselves? We'll soon have three kids, Gabriel, and we can't bring them up right in a circus like this!" Gabriel knelt before her, resting his head between her thighs. "If we were all by ourselves, we'd be so poor! We're better off here!" He heard a sob catch in the fat woman's throat. "But who says that we wouldn't be happier, Gabriel? At least it'd be our own poverty! Here, I feel as if nothing belongs to us! Not even that! They took away my responsibilities, they took away my children, and now, I can't even spend ten minutes alone with my husband! At night, you're at the printshop; and in the daytime, we have to be careful because our room opens onto the dining room.... And when the baby's born, we'll have to keep it in here, in our room, and it'll grow up in the dark!" He promised his wife everything then: a new apartment, a new life, a new job for him where he'd work days; everything she'd been asking for since they'd come here to this house that was too small, between his mother, who was fond of him but only had eyes for Edouard, and Albertine, who'd never forgiven him for marrying for love, who constantly told anyone who would listen: "They didn't get married for love, it was just so they could do *that*," knowing very well it was precisely the absence of "that" from her own marriage that had nipped it in the bud. But Gabriel knew he didn't have the courage to condemn his family to the hovel his starvation wages would impose on him if they left, nor the thin soup and constantly needed clothes — a whole way of life so boringly melodramatic that he'd try at all costs to avoid it, a humiliating poverty that would drain all his courage and give rise to weakness and self-destruction. Here, at least, with the money he contributed, Edouard's board, the money that Paul sent Albertine, and their mother's lifetime hoard of small savings, they all managed to live decently enough, eating their fill and eating well and often, sleeping in clean, comfortable beds, keeping warm in the winter, and sometimes even having some fun at mealtimes. Gabriel feared that he wouldn't be able to give up all that for some hypothetical future. But he promised, knowing very well he was doing so only to gain time. He started: someone had just tapped his shoulder and the bitter smell of ill-digested beer and the stink of unwashed clothes tickled his nostrils. Willy Ouellette, a mouth-organ player, as famous for his dead-on retorts as for his approximately accurate music, was leaning over him, saying with a smile: "Maybe you aren't my very best friend, but that's no reason to act like you don't see me!" Without waiting for Gabriel's invitation, Willy sat down at his table, placing before him his harmonica and the beggar's bag that he carried with him everywhere, which contained everything he possessed: an unlikely series of handkerchiefs for the cold that he'd been trying to cure for a good twelve years now and a collection of threadbare underwear which he washed regularly in the wash basin in the tavern bathroom and then put to dry on the radiators in winter, or spread on the grass in the parks in summer. Otherwise, he was rather repulsively dirty, thank you, his disgusting smell discouraging any conversation longer than ten seconds, responding automatically to any reproach that he might receive because of his smell: "I ain't that dirty, you stinking fart. I got a whole set of clean drawers!" Then, he'd take out several pairs of underwear and wave them under the nose of his interlocutor. "You know any French Canadian with this many drawers? Don't you worry now. You might think doctors look clean, but go check in their pants. It isn't so pretty! Maybe my hands don't shine like a mirror, but my ass is as white as snow!" Willy Ouellette seized a glass of beer and drained it in three seconds. He wiped his mouth on his shirt sleeve, belched and smiled. "Say, you got a grin like the cat that stole the cream. You just screw your wife?" Gabriel burst out laughing and pushed the three remaining beers at Willy. "Play me a tune, Willy, and make it a long one. I've got a lot to forget!" Willy literally pounced on the three beers, drained them in record time, then got up, shouting to the world at large: "Listen, everybody, Gabriel's just gone from being an acquaintance of mine to being a real good pal—and I'm gonna celebrate by playing something I haven't played for years, because it used to make my mother bawl. She died asking me to play it for her, but she didn't get to hear it, because before I could get my mouth-organ, she passed away like a little chicken, with her head dropping on her chest and her hands clutched over her stinking goddamn heart that'd just given up the ghost: that song's called 'Clair de Lune,' by Débussy, or maybe Ravel, who knows—anyway, by some Frenchman." Gabriel shut his eyes and let the music lull him. His motor had just started up and he'd have needed his four other beers to take off, but he decided that the music would do the job just as well, so he began religiously following the wrong notes that Willy produced with serious aplomb, mixing "Clair de Lune" and "Summertime" with disconcerting sincerity. But a completely unexpected notion occurred to Gabriel, who opened his eyes at the shock: "Deep down, Gabriel, you're nothing but a goddamn crybaby. A goddamn crybaby—and lazy on top of it!" Without waiting for the end of the piece that Willy Ouellette was murdering so effectively, he shouted: "Waiter! Four more!" And Willy Ouellette interrupted his concert just long enough to yell even louder, a resounding: "Make that eight!" which made the seven or eight drunks who'd come to sit near the new-found friends burst out laughing.

Everyone on la rue Mont-Royal—storekeepers, workers, deliverymen, salesmen, waitresses, even the man who tore tickets at the Passe-Temps—knew Victoire, or at least they'd heard of her, the older ones often saying to the younger ones who'd been recently hired: "We can complain all we want about what a pain in the neck our customers are, not one comes anywhere near Ti'-Moteur! Now, there's a pain in the neck! She'd come in here and buy nothing more than a peanut, but she'd drive everybody crazy, knocking things over, saying we hid the best things for the rich ladies from boulevard Saint-Joseph, and most of the time, she'd walk out without buying a thing, leaving us to clean up her mess! We were so scared of her sometimes, we'd call the other stores and tell them to pretend they were closed! That's the truth! We were doing them a favour! Ti'-Moteur would take la rue Mont-Royal all the way from de la Roche to Papineau, both sides of the street, and turn it upside down in one afternoon, then afterwards, she'd go back to la rue Fabre with one pair of stockings in her brown paper bag or a one-cent sucker stuck in her mouth like a trophy!" Françoise, the head waitress at Larivière et Leblanc's lunch counter, would tell at the drop of a hat about "the time that crazy bitch Ti'-Moteur ate three butterscotch sundaes and after every one, she told me I'd forgot to serve her, and then she left without paying, shouting at the top of her lungs how she'd never set foot again in a place where you wait hours for your sundae and never even get a whiff of it!" That time, in fact, Victoire had realized she'd forgotten her change purse and, too proud to admit it, she decided to gain some time by eating sundaes until some solution occurred to her. After the third sundae, when she was about to retch and a migraine was sawing through her skull, she suddenly straightened up and started giving hell to Françoise, almost without realizing it, as if she were having a nightmare, scarcely knowing what she was saying, but saying it with conviction. Luckily for her, it worked: she left the store unscathed, her reputation still intact, or so she thought — and feeling not a shred of guilt. "Don't tell me three butterscotch sundaes are going to break Larivière et Leblanc! I'll never believe that!" And when Ti'-Moteur disappeared from circulation, stories started going around about her, each more harebrained than the next — all over Plateau Mont-Royal. They started by saying that she'd simply moved and so much the better, but this too-easy conclusion didn't satisfy anyone; they needed something they could get their teeth into, a tragic end or at least some great misfortune, to fill the gap caused by her absence from the life of la rue Mont-Royal. Monsieur Applebaum, the manager of Grover's on the northeast corner of Fabre and Mont-Royal, claimed that he'd seen Ti'-Moteur get hit by a garbage truck, but nobody ever believed anything said by Monsieur Applebaum, who had a reputation for exaggerating, and anyway, there was something a little too categorical about this explanation. They preferred stories in which the words "mysterious disappearance" replaced the word "dead," because that way it was easier to imagine Victoire unhappy, in pain, repentant. Dying but not dead. No matter how much you believe in the fires of hell, the final and irrevocable punishment for a dissolute life, a good thrashing in some backyard, a devastating fire or an incurable disease are a lot more frightening to contemplate and a lot more exciting to wish on your enemies than the Devil's forked tail and ridiculous sniggers. The news got around then, that Ti'-Moteur's house had been razed by a tremendous fire, that it had driven her completely mad, poor old woman, and now, she was in an insane asylum, "at Longue-Pointe, with the hopeless cases," victim of a disease resembling leprosy; but a lot more painful and, in particular, horribly ugly to look at. A visible cancer. Purulent sores. Scabs. Buboes. Françoise, for her part, refused to listen to such nonsense. She preferred to imagine Victoire lying on the operating table, tied down and wide awake, stuffed with ice cream and butterscotch sauce, showered with insults and bodily blows. And so, when Victoire and Edouard, an odd couple if ever there was one, emerged on la rue Mont-Royal, turning left towards la rue Marquette, Victoire suddenly straightened up and then hunched her back like a beaten dog, as a strange silence fell over the neighbourhood. It was Saturday afternoon: la rue Mont-Royal was teeming with housewives doing their shopping, whimpering children drooling onto their mothers' skirts, drunks sitting or, rather, laid out in the tavern doorways. No adolescents. No young men. Or hardly. The few young men cruising la rue Mont-Royal that afternoon did so on the arms of pregnant women, whose presence served as alibi to their country in time of war, as guarantees of their honesty, and most of all, their innocence. Abandon a pregnant woman to go traipsing around the Old Country! Never! Victoire and her son hadn't taken thirty steps along the sidewalk when, already, heads began to turn and salesmen came out of stores with measuring tapes around their necks or tailor's chalk in their hands. When Victoire and Edouard walked past his store, Monsieur Applebaum from Grover's was waiting on a skinny woman who insisted on finding some cloth to match the colour of her hornrimmed glasses. Monsieur Applebaum almost dropped the roll of red-and-brown spotted fabric he'd just unearthed in the back of the store and ran to the door as if someone had kicked him in the butt. "Criminently, she isn't dead!" A sardonic little smile appeared on Victoire's lips. She glanced furtively to the left and right to see the effect that their presence was having—and her eyes wrinkled with delight. "Two years now, and they haven't seen hide nor hair of me. And I bet my nightie they all thought I was dead!" As for Edouard, he wished he were, indeed, dead. He knew his mother's reputation all too well, his own career having started as a clerk in a shoe store on la rue Mont-Royal. He'd heard people talk about her in terms so appalling that he'd never admitted she was his mother. And amazingly, for years Victoire played along: whenever she came to the store where her son had managed to land the manager's job through flattery, compliments and scheming, she pretended not to know him either. She treated him just like the others, yelling at him, threatening him, making abundant use of the words "cheat" and "thief," trying on fifteen pairs of shoes and buying nothing; sometimes, even going so far as to tell him in front of everybody: "I pity the woman that brought you into the world!" or: "If I had a numbskull like you for a son, I'd kill myself!" or again: "You should be wearing a shoe on your head, not a hat!" And when Edouard came home at night, she would literally throw herself at him, cover him with kisses, laugh so hard that she had to wipe her eyes with her handkerchief. "By God, I had a good laugh! You should've seen the look on your face! Like a potato about to sprout!" Edouard never really understood why his mother behaved like this. Enraptured of him as she was, she should have been delighted that her son was manager of a shoe store, that he had a position of trust, with heavy responsibilities on his shoulders; but instead, she humiliated him before everyone, even going so far as to express pity for his mother! How, though, could he understand the affront this manager's job represented to Victoire, compared to the ambitions and dreams that she'd entertained, maintained and nourished for him since his birth? How could he guess that she desired power for him, poor child, a lost cause, a hopeless case; he, who had always let himself be shunted about, bereft of any idea of grandeur, knowing nothing of the thirst for power until the day when, suddenly, everything came to him at one blow — desires, thirsts, dreams, ambitions — the cursed day when he realized that he was different, in a society that condemned any disposition, tendency, talent, taste that didn't fit its criteria of normality and where he had hidden his "abnormality," stuck it away beneath a mask of indifference, in the character of a store manager? How could he imagine that his mother knew he wasn't like the others and that the shame she felt because of it, since he was unable to assume his difference in her presence, could turn to pride only if he worked up the courage to talk to her about it? Victoire knew that Edouard became someone else when he walked out the door and she never forgave him for that. The shoe store manager was a stranger to her because he was too different from everything she'd always dreamed of for her darling son, her heart's delight, her baby, who was full of talent, but blind. Or fearful. Hadn't she given birth only to a handful of gutless wonders? Gabriel, who'd taken refuge in the bosom of his fat wife, Albertine-the-victim, and Edouard — *a manager of a shoe store?* Clinging to one another on the sidewalk along la rue Mont-Royal, Victoire and Edouard had never looked so much like strangers. She was sure of the effect she was having and relished every moment of it, while he, even though he'd left the neighbourhood long ago to go and sell shoes in the west end of town, at Ogilvy's, where rich people shopped and he was the only French-Canadian salesman on the floor, completely bilingual now, so that even his boss called him Eddy and customers always addressed him in English, still he felt the burning humiliation represented by this so-called innocent walk on the arm of the most hated old woman on the street — his mother. At the corner of la rue Marquette, Victoire stopped in front of a jewellery store window. She dropped Edouard's arm and leaned against the glass. Edouard stepped back a few paces. It was as though la rue Mont-Royal had stopped living. Everyone, customers as well as salesmen, came out of the stores to look at Victoire staring at the jewellery. Edouard folded his arms over his big belly, looked down, and finally, leaned against a telephone pole. Die. Right there on the spot. Never feel again those mocking looks. Or else survive and confront them. Whirl around and laugh in their faces. "Good joke we've been playing on you all these years, eh, you jerks? We had you fooled all this time and you let us play our game and never suspected a thing..." No. No courage for that. Withdraw. As usual. Shame. The man who tore tickets at the Passe-Temps came out too, and he was shouting: "Edouard! Edouard! At last, you got yourself a girlfriend!" Victoire turned around and walked over to her son. All this hypocrisy on top of everything else! "I'm hungry!" They crossed la rue Marquette as la rue Mont-Royal looked on in amazement. Victoire kept nodding at all the people whose paths they crossed, sometimes murmuring a scarcely audible "Bonjour" or: "Comment allez-vous?" At the corner of Papineau, they turned right and crossed Mont-Royal. Françoise, the head waitress, was watching them through the window of Larivière et Leblanc. Victoire gave her a big smile, as if she were a friend she hadn't seen for years, and hurried into the store. She faced Françoise, unflinching and happy, and said in a very loud voice: "Three butterscotch sundaes please!"

"Thérèse, that's a nice name. I don't hear it very often." "Yes. My mother used to read a lot of French novels before she got married and she decided if she ever had a daughter, she'd call her Thérèse. I'm the only Thérèse in grade six at my school and there's three classes of thirty-one pupils!" Thérèse was comfortably settled on the big green wooden bench, her feet barely touching the ground. Gérard Bleau, the playground attendant, rolled cigarette after cigarette, frowning when it was time to strike a match, as if this were a difficult task requiring concentration almost beyond his capacity. "There's three Jeannines, just in my class. And two Claires. Claire Côté and Claire Thivierge. There used to be four Denises, but one of them left because her mother needed her to take care of her new baby brother." "What about your little brother? How come he's like that?" Captivated by the beauty of the young man's face and by the hunt from which she had emerged victorious, an inevitable victory that delivered her victim to her bound hand and foot, Thérèse had forgotten Philippe and Marcel for a good half-hour, so she was a little startled by the attendant's question. She looked towards the ladders where she had left her brother and cousin. "Don't go looking for them. They're under a tree. For a kid with St. Vitus' Dance, I'd say your brother calms down pretty fast when he sits down! The minute he was under that tree, he stopped twisting and turning—just like that! And he stopped shaking all of a sudden too. Is he always that way?" Thérèse wondered if the attendant was laughing at her, if he'd already seen through their little game, but there was no irony in Gérard Bleau's grey eyes: they were innocent, pure, wide open—and yet, astonishingly empty. "I guess he isn't too bright." Before she spoke, Thérèse coughed nervously to conceal her emotion. Really, he looked better and better. "No, he isn't like that all the time. Depends on the day. He's tired today. Sometimes, he's a real pain in the neck and nobody can stand him, but today he isn't bad at all." Thérèse laughed. A chilly little laugh. "I say whatever comes into my mind." She had circled the attendant long enough before the attack. First, she pretended to be playing hide-and-seek with her brother and cousin, then hopscotch, but when she realized that Gérard wasn't paying attention to her, she started walking around the bench in ever smaller circles, never taking her eyes off the head of the young man who went on smoking, unaware of her presence, glancing absentmindedly every now and then at the few little girls on the playground. "I'm a big spider. A big black spider with hairy legs and scissors for a mouth! And a great big fly just got caught in my web! Mmmmm. . . . Now, let's go up to that fly nice and slow. We don't want to scare him right away. . . . And when he finally sees me, it'll be too late. . . . I'll throw myself on top of him and eat him in one bite. . . . No, no, maybe I'll take my time instead." When she walked behind the attendant, she felt a pang in her heart and her breathing became faster. "My Lord, he's gorgeous!" He had unfastened the two top buttons of his shirt, revealing a scrawny chest adorned with a bit of fuzz. "Just like a movie star!" Once, he looked at her. Smiled. Thérèse immediately looked down and turned her head away. She'd often been told never to stare at men, that it might put ideas in their heads. "Ideas?" For the moment, she was the one who had the ideas. . . . "I'm a mother cat that's just had babies and he's a mouse that wants to eat them up. . . . Here, mousie. Just try and touch them, you mean rotten mouse. . ." But it was she who approached him, spider-cat, with confused desires, uninformed foolhardy little girl, for whom men were beautiful objects whom you parade around and show off, then put away when you don't want them any more. "When I'm finished with you, your own mother won't recognize you!" She thought of her own mother for a few seconds: her mother bending over her, scrubbing her mouth with a soapy washcloth. "I'll tell you when you're ready to wear lipstick! Eleven years old! Next thing we know, you'll be asking for high-heeled shoes and nylons! Do you want the men to run after you like a chippie?" But she refused to explain what a chippie was. "If I tell you that, I'll have to tell you other things and I'm not in the mood." But the memory of her mother vanished when Gérard Bleau slipped his hand inside his shirt to scratch his chest. "I wish he'd take his shirt off!" Amazed at this thought, Thérèse came to a stop. "I wonder why?" No reply occurred to her. She just wanted him to take off his shirt. But her desire troubled her deeply and she was unable to resume the hunt. "It isn't just that. There must be something else." Suddenly, she saw herself in Gérard Bleau's arms, her mouth almost glued to his, like in the Ipana toothpaste ad that she'd cut out of one of her uncle Edouard's English magazines, the ad that showed a man and woman with their arms around each other, just about to kiss... "So that's it!" In two seconds, she'd crossed the ground separating her from the handsome attendant, sat on the bench facing the one where Gérard Bleau sat calmly smoking, and asked point blank: "What kind of toothpaste do you use?" The hunt was over. She knew what she wanted. She saw in Gérard Bleau's astonished expression a hint of fear that flattered her. He replied: "Pepsodent," without laughing, and she said, "Ipana," her ulterior motive as big as a house. That was when he asked her name. And she was proud to tell him. And then, they were off. "He wasn't born like that, you know.... He fell from the second floor when he was little .... He didn't get hurt, but it did that to him..." Anything at all. Just as long as the conversation went on. But how could she bring him into it, guide him along that mysterious road of which she knew absolutely nothing? What made a man want to kiss a woman? A woman?

Thérèse saw her mother again. "You haven't got any problems. You're just a little girl. Enjoy it! And stay that way as long as you can. You don't know how lucky you are!" Lucky! She cursed the "luck" that made her powerless, ignorant, completely disarmed and bereft in the face of a desire that she didn't understand, a new desire that, against her will, made her heart pound, a hunger that she didn't know how to appease, an unfamiliar thirst that frightened her, but fascinated her too. "Why don't you want to play with the others?" Suddenly, an insult. A kick. As usual: Go and play. Don't bug the grown-ups. Play with your dollies. Look after the baby. You're too young to be here. "They're asleep. . ." Gérard Bleau threw his cigarette butt to the ground and stepped on it. "They'll have to wake up some time!" Something about this clinging little girl was starting to get on his nerves, but he didn't know what. Her insistent gaze, perhaps, her piercing eyes. Yes, that was it. Her eyes. He was surprised to find himself buttoning his shirt again. The way she stared at him. As though he were a mannequin in a store window. A toy. He felt like a toy. Unconsciously, he picked up his tobacco pouch. He was trembling a little. "I told you to go and play!" He had raised his voice without realizing it. She frightened him. He was afraid of this little girl of — what? — ten, eleven? He shrugged. Just then, Thérèse leaped up, grinning. "Today's my birthday! I'm twelve years old!" "Oh yes? Happy Birthday." "Usually when it's somebody's birthday, you give them a kiss!" Without waiting for him to reply, Thérèse took two steps and stood between the attendant's knees. He moved his head back a little. "Let's have a little kiss." She bent over, serious now, and kissed him on the mouth. It was very brief, but Gérard felt the beginning of profound anguish; more than that, he felt fear, the real thing, mixed with guilt and remorse, total panic, as if he'd just committed some irrevocable act that cut his life into two distinct parts: the part before the little girl and the part after. But *he* wasn't the one who had committed the act! It was the girl! *She* had kissed him! It was not him! He was innocent! His erection surprised him in the midst of his terror and he bent double as Thérèse ran away. "I'm such a dope! My birthday! A birthday kiss doesn't count! It isn't a real kiss!" She'd have to start all over again.

He'd taken refuge under a balcony, any balcony at all, the closest one, he'd slipped into the first dark hole he saw, he'd lain on his side, shaken by spasms, his gouged eye dripping onto his muzzle. He didn't even have the strength to lick his wounds. He took short breaths because of his broken ribs. He didn't understand. He couldn't accept it. All this pain. This useless suffering. Gratuitous. Godbout had seized him in his jaws and shaken him like some ugly old rag, then thrown him up in the air and jumped on him. First, Duplessis tried to explain that he only wanted to walk past, that was all, that he had business in Parc Lafontaine, that he didn't feel like walking around the whole neighbourhood...but Godbout kept a jealous eye on his territory and never, never would he let Duplessis past. "I took over your area because you were too gutless to hold onto it, so tough titty, Kitty! You've got no business here! Scat! Shoo! The south side of Mont-Royal doesn't belong to you any more, so you can take de la Roche or de Lorimier if you want to get to Parc Lafontaine. I don't want to smell your piss on one of my posts or on my hydrants! Because I wouldn't put it past you to start marking out your territory behind my back. I know you, I've been keeping an eye on you for months, whenever you put on one of your scenes in the neighbourhood! I can see you sniffing around your old tracks and hanging out around your favourite spots. . . . And don't think you're going to come up on me from behind and chase me out of here like some vulgar beggar. Oh no! This is my territory now and I'm staying! J'y suis, j'y reste!" The confrontation that followed was inevitable. But Duplessis didn't hold his own at all. At first, he was surprised by Godbout's aggressiveness: the dog had no reason in the world to be annoyed with him; on the contrary, he'd beaten him to a pulp only a few months before, so now he was master of a neighbourhood rich in restaurants and well supplied with garbage cans. . . . But then, Duplessis told himself that it was normal for Godbout to be afraid of him still. "He knows very well that I'd never give up for good. That I'm getting ready for a comeback. He's no fool. In his place, I'd do the same." And Duplessis moved clumsily. Godbout went through the motions of biting him (a warning), but Duplessis clawed him in earnest. And that was what started everything. A mistake. As soon as he felt the blood on his muzzle, Godbout went wild with rage and the carnage began. Duplessis was a strong cat though, and aggressive too when he had to be, alert, lively and agile, but Godbout's obstinate anger went beyond the bounds of caution and common sense and the cat could see in the dog's eyes that for one of them this battle would be the final one. But Duplessis wasn't in the mood. Not today. He defended himself, of course, but his heart wasn't in it. Right in the middle of the mêlée, when he was clinging to one of Godbout's ears while the dog shook his head in every direction, trying to dislodge him, the cat mentally shrank back. For a moment, he saw the scene from the outside, completely detached, and the absurdity of the situation hit him in the face: a flea-bitten cat and a mangy dog fighting over a right-of-way — how silly! While a little boy who was madly in love with him was waiting at Parc Lafontaine, he was demeaning himself in this squabble with a narrow-minded brute who'd sell his mother (or kill her) for a chicken bone, which would then get stuck in his throat. He let go, landed on his paws, hesitated briefly (what he really wanted to do was run away and too bad about his reputation. Love is more important) — and that was fatal. Godbout sprang to his throat, clipping his eye on the way so that it burst like a grape, and Duplessis felt the shadow of fear pass over his soul. Duplessis jumped with pain and meowed to signal that death was near. "Die! Die rather than suffer like this!" Godbout lay down on the other side of the garden fence where Duplessis had taken refuge, watching the cat as he licked his blood-reddened claws. "At least you could let me die in peace." "No, I want to be good and sure that you're dead. I want to be the first one to announce it." "If the gate wasn't closed, would you come and finish me off?" "No. Anyhow, I could jump over it. I'd rather watch you die nice and slow, nice and easy. And enjoy every minute of it." "You hate me that much?" "Yes." And Duplessis knew that Godbout would start howling the moment he was dead. That he'd howl the news of his final victory, his irrevocable dominion. That people would come out on their balconies and say: "Somebody just died. I hope it's nobody we know!" and eventually, a child would shout: "Doesn't matter. It's just a cat. I can see it. He's under the balcony..." Just a cat. A foolhardy cat. A cat in love who, without really feeling anything, had just spent two whole nights paying honour to a crazy lady cat who was fulfilled now. Detached. A cat who had detached himself from that hygienic act just as he'd detached himself from this mortal battle. He stretched his head a little so that it jutted out from under the balcony. "If the little boy that smells of dried peepee comes by, my life, my love, my heart's delight, at least I'll see him before I die."

"You really think I'm too hard on Marcel?" In the middle of her Saturday afternoon dusting, Albertine had stopped in front of the open door to the fat woman's bedroom; the latter had invited her in. Albertine sat on the foot of the bed, as did all the visitors who came to see Gabriel's wife. Legs squeezed together, duster on her lap, she didn't dare look her sister-in-law in the eye. The sounds of Gabriel and his wife making love were still too present in her memory, too fresh, so if she looked the fat woman in the eye, the latter might be able to read there envy, disgust, contempt, respect — too many feelings all jumbled together, hesitant, shaky, all different. The fat woman waited for Albertine to speak first. She felt one of her sister-in-law's rare confidences coming on, a confession as brief as it was sudden, that Albertine would let drop in the most incongruous places and at the most unexpected times: over the stove on Christmas Eve as they were making doughnuts; coming out of Mass one July morning when everyone else was in raptures over the beautiful summer day; or once, when she was bringing the mail to her room on a pleasant morning when it seemed nothing in particular was going to happen. . . . Brief, choppy sentences; voice low, a murmur. Everything expressed in fifteen secods — with no warning at the beginning or at the end. This time, though, only one question came out. The fat woman waited two long minutes before she replied. Just in case. Then, realizing nothing else was

147

coming, she leaned a little to the right so that she could take her sister-in-law's hand. Albertine had anticipated her gesture though and avoided it by placing her hands on either side of her on the bed. And the fat woman found herself holding a dirty rag. She picked it up, squared her shoulders and began dusting the arm of her chair, the place where she always rested her elbow, where there was never any dust. "Why are you asking me that out of the blue?" Albertine then told the fat woman of her conversation with Thérèse the night before. And her promise to try in the future to be nicer to her youngest child. The fat woman smiled. Albertine sighed. "I don't think I'm all that mean." The fat woman answered with another question. "Bartine. . .do you really think I'm too old and fat to have another baby?" Albertine jumped as if someone had pricked her. Then she looked her sister-in-law in the eye and everything came tumbling out so fast and with such force that even when she'd finished her voice still rang in the fat woman's ears. "Yes! Yes, I think you are! Yes, you're too fat! And too old! You know what people out on the street say about you? Eh? They say you're filthy! They say only somebody really filthy would want a baby after forty! They say when a woman gets to forty, it's time for her to rest! That it's too late to start washing diapers and bringing up children! And I think so too! When that kid starts to school, you'll be fifty! When other women are fifty, they're grandmothers, dammit! And do you want to know what you'll look like when you start to take him out? Like his grandmother, that's what! His grandmother! People will tell you: 'You look young for a grandmother! And you'll have to tell them: 'I'm not a young grandmother. I'm an old mother!' You can't wait, eh, you just can't wait! People will point at you and it'll be your own fault! And if you keep on. . .if you don't stop. . . . Anyway, if you go on doing what you did this afternoon, on top of everything else, you'll be having even more! Lord Almighty, do you really want to rip your belly apart like that till you're fifty? And on top of it all, another baby in the house will make too many people. It'll drive us all crazy. And if it takes you a long time to get over having it, who'll be stuck with it, eh? Me, that's who! I'm the one that'll wipe his behind and wash his diapers! But did you ever ask me what I thought when you decided to have that baby, you and your handsome Gabriel? Eh? Oh, it's fine to have babies, but you have to be able to take care of them. And let me tell you, I'm nobody's servant. Ever since you've been stuck in here, I've done everything in this house. But don't think for one minute that I enjoy it. Besides wiping up after the whole house, I have to clean you up too, just like a baby!" Albertine got to her feet as she spoke. She bent over her sister-in-law, who had looked away from her. She stopped speaking as abruptly as she'd begun. The good smell of homemade soup was beginning to drift through the house. The clock in the dining room sounded five o'clock. The fat woman shut her eyes. Albertine picked up her duster. "If you feel ashamed of yourself, just try and imagine how the rest of us feel when we go out on the street!" The fat woman opened her eyes again. "You just answered your own question, Bartine. About Marcel. And everything else."

Germaine Lauzon burst into the house of her sister, Gabrielle Jodoin, just as Roger Baulu was announcing on the radio that the time was five o'clock and that the news would follow. "Five, already? Well, I won't stay long. I've got the supper to get ready and Arnest doesn't like to wait." Germaine Lauzon gave her brother-in-law a big

149

smile. "Bonjour, you good-looking bugger! Off work today?" Mastaï Jodoin was whistling as he peeled his third
potato. "I was done at 4:07 today and I don't go back till
5:18 Monday morning." "You drive me nuts with your
hours and your streetcars! Why can't you start at eight
and finish at six like everybody else?" "If we started and
finished at the same time as everybody else, how do you
think they'd get to work, dingbat?" Gabrielle Jodoin took
the potatoes, ran them under the tap and tossed them into
a pot. "Now, don't start tearing each other to shreds, you
two, or there'll be no end to it!" Germaine sat at the end of
the table, puffing. She was much fatter than her sisters,
Gabrielle Jodoin and Rose Ouimet, and her pregnancy
(eight months gone, like them) was giving her some trouble. "I'm going to have a little sit, otherwise, I'll bust!" She
patted her belly, trying to put to sleep the child who had
just kicked her so hard that she could feel it. "I can't do a
thing any more. I get out of breath right away. I'll tell
you, I just went over to Souci's for a quart of milk and I
feel as if I'd been running for two hours! And I wasted my
breath anyway because they were out of milk..."
Gabrielle opened a cupboard. "Anyhow, I hope you didn't
come here looking for sugar! I'm right out! It's hard to put
your hands on any these days." She took down two soup
bowls, two spoons and the salt and pepper. Germaine
shrugged and ran her hand over her brow. "You think I
just come here to borrow things?" "Want some soup? The
rest won't be ready for an hour, but Mastaï's hungry."
"Oh, why not? A little soup before supper never did any
harm!" Gabrielle took down a third soup bowl and placed
it in front of her sister. "What kind is it?" "The soup?
Barley." Mastaï was rolling himself a cigarette now. He
spoke gently, evenly, as though nothing were happening. "I'm taking your sister to the theatre tonight." A
small bomb. He was sure of his effect and watched his

sister-in-law react, a mocking smile coming to the corner of his mouth. Germaine stiffened and turned first red, then white. The theatre was her great passion (throughout her childhood, she told anyone who would listen that, some day, she'd be going to Hollywood or Paris, that she'd be a great actress. . . the drama of a child with no imagination, whom everyone finally tired of, and whom the family nicknamed "The Actress," a nickname that stuck, that she detested now like some shameful sin or a birthmark), but her husband Ernest Lauzon, a mechanic at Canadair, a young man completely bereft of fantasy, whose sense of humour consisted of looking at the comics in the weekend papers with an imperturbably serious expression, some-times murmuring: "I don't get it!" or: "That's dumb!" that drove Germaine absolutely mad with rage (she liked the comics too). Ernest Lauzon, then, forbade his wife to go to the theatre on the pretext that it would get her too worked up and put ideas in her head. What ideas, he would have found it hard to say as, to him, the very word "idea" represented mysterious needs that he didn't know, wasn't interested in and never thought about. The only thing he knew was that when Germaine came back from the theatre, she looked right through him, glassy-eyed with joy, as though he didn't exist. He'd once confided to his brother-in-law, Mastaï Jodoin: "When she comes home, she talks about Jacques Auger as if he was the good Lord in person and she talks about Albert Duquesne as if they'd made a date to meet in the back yard at midnight the next day! I can't get over it! We only been married two years and I'm sure as hell not going to let her spend her nights dreaming about Albert Duquesne! She says he's got a beautiful voice! Why shouldn't he? He hasn't got anything better to do!" Germaine plunged the spoon into her soup without a word. Mastaï put down his cigarette, which he would smoke later between the soup

151

and the rest of the meal. "I'm taking her to the National. La Poune's playing. And Juliette Pétrie." Germaine blew on her soup, making as much noise as she could when she swallowed so that she wouldn't hear her brother-in-law, then she added a little salt. "Good soup. Barley's good. But Christ, it's hot!" And Mastaï slurped too as he ate his first spoonful. "There's two shows. Six hours altogether." Gabrielle Jodoin looked at each of them in turn, her husband whom she loved so much, her reason for living, and her fat sister whom she'd got to know better since they'd both become pregnant (Germaine and Gabrielle had grown much closer in the past seven months, while their sister Rose, who was pregnant as well, had withdrawn into herself, hiding away in her house and using every means to conceal her pregnancy) and she felt that twinge of jealousy that she experienced when they got on each other's nerves, like children, something that happened often; it wormed its way into her, making a hole, a void, in place of her heart. "They fight and pick on each other just like an old married couple! I'm the one that seems like the sister-in-law when they get together!" Germaine still acted as though Mastaï had said nothing and went on eating her soup. Only a slight trembling in her hand, which she tried in vain to repress, bore witness to the furor inside her. In fact, she wanted to claw her brother-in-law, cut him into bits and stamp on the pieces. "He knows that pisses me off! So why doesn't he cut it out?" But Mastaï kept his trump card till the end, as always. (He had a way of setting up tricks and a sense of timing that made him a peerless storyteller and a player who was highly skilled, to say the least: when you least expected it, when you thought everything was over, when you thought that you could finally laugh at his joke or submit to other people's mockery, he was always there with something unexpected that was even more hilarious or infuriating. "I bought tickets for you and Arnest too, but then I remembered your lord and master doesn't like the theatre, so I gave them to a bum that was walking past the National. He was real glad. He even promised to give himself a wash before he went to the theatre, so we wouldn't get sick to our stomach. It would've been dumb to waste good tickets like that, know what I mean? Best seats in the house!" Germaine Lauzon slowly put her spoon in her soup bowl. "I was coming to ask you over to play cards tonight. Rose and her husband will be there. And Momma's coming too — with Pierrette. If you feel like it. . . . You just have to walk across the street. Thanks a lot for the soup." She got up and walked down the hallway, as her brother-in-law roared with laughter. Gabrielle followed her sister to the front door. "Maybe we'll come, Germaine, but I don't know for sure. If we aren't there by eight, it means we won't be coming." The door closed softly. Neither Mastaï nor Gabrielle saw the tears on Germaine's fat cheeks, but Gabrielle knew they were there.

"Why do you think we all voted 'No' in the plebiscite last week? Because we all got a yellow streak? Well, we haven't! But we don't want to go and get killed in a war that's got nothing to do with us!" A dozen men were sitting around Gabriel as they did every Saturday afternoon — labourers, retired men and even a few rubbies who came to finish off the day in the tavern, knowing very well they'd have to listen to what they called, among themselves, "Gabriel's sermon," the inevitable political harangue that the fat woman's husband launched into right after his eighth or ninth beer, which could last until very late at night if the speaker was in top form and his audience was attentive. Gabriel had earned the affection and respect of all the establishment's clients because of these speeches, which were always naïve, but expressed perfectly well the preoccupations that got Quebeckers worked up in these days of insecurity, hesitations and questioning. His influence was even beginning to take on a certain importance without his realizing it, the men often waiting to know what he thought about some social or political question before they expressed their own opinions. He had even, to a large measure, been responsible for the official "No" with which all the men in the neighbourhood had answered Mackenzie King's plebiscite. "If Canada wants to give England a hand, it's their funeral! But I don't want to murder people and lose my limbs for a country that never did nothing for me!" The men applauded. But Willy Ouellette, still sitting across from his friend, didn't know what to think. "Isn't that right, Willy?" Willy Ouellette seemed to be dozing in his chair, holding his mouth-organ. His thinking wasn't clear, far from it, but something was nagging at him. "I just think . . ." He ran his sleeve across his mouth where there was still a little foam from his beer. "I just think it's too bad about France. If you ask me, we gotta save France . . . our mother country . . . our roots . . ." Gabriel got to his feet and came and stood before Willy Ouellette, who moved back in shock. "France! France abandoned us! France sold us down the river! Save France so it can go on shitting in our faces afterwards and laugh at the way we talk and think they're better than us!" Without really knowing why, Willy Ouellette decided to stand up to Gabriel, perhaps so as not to lose face; perhaps too, because, in his heart of hearts, a small fleur-de-lys flag was still feebly waving. "I think you're laying it on a little thick there, Gabriel! Just because France dropped us a few hundred years ago, doesn't mean we should let her die at the hands of the Nazis!" "It's no reason to go and die for her either! I don't want to die for France and I don't want to die for Canada either! And I sure as hell don't want to die for England! So why should I go? Can you tell me? Can you see yourself fighting in the middle of a bunch of Englishmen and Frenchmen from France that always turned up their noses at you, against a bunch of Germans, squareheads that never did nothing to you?" "If we leave the Germans alone, they'll invade the whole place, even over here, and turn us into atheists and pagans!" "That isn't true! The Pope in Rome, what side do you think he's on, eh? He's on Mussolini's side — and Hitler's!" "Now Gabriel, don't tell me you're on Hitler's side, and Mussolini's too!" "Of course not, I didn't say that. . . . I'm no Fascist. . ." Gabriel would soon be out of his depth, he was well aware of it, but he couldn't find a way to get back on his feet. And in addition, this was the first time anyone had dared stand up to him. He pounded the table with his fist, a gesture that was usually effective and final, but this time, amazingly, it left no echo. "I'm not going to go and die for nothing, for some country that's always made fun of me!" "Maybe it's better to die for nothing, like a man, Gabriel, than have everybody think you're yellow-bellied for the rest of your life. . ." Gabriel paused, the first pause since the argument had started. Willy Ouellette took advantage of the pause to rise. "One thing for sure, we're all going to look like a bunch of goddamn cowards! You think Canada's going to believe the only reason we don't want to go to war is because we think it's none of our business? Don't kid yourselves! The Province of Quebec's the only part of Canada that voted 'No'! All the others said 'Yes' except us! So now they've got another good chance to laugh in our faces. They're already saying we make babies just so we won't have to fight, because men

155

with families don't have to go—and now, we come right out and refuse to pass a law to make all able-bodied men go and fight for England!" "They promised us we'd never have to fight for England!" "Sure they did, but then they changed their minds. What do you expect? It's them. It's the government that's in charge! And we're the only ones that voted 'No,' so now we'll have to go and fight anyway." Gabriel suddenly sat down again. The roles had been reversed without anyone wishing it. Willy Ouellette hadn't wanted to take the wind out of Gabriel's sails. He didn't know where his arguments had come from; he hadn't even looked for them or thought them out. There he was, suddenly, almost the winner of the argument, facing a Gabriel he didn't recognize, who seemed to want to run away, step back, give in. A painful silence fell over the tavern. Gabriel picked up the last beer on the table and drained it in one gulp. Then, the decisive question, the coup de grâce, came from Ti-Paul Boudreau, the waiter: "I hear your wife's expecting, eh Gabriel?" Gabriel leaped to his feet and the words poured from his mouth, distorted by emotion, disfigured, hoarse, broken. Pleading. "I didn't get my wife pregnant so I wouldn't have to join up! Please, don't think I did that! I got her pregnant ...because I love her...and she wanted another baby!" Gabriel retreated before his obviously incredulous audience and ran away like a beaten dog. The saddest, most confused man in the whole matter was Willy Ouellette who, without wanting to, had just humiliated the greatest tavern orator in the neighbourhood, his new friend, and sown doubt—that sore, that incurable wound—in the hearts of his brothers.

Violette had been back at work for several minutes: purl one, knit one, green yarn, blue yarn — or yellow, or pink — glance down at the street between two booties or sip some cold tea, but something about her behaviour had changed. Her hands weren't so agile. She wielded the needles with some uncertainty and most of all, the booties that she was knitting were really too small now. They were ridiculous balls of wool with no precise shape that wouldn't fit the foot of any baby, no matter how puny. Florence saw all this, but said nothing. She would have to wait until night, until bedtime, when it was completely dark, with only the blind eye of the moon as witness, before she spoke. . . . Only then could she sit by her daughter's bed and tell her. Everything. Explain? No. Tell. Victoire's family. The generations, the waves of individuals, clans, relatives, the prolific love-matches between blood relatives, the barren marriages of convenience, the new branches, the dead ones that needn't be cut off because they fell off the tree by themselves, Victoire's great-great-grandfather, Thomas-le-Fun, who had fought against the Americans, thereby gaining a wooden leg on which he had carved the words: "Sacrificed at Saint-Denis," his son, Gaby-Gaby, who never stopped growing and who finally died from it, his bones bursting, disjointed, his daughter, Nénette, who had twenty-seven children in twenty-seven years and died giving birth to her last daughter, Victoire's grandmother, cursing her husband, her fate, her curé, her body, and the role of generative servant that was reserved for women, a saint who was refused the last rites and who hadn't been buried in consecrated ground, a witch who dared speak out, a cursed woman who had spattered the village with her imprecations until the curé himself threw himself at the feet of his bishop, exclaiming: "Come and wash the sky of my village, Monseigneur. The sun's gone away and it's black everywhere!" and Victoire herself, yes, she'd tell her about Victoire, about her youth, about her loves (especially Josaphat-le-Violon, her brother, the one great passion in her life), about how she'd been torn apart, heartsick, when she had to move to Montreal to follow the man she didn't love, but who adored her, Télesphore, so gentle but so soft, and her life as a recluse on the second floor of the house on la rue Fabre—and finally, about themselves: Florence, Rose, Violette, Mauve, who had followed beside it all, straddling the generations, perpetually tending and knitting, hidden watchers, surveying and looking on, united, protecting cradles from afar, counting the births, but not the deaths—and happy? Happy. They, who patiently knit up time. They, who watched over Victoire's family from the very beginning and would watch over it until it was extinguished. Why? What did it matter? She might even, perhaps, tell Violette the future: the fat woman's multiple child, all the simultaneous births on la rue Fabre: Rose Ouimet, Gabrielle Jodoin, Germaine Lauzon, Claire Lemieux, and that other birth, to Marie-Louise Brassard, who hovered behind the lace curtain in her living room, wild with fear, who thought her first child would come out her navel. But Florence thought, she'd keep that all for herself. To put Violette to sleep, she would tell of the past. She would keep the future for herself. What was the good of telling everything? Knitting as she went along, keeping her eyes open, offering no interpretations, rejoicing or suffering with Victoire, with Gabriel, with Albertine, with Edouard—and later, much later, recreating it all with the boy-girl child who would be born to the fat woman, suffering with him, taking refuge in sounds and images, reliving his family's past, for fear of seeing it extinguished by general indifference—this was their lot, the lot of Florence, Rose, Violette and Mauve. But predictions?

No. And yet, Florence knew everything that would happen — or almost — but she refused to consult it. Wait. Watch. Knit. Baby booties to perpetuate the line. Violette burst out laughing, a harsh laugh, nervous, and bringing her hands to her mouth, she dropped her knitting. "Momma, I closed up my last bootie! I was daydreaming and I knit it shut. . . . I knit a perfect circle!" Florence took the circle in her right hand and dropped it into her apron pocket. "Go get supper ready, Violette. I'll take your place." "It isn't my turn." "Go make supper."

Marie-Louise Brassard had gone into hiding behind the lace curtain in her living room. Throughout her pregnancy, for seven months, as long as a tunnel where nothing moves, where everything is frozen, hollowed out in the midst of the void, leading to nothing but fear, Marie-Louise had taken refuge at her window, as though seeking help there. Sometimes she stood, but most of the time, she sat on a straight-back chair that she brought from the kitchen and placed sideways, the seat and the chairback grazing the lace, while she sat, always bored, except when she was afraid. She took her place at the window every morning with a cup of tea in her hand. Her body faced the wall where a huge crucifix reigned between two electric vigil lights, but her head was always turned towards the outside, towards life. She rarely moved and she let her tea get cold on her lap, occasionally bringing the cup to her lips, an automatic movement performed almost in spite of herself. Sometimes she turned her head towards the living room, but then she would quickly look back at the street again. She had hung a curtain between herself and life and she watched life from

159

between the cotton flowers. Unlike Marie-Sylvia, who spied and interpreted every movement on the street, Marie-Louise Brassard was content just to take note of everything—the gestures of the passersby, the way the light changed when a cloud passed over, even the sound of an occasional car—but she never recorded a thing. All was forgotten as soon as it passed. At noon, she got up, went to the kitchen and ate a devilled ham sandwich or a fried egg, then came back to sit behind her curtain for the rest of the afternoon. When the baby kicked, as it did more and more often now, Marie-Louise would stare in fright, wondering if her time had come. Every time. Because Marie-Louise Brassard, perfect product of the ignorance and intolerance of a rural society that imposed silence where explanations were vital, a society that fostered envy, hypocrisy and guilt as three essential virtues, and that, most of all, considered sexuality a necessary evil (not simply a sin, but *the* sin, the sole and ultimate one, to which women must submit in order to assure progeny for the race), was lost in fear of her child. No one had ever told her anything about sexuality, she, who, on her wedding day, still thought babies were delivered by the Indians from Caughnawaga, had been not surprised, but horrified when Doctor Sanregret, whom she'd gone to see about her nausea and stomach aches early in her pregnancy, told her she was "carrying" a child, a child that would be born early in the summer. She hadn't dared ask any questions, as her mother had told her that one doesn't ask questions, ever, about anything between the belly-button and the knees, but, by sitting on her chair and thinking things over, by frightening herself and questioning her ignorant body, by muttering bits of conversation that she'd overheard at home when she was little and too young to understand, she finally reached the conclusion that her baby would come out through her navel. All her terror, then, was concentrated there, in the middle of her body, and when her child struck out with its little feet to remind its mother that it was there, alive and happily preparing for its arrival in the world, she thought, every time, that the doctor had lied to her, that the little devil would rip her belly apart before summer. There were drops of sweat on her forehead, her breathing became jerky, choppy. She was overcome by fear. Often, she would put both hands over her navel, as if to plug it, and she would croon, bent over: "Go away, go away, you bloody nuisance. Your mother doesn't want you and your father's out of his mind." Léopold Brassard, like Gabriel, worked nights and slept during the day. In fact, they both worked in the same shop (Gabriel was a pressman, Léopold a linotypist), but they never spoke, merely greeted one another with a timid "Bonjour!" when they punched in together or at the beginning of their half-hour lunch break at ten o'clock at night. If they left for work at the same time, each would keep to his own side of the street, parallel roads that refused to cross. They avoided looking at one another at the corner of Fabre and Mont-Royal and never sat together in the streetcar.... And when Léopold came home from work around two in the morning, he never went to bed. He would wander through the house, reading the comics, making something to eat, big meals (excellent, as a matter of fact; he was a better cook than his wife and it was he who prepared their food at night), which he ate as he watched the day break. Then, he would wait for his wife to get up before going to bed. They had never been able to get used to each other. Léopold was as ignorant as Marie-Louise and when this large snivelling person that he didn't know what to do with arrived in his bed, it had been the greatest humiliation of his life. They took turns, then, in the conjugal bed. His wife's enormous belly was as great a source of amazement and terror for Léopold as it was for Marie-Louise. The child was the fruit of their wedding night, the only night that they'd spent together, horrible, Léopold scarcely knowing what to do and doing it badly; Marie-Louise scared to death when that thing she'd always seen flaccid on her little brothers penetrated her and she didn't know why. She even went so far as to think Léopold wanted to piss inside her, because he was drunk and didn't know what he was doing. Léopold and Marie-Louise Brassard moved to Montreal immediately after their honeymoon (a weekend in Quebec City, during which he hadn't once been sober and she hadn't once stopped crying), because Léopold got a job at the Laprairie printshop on rue Sainte-Catherine. Marie-Louise was cut off from her village and transplanted onto this foreign street where she knew she'd never put down roots. And like a poorly tended plant, Marie-Louise was dying at her window — from boredom and from fear. In the midst of a maelstrom of passion, joy, cries, jokes, weeping and laughter from the street, she was totally motionless. La rue Fabre was stifling her like an asphalt cloak.

At the hour when the sun was beginning its slow descent over the wealthy neighbourhoods, Parc Lafontaine began to look like a forest at dusk. The shadows grew longer, creeping onto the lawns where now, in early May, there grew only frightful little signs that read: "Keep off the grass," while the squirrels, less timid, came out of their hiding places and frisked about, chattering wildly; and hydrangeas, like bouquets, formed darker spots in the shadows of the trees. The air was cooler, rather damp, and everything was covered by a weighty calm. It was as though nature was waiting, as though something important was about to happen. In the slanting rays of the setting sun, everything seemed to be in profile. Béatrice too. She was leaning over the railing, standing in the middle of the bridge that joined the two artificial lakes which hadn't yet been filled with water and looked like garbage dumps, they were so full of greasy papers and beer bottles. It was the first time she had seen the lakes empty and it made her sad. "People are pigs! When will they learn not to dump their garbage wherever they happen to be standing?" She would have preferred not to know that the lakes were artificial, holes that had been dug and filled with cement, basins that had to be drained of their water in the fall and their garbage in the spring, and that the fountain in the middle of the smaller lake was filled with cracks, split open, on the verge of being no longer usable. In summertime, on splendid silky nights, the lake, crowned with its fountain that changed colours every thirty seconds, was magical. Everything in the park was beautiful, easy, perfect. But, on this late afternoon, in the golden light of a sun whose journey was coming to an end, its ugliness was hard to bear. "When you look on the other side of the lake, it's as pretty as a picture and you'd think you were in the middle of the woods, all by yourself and happy, free, but then, you look down and that dump hits you in the eye and you know there's no hope." Béatrice had given up any hope of finding Mercedes in Parc Lafontaine. She didn't know where to go. Above all, she didn't want to return to the apartment on la rue Fabre. "I'm flat broke. I haven't got a place to sleep. I mean, I've got one, but I'm scared to go there. All I've got is what's between my legs. It's all I've ever had." She thought that she'd combed the park, but she'd gone right past Mercedes and Richard four or five times without seeing them, perhaps hearing bits of Richard's confession, but unable to imagine that those sobs, that breaking voice, the moans and whispers that she heard, were addressed to her friend whom she could more readily picture in the arms of a client on the verge of apoplexy than bending piously over the suffering of a little boy. She had gone up and down all the paths in the park, all the alleys. She'd seen timid lovers looking down as their hands brushed — and bolder lovers coming out of the bushes, scratched and pink with guilty pleasure. She'd seen pale old men smile at the sun and even greet it, and children playing noisily in the playground. She'd seen a young girl kiss a man on the mouth (her father? the park attendant?) and two little boys fast asleep, neighbours from la rue Fabre, under a tree, arms wound lovingly around one another, breaths mingled, calm, serene, abandoned. But not a sign of Mercedes. Nor of any clients either. She lay in the shadow of a maple tree for an hour or so, just thinking. Had the three soldiers kidnapped Mercedes, killed her? Or had the police finally come and raided them (they'd been expecting it for so long)? Who sent the note that she'd found under her door? And what would become of her? Where could she go? Back to her aunt, Ti-Lou, to tell her everything? In the end, all these questions put her to sleep. She dreamed that she was putting on a show in the big hall and that she was on stage, stark naked, but pretending not to take notice of it and going on with her performance in the midst of the mocking laughter and jeers of a jubilant audience. She awakened soaking wet, lying in the sunlight, exhausted, as if she had just spent one of those agitated nights that are more tiring than restful, so she decided to come and watch the sun die behind the trees in the park. "There's a time for everything. Like Grandma used to say. 'Nothing's as important as the only free show the good Lord puts on for us. If you've got any problems when the sun goes down, just forget about them and let yourself go over the orgy of colours your Creator gives you every night. It cheers you up and cleans you out and purifies your soul!' The old witch was right too. Sunset is like a knife that slices the day right in two! When you look at it, you aren't either happy or unhappy. You're just small." She waited anxiously for the moment (in one hour? two?) when, for a short time, she'd no longer feel anything, neither fear nor sorrow, nor concern, nor that sense of destitution in the face of a problem that wasn't really all that complicated, but which disarmed her because she didn't understand it. Leaning against one of the artificial cement tree trunks that served as armrests for people crossing the bridge, made of imitation field stones (cement again), Béatrice began to hum.

Victoire finished her butterscotch sundae and wiped her mouth on the corner of her paper serviette. "Get a move on! We're going to Parc Lafontaine!" Edouard's ice cream almost went down the wrong way. "It's five o'clock, Momma!" Victoire had taken a dollar bill from her purse and carefully placed it on the counter, looking at Françoise. "We never eat before six-thirty, seven, on Saturday in the summer, so we've got all the time in the world for a little walk." "It isn't summer yet." Victoire looked at Edouard for the first time since they'd sat down at the counter. "If we miss supper, we miss supper, that's all! I haven't set foot outside the house for two years and I feel like taking a little walk in Parc Lafontaine! Can't you get that through your thick skull?" She drummed on the counter with her fingertips to attract the attention of

Françoise, who was chatting with a customer, leaning forward, her hands spread on the cold marble. Then Victoire turned back to her son, a glimmer of pity in her eye. "Don't worry, I'll walk faster and you'll be back in time for your soup. Now, don't tell me you'll be ready to eat again in half an hour!" Edouard looked at her, amazed at the change in her tone of voice. "Don't answer, Edouard. I can tell that you'd say yes and that's depressing." Françoise added up the bill and took the dollar from the counter, then she muttered, very low, just loud enough for Victoire to hear. "Look at that! She's paying her bill!" Victoire looked her straight in the eye without replying. The bill came to fifty cents. Françoise brought back the change in dimes, in the hope that Victoire would leave at least one of them as a tip. When she saw the five ten-cent pieces, Victoire smiled. "Could you change these for a fifty-cent piece please?" Françoise went back to the cash register muttering about customers who preferred their change in large denominations. "They think it looks better to take out a fifty-cent piece than a bunch of nickels and dimes. Cheapskates!" She brought the fifty-cent piece to Victoire, who immediately put it safely away in her change purse. The old woman hissed in Françoise's direction: "If she thinks she's getting one red cent from me, that one, she's sadly mistaken. If there's one thing I can't stand, it's waitresses that talk behind your back!" Edouard had noticed none of these goings-on, as he was busy scraping the last of the butterscotch from the bottom of his glass dish. Victoire tapped his arm and got up. "No use scraping the bottom, my boy. It's all gone!" Françoise stood, frozen by what Victoire had said. She would have liked to leap over the counter and snatch the ridiculous straw hat off the old witch's head, but lately her aggressiveness had been causing problems (she'd slapped one client who tried to untie her apron and told a

Madame from boulevard Saint-Joseph to fuck off when she claimed the rice pudding tasted burnt) and she swore she'd keep her head, no matter what — at least until the end of May. Edouard followed his mother, docile as a great flabby dog. Françoise followed the curious couple all the way down the counter, as far as the front window. "If it wasn't for this counter, she'd've been dead a long time ago, the fucking old bitch! That's right, drag your dimwit son around after you! I should've thought of it before that you two knew each other. You've got the same nose! Like a grotto! With no Blessed Virgin in it! No wonder their noses are turned up like that, they're always looking for shit!" Without knowing he was Ti'-Moteur's son, Françoise had never been very fond of Edouard. After all, he was the only man on la rue Mont-Royal who never flirted with her! All the men in the neighbourhood found the buxom waitress from Larivière et Leblanc a tempting morsel and not a day went by without one of them asking her for a date, or even for something more specific. Françoise fulminated and distributed slaps and insults, but deep down, she was very happy. When Edouard came in for lunch though, when he was still working for Giroux et Deslauriers, he never spoke to Françoise, except to order his meal. He didn't even look up at her. Finally, she felt an aversion to this obese individual who seemed to prefer fat food to women. But as he always left a generous tip, she never said anything nasty to him. Françoise watched Victoire and Edouard turn the corner, arm in arm, the old woman hobbling after the fat man, ridiculous in the get-up that, instead of making her look younger, made her appear even more worn-out, like someone from another age, a creaky, elderly phantom that gropes and gesticulates more than it shocks or scares; and the obese man, her son, standing beside her, stiff with shame, or with embarrassment at least, turning

167

his head away a little when she spoke to him, as though nothing she had to say concerned him or, even worse, as though he were nothing but a cub scout helping his first little old lady cross the street. Françoise folded her arms over her opulent bosom. "Wonder what her husband was like to make an elephant like that?" After this profound reflection, she turned away from the window, attempting to chase the two customers from her head with a wave of her hand. Françoise tended to settle everything in her life this way: her difficulties in love, as well as an aching shoulder, or even her emotions when they were too strong, on the verge of being uncontrollable. When she was very young, she'd developed the habit of erasing things that irked her by running the back of her hand across her forehead, the only gesture that betrayed the great weariness she tried to hide beneath a cosmetic layer of feigned good humour and a tone of voice that was just a bit too imperious to be truly dangerous. This time, though, her gesture was no help at all. Victoire and Edouard kept scurrying through her mind. She leaned against the counter for a moment. "It wears you out, hating people like that. Life's too short. But it's hard to forget them, that's the trouble!" Victoire and Edouard were heading south now, down la rue Papineau, which crackled with the cries of countless children abandoned to their fate on the sidewalk of this dangerous road and with the noise of metal rubbing against metal, of streetcars rattling past, spitting sparks at regular intervals. At the corner of Marie-Anne, Victoire paused briefly. "Want to go home, Momma?" "No, I'm not tired. Just my paw dragging a little." She looked east, towards la rue de Lorimier, towards la rue des Erables. She thought of her sister, Ozéa, whom she hadn't seen for two years, who was probably out rocking on her balcony, a Saturday paper open on her lap. "Your aunt Ozéa's a heartless bitch." She said nothing more and crossed la rue Marie-Anne with no help from her son. Edouard had said practically nothing since they left the house. He was too afraid of giving in to his rage, which would have made Victoire very happy. He was afraid of saying things to his mother that he'd regret later, things which would have delighted the old lady. As he watched her limping, clinging to his arm, he shuddered and wanted to scream. This exhausting relationship with his mother had undermined his life and only now that he was over thirty-five was he beginning to realize that he was no more than a silvery-coloured fish, an object wriggling in Victoire's aquarium, as she feasted on his prisoner's life, giving him only leftover scraps of love to nibble on and changing his water only when he really didn't have enough oxygen. Contact with his mother electrified him, obsessed him, drained all his energy — and yet, he needed it. His evening flights, the nights that he spent partially outside, in other places, other arms, were basically only unimportant episodes, intense interludes, of course, that left him deeply marked by experience (furtive sulphur-scented touches, small closed infernos that were consumed in a few hours, then quickly transformed into memories it is pleasant to think of as blasphemous), but they remained only interludes, in fact, for the most important part of his life was lived within the walls of his mother's house — the squabbling, the fights, the duels, the reunions that he thought he hated so much, were really his own skeleton, his nervous system, his heart and blood. As long as his mother was alive, he could only move around on the fringes of her will, circling her like a dependent satellite, submissive to laws that were not his, totally stripped of any self-determination and, most of all, of choice; and the day she ceased to live he would, perhaps, die with her, disarmed, disconnected, at loose ends, a dismembered puppet forgotten in a corner, gathering dust and indifference—unless he were suddenly to blossom, experiencing all his springtimes at once, exuberant, overflowing, broken down by delight, drunk on freedom, in control of himself at last, holding the reins with a firm but mad hand, and riding hell-bent for leather to make up for lost time. He knew only too well that he'd be offered this choice one day—he dreamed of it—but no matter how often he told himself that his mother's death would be a deliverance, the very notion of being deprived of her—her voice, her expression, her odours—terrified him. Victoire had taken her son's arm again, though he didn't realize it, lost as he was in his unfathomable dilemma. As they passed the church of L'Immaculée Conception at the corner of Papineau and Rachel, Victoire suddenly emerged from her thoughts as if she'd just found the solution to a very important problem. "No wonder Ozéa's crazy, the whole parish is full of lunatics! Priests that plant corn out back of their church aren't priests! Even the curé back home in the country wouldn't do a thing like that, for Chrissake! They ought to be looking after my sister's soul, instead of their tomatoes!" She had spoken loud enough so that the two priests, who had just spent the afternoon trying to dig even furrows in the rich earth of their future garden, could hear. They looked up at the old woman and smiled. One of the priests took out a big checkered handkerchief and wiped his forehead. "Give us your sister's address, Madame, and we'll drop our tomatoes right away!" Victoire shrugged. "Oh, never mind. You don't seem bright enough to know the difference between a tomato and a cucumber anyway! I wouldn't be doing my sister any favour!" The two priests burst out laughing. "I wonder where they dig up these new priests nowadays? In the loony bin? Come on, my boy. They're too depressing." On the other side of la rue Rachel, Parc Lafontaine stretched out. For a long time,

170

Victoire looked at the trees, then she crossed the street. At last, she looked at Edouard. Her eyes were misty. "Here's where I made you, my boy. Come on, I'll show you the place."

Gabriel came and stood beside Béatrice on the bridge in Parc Lafontaine. He had recognized her in the distance, in the pale green polka-dot dress that she usually wore on Sunday afternoon in the summer, when she and her friend walked back and forth past his house, laughing, singing and shocking just about everybody with their insolent manner and their garish makeup in these difficult times. Albertine would say of them: "They ought to be shot like criminals! As far as I'm concerned, I have to hold myself back to keep from smashing their windows with a handful of rocks!" Victoire merely smiled, occasionally muttering something like: "Must be times when they'd like to smash *our* windows too! We don't make life any easier for them. If they weren't such floozies and you were a little more like one, the house'd be more fun — and the rest of the neighbourhood too!" Béatrice had seen Gabriel coming, bent over, staggering a little. She also recognized her neighbour, whom she thought was such a nice man because he was so discreet and because he always seemed embarrassed. She wondered if he might be not quite so shy when he'd been drinking. But Gabriel didn't approach Béatrice and Béatrice didn't move, purposely; she went on humming some old hit of Damia's or some new one by Charles Trenet, she wasn't too sure which. She wondered if he'd dare speak to her. But Gabriel kept his head down. Without saying a word. The light was more and more golden and now there was some green mixed with the

171

blue of the sky, a fleeting green that disappeared if you looked at it directly, but reappeared as soon as you looked to the side, bright, vibrant and soft, all at once. Gabriel was thinking of how he himself had just fled, run straight here, mostly because he'd been defeated on his own ground by some bum who didn't even know what he was talking about and whom he himself had just stuffed with beer and given a show of friendship. Ten times, he thought of returning to the tavern to smash the jaw of that stinking bundle of rags, but each time, the shame of being seen by his friends held him back. Another day, perhaps, next week or the week after that, but not now. He was suffering too much. Finally, Béatrice spoke first, not looking at him, however, but staring off towards the tops of the trees that circled the lake. "You don't look so hot." "When a man gets called yellow, it messes up his day." "Who called you yellow?" "Somebody that might have been right." He seemed to hesitate for a moment, then suddenly, he approached her. "Is that what you think? You know a lot about men, even though you're still pretty young? Do you really think we got our wives pregnant so we wouldn't have to fight in the war?" Béatrice looked at him for the first time since he'd arrived. "Yes. And I think you did the right thing." She went back to the treetops, just as Gabriel, in turn, looked at her. She kept speaking, but very softly, as if she were speaking to herself. "I don't know why men go and get themselves killed over on the other side. I don't understand a thing about the war." "If you really want to know, neither do I. Only thing the war does is move the pile of shit from one place to another! Doesn't matter which side wins. How's it going to change things for you and me, will you tell me? We aren't important enough, neither one of us, and we're too far away from it all for our lives to be any different if the Germans win or the Allies! Everybody tries to scare us by saying the Germans and the Wops'll come over here if they win the war.... Now, come on! It'll take them forever to put Europe back together again. They won't have any spare time to be thinking about us!" With the help of the beer, he gradually became impassioned. (He was standing in the middle of the tavern surrounded by his friends who asked nothing more than to let themselves be convinced that what he said was justified — and he was getting ready to spawn one of those endless speeches that had made him a local hero. He'd let himself go for hours, winning them over one by one, reading on their faces now surprise, now anger; he'd make them laugh, weep, applaud; he'd descend to the darkest melodrama to draw gasps of pain from them, then, suddenly, he'd ascend to summits of promises and good faith, hand on his heart and head held high; for a long time, he'd soar, following the winds of his inspiration, repeating the same thing a hundred times — but in a hundred different ways; and, once again, he'd be Gabriel, king of the tavern orators, the most listened-to and most respected man in Plateau Mont-Royal!) "I didn't get my wife pregnant so I wouldn't have to go and fight on the other side, but I'm glad she's pregnant anyway! And I got a feeling that's why she did it! Maybe she's even risking her life for me!" He didn't believe a word he was saying, but what difference did it make. He was talking! And talking well! "Let them do whatever they want, this side or over there. I know I'm yellow. I likely shouldn't've got her pregnant because I know very well she's too fat and too old.... But I did it. And now, she's been stuck in the corner of that room for months. She can't walk, can't even get up.... When Doctor Sanregret comes over, he looks at me like I'm the world champion jerk.... But I'm not! I love my wife! And I want that child! Can you understand that?" Béatrice cut him off with an abrupt gesture. "He's just like all the others! When he's sober, he's too ashamed — and when he's tied one on, there isn't an ounce of shame left!" Gabriel, surprised, pulled himself together and apologized. "I'm a bit drunk. Had a lot of beer. Too much. Thought I was back in the tavern with my buddies." Béatrice ran her right hand over her skirt as if she were brushing off imaginary crumbs. "That's the trouble. Whenever a man talks to me, he thinks he's talking to somebody else — his wife, his friends. He gives me his confession as if I was a priest, but no man ever just takes me for myself!" Suddenly, she didn't want to see him any more. She wished he'd disappear like the others after they'd taken their pleasure and paid for it. She wanted to be alone in the sunset and forget everything. She straightened up, took a few steps and came back to him. "There's men that pay me to listen to what you've just told me, so I don't see why you should do it for free!" "You're the one that asked me what was wrong . . ." She turned around and walked to the other end of the bridge. He followed her. "I'm sorry. If you're going back home, at least I can walk with you. And you can tell me your problems too . . ." "You'll lose your reputation as a good family man if anybody sees you with me." "After this afternoon, I haven't got much of a reputation left to lose. Anyway, let people think whatever they want." And Béatrice realized that she was getting ready to tell this man everything. Maybe he wasn't as mean as the others, after all. And though they'd talked for a good ten minutes, he hadn't made the slightest dirty remark. So Béatrice prepared to unburden her heart. But as they were crossing la rue Calixa-Lavallée, Gabriel noticed Thérèse, Marcel and Philippe leaving the playground. Philippe was walking very strangely, as though he were sick, and Gabriel began running towards him. "Flip, what's wrong? Are you sick?" Béatrice watched him move away. "So soon . . ."

174

Albertine slammed two empty bottles on the counter. "You there, Marie?" Marie-Sylvia's voice came to her from the very back of the shop. "Yes, yes...coming." Albertine heard the toilet flush, then saw Marie-Sylvia emerge from the storeroom where she had her washroom and toilet, carrying two molasses cookies and a big glass of milk. "You eat in the toilet?" "If I pour myself a glass of milk when Duplessis's here, he bugs me till he gets one too, so I started having my five o'clock snack in the bathroom. It's no dirtier than anywhere else, you know.... If the bowl's clean..." "Cut it out, I'm going to throw up!" Marie-Sylvia put her cookies and milk beside Albertine's empty bottles. "I'm going to let you down, I'm afraid, ma pauvre Madame.... I'm right out of Larose spruce beer.... Sold the last bottle to Monsieur Brassard this morning. You know what it's like. There's a war on.... I don't know if they're running out of spruce trees or not, but we're having a hell of a time getting spruce beer." "You blame everything on the war! For three years now, all the lazy slobs in the world have been trying to make us believe that if we can't get anything any more, it's because of the war!" Albertine picked up her empty bottles. "My weekend's shot to hell now. That's my Sunday treat — to sit out on the balcony with my two bottles of Larose. You know that! So how come you didn't keep me one, at least? I've been a customer here longer than those two rats that hide inside their hole because they're so scared of the big city!" Marie-Sylvia was standing with her elbows on the counter. She looked at her milk and cookies. "You don't even listen when we complain, Marie. We'll end up taking our business somewhere else!" Albertine turned and headed for the door. Marie-Sylvia looked up suddenly. "Have you seen my cat?" "He clawed me and then he took off, the little beggar!" Albertine turned to her as she opened the door. "Generally, you're the one that knows where everybody is. . ." "I've been keeping an eye out for him all afternoon. . . . I saw the two floozies go by, one after the other; I saw your kids going on their picnic; I saw Madame Ouimet going off to boulevard Saint-Joseph and coming back; I saw. . ." "But you didn't see your cat." "No. He's just been gone for three days. You know what it's like, nature. . . . But usually, he comes home to stay afterwards, for practically a week, all tuckered out. . ." "I didn't see him either. I was in the house the whole blessed day. . . . But I've got better things to do than look for cats!" She slammed the door behind her. Marie-Sylvia shrugged. "Charming as ever. . ." She was preparing to go back to the bathroom when the door opened again, making the little bell above it ring. Albertine stuck her head inside. "How many bottles did Monsieur Brassard buy?" "Four. That's all that I had left." Albertine disappeared without thanking Marie-Sylvia, who settled comfortably into her armchair. "For once. . . . After all, Duplessis isn't here. . ." Even as she ate, her head was turned towards the window. Albertine was walking purposefully across the lane towards the house where Marie-Louise and Léopold Brassard lived, the second house from the corner, just across from her own. From their balcony, Florence, Violette, Mauve and Rose saw her open the gate in the wrought-iron fence. Mauve looked at her sisters, then at her mother. "Will you tell me what she's doing there?" As Albertine walked past the living room window, she saw Marie-Louise's shadow behind the lace curtain. "She's nailed down in there, if you ask me!" Marie-Louise had become a sort of legend on la rue Fabre. She was a familiar ghost people had grown accustomed to, knowing she was always there, but not concerned about her. When people passed her house, they knew she was there at her window, but they no longer even bothered to check. If they said hello, she didn't answer, so they didn't say hello. Richard called her "the eyes in the curtain," a name that had the good fortune to terrify Marcel, who imagined there were, in fact, eyes sewn into the curtains at that window. When Marcel got on Richard's nerves too much by playing on the sidewalk, the older boy would say to him: "The eyes in the curtain will pick you up and eat you!" Marcel would stand there, paralyzed, and look anxiously on the other side of the street. "Whose eyes?" "Nobody's. The eyes in the curtain." Albertine rang three times before the door opened. "They're dead. He polished off his four bottles of spruce beer and blew up!" After two long minutes, a small silhouette could be discerned behind the door. Marie-Louise. "I wanted to talk to him in person, but oh well." Marie-Louise opened the door a crack and looked out timorously. She said nothing, simply watched Albertine, who stood there for a moment not knowing what attitude to assume. "Maybe she's dumb. Or deaf. Or crazy. Or maybe all three!" She cleared her throat and raised an empty bottle to the level of Marie-Louise's eyes. "Bonjour, Madame Brassard. Sorry to bother you right at suppertime, but, you see, I just went over to Marie's to buy my spruce beer and she tells me she just sold the last bottle to your husband, Monsieur Brassard. Four bottles. So I was wondering if you could sell me one. . . . I wouldn't think that the two of you would drink all that by Monday. . . . Marie said she'd be getting a carful — no, a boatload — on Monday morning, but that's too late because I only drink it Sunday afternoon, out on the balcony and . . ." Marie-Louise had already disappeared, leaving the door ajar. Albertine stuck her nose against the glass and looked inside. "What am I doing here? Is she going to fork over or not? Now I don't know what to do!" A few moments later, Marie-Louise was back with a cold bottle of spruce beer, which she handed to Albertine through the half-open door, then took one of the two empties Albertine was holding, and gently closed the door. Albertine was flabbergasted. "Maybe I wanted to pay!" She bent down and slipped a quarter into the mailbox, a slot at the bottom of the door. "Keep the change and buy yourself some manners!"

The fat woman had tried to go back to *Bug-Jargal*, but the lines of print danced before her eyes and she knew, in any case, that she'd never be able to concentrate enough to follow the story. "Too much is going on today. Escape's out of the question!" Even the name Acapulco, printed in her head in iridescent letters, couldn't make her dream. "It's silly to dream about Acapulco when I can't even get up to pee!" Her conversation with Albertine, or rather, the long list of insults that her sister-in-law showered on her, convinced the fat woman of the validity of the suspicion that had been gnawing at her conscience for some time, but which she'd dismissed or repressed, because she was afraid of it and didn't want to face it. She knew that members of her family and Gabriel's family, the women in particular, denounced her pregnancy as obscene, a scandalous state of affairs, a blot on the family's honesty and integrity, an attempt to provoke fate, which, in turn, would punish her, they all sensed it, when she least expected it, giving her a deformed or an abnormal child, but, at any rate, certainly taking revenge on her. As for the men . . . she knew so few of them, if the truth be told.

And it was so hard to know what they were really thinking. Her brother, Léo, had come to see her a few weeks
earlier and had looked at her strangely, concentrating on
her face and avoiding her belly, his lips stretched out in
an improbably sincere smile. He even looked her in the
eye and told her how thrilled he was, but everything in
his expression contradicted him. She would have preferred it if he'd shouted insults at her too, then at least she
would have been sure how he felt and been able to try to
explain everything. . . . But no. His feigned good temper
made contact impossible and Léo left wearing the same
false smile. Edouard, at first, seemed embarrassed when
he found out that another squalling voice would be added
to the ones that were already polluting the house a bit too
much for his liking, but gradually, perhaps out of pity for
the fat woman as he saw her body changing shape from
day to day, uncomplaining, except sometimes late at
night when the tension became too great and a fit of rage,
brief but devastating, would shake her for several
minutes, unleashing floods of tears and cries that she
would try to hide behind hands that she joined over her
face; or perhaps because he sensed without understanding
it that she really wanted this child, that she needed it to go
on living, and he began to talk to her in the morning
before he left for work, and in the evening when he came
home, even going so far as to serve her breakfast or supper, telling jokes and making faces to amuse her (she who
was so fond of such things), and morning and evening,
running his hand over her stomach, saying: "He's going
to weigh two tons and we'll have to buy a whole herd of
cows!" Her husband, Gabriel, the big child she'd been
protecting for twenty years and guided still, though he
was unaware of it, keeping her most serious concerns to
herself so that he never suspected their existence, always
singing when he got up in the afternoon or late in the

179

morning, though tears would often have been normal, and even necessary; her husband, so understanding that it sometimes bowled her over, had given her this gift without asking any questions, gladly complying as soon as she told him that she wanted another child and rejoicing when she told him that it had worked, that the baby was "on the way" and that she was happy. At times, the fat woman wondered if Gabriel was hiding as much from her as she did from him, if he wasn't far sharper than she thought. "Maybe we hide the same things from each other without knowing it and we settle our problems twice, each one in his own way, thinking that the other one's completely in the dark." She smiled at the thought. In fact, she really enjoyed this complicity in camouflage. But was Gabriel happy at the prospect of another child? She couldn't say. "Yes, maybe. Of course he is." The only one in the family who seemed truly pleased at the news was Victoire's brother, Josaphat-le-Violon, who had hugged the fat woman with his knotted, still powerful arms, not saying a word but showing her that he understood, encouraging her, letting her know that he would even back her up in her struggle, support her against the others, defend her and help her as much as he could. But she already knew all that. She lived it every day. She'd finally become almost immune to it. But what Albertine told her confused her, even though she was expecting it — what la rue Fabre, their neighbours, friends, acquaintances were saying about her. This sentence, with no right of appeal, this refusal to accept such a vital need, this crass ignorance that put restraints and limits on her freedom and spat upon her choice — yes, her choice — to procreate, to gestate, to give birth, despite the fact that she was over forty, insulted her to the very depths of her being. What right did a neighbourhood have to decide when and where a woman was entitled to have children? What right did they have to decree that a forty-year-old woman who wanted a child was automatically filthy? Who dared to say that being pregnant was ugly? She wanted this child. She needed it and she was beautiful! Her stomach contracted suddenly and the baby kicked her. The fat woman uttered a small cry of delight as she brought her hands down to her thighs, running them gently over her belly, touching, trying to guess where the head was, where the limbs were — laughing, happy, thrilled. "You're going to put me through the wringer, you little devil, but I'll be glad to see you anyway!"

"It was a wonderful day! People everywhere. The paths, the streets, even the grass. Just that once, Parc Lafontaine was full of beautiful women wearing long dresses and men got up like waiters in a fancy restaurant. . . . You see, the people that arranged the party had asked all the women to wear white. The rest of us — my sister and me, for instance — we didn't have white, so we wore the palest-coloured dresses that we had." Victoire was taking small steps; she was transformed, rejuvenated. "Back then, you see, Parc Lafontaine wasn't like it is today. It was a lot prettier. In 1906, the streets had hardly been paved and there were hardly any cars in Montreal! Every Sunday afternoon, your aunt Ozéa and I, we'd come and sit by the refreshment stand and watch Montreal's high society parading past us in their calèches. . . . People took their time in those days — they didn't shoot across the park the way they do now, like an accident looking for a place to happen!" Edouard listened to his mother, his hands clasped behind his back. He knew that she could walk without his help now. She was two or three paces ahead of him and, from time to time, she would turn around, talk to him, wait, then dart off again. A different woman. "You'd've thought you were in the middle of the country! You can't imagine what it was like! At the edge of the lake there, if you shut your eyes. . ." Victoire stopped, closed her eyes, took a deep breath, as if she were seeking some odour that had vanished, dissolved, flown away long ago. "Nowadays, you can always hear some car shrieking or the french fry wagon whistling!" They crossed la rue Emily Duployé, heading west, and they entered the section of the park that was calm, reserved for pedestrians. Everything seemed ablaze in the setting sun. Victoire laid her hand on her son's arm. Her voice became confidential. "When I see more than ten trees together, my heart explodes, as if I was going to die. . . . I've been a prisoner in the big city for forty-five years now and I still haven't got used to it!" Edouard, overwhelmed, wanted to make some gesture towards his mother, but she turned away and regained her lead. "The city of Montreal was putting on a big party to inaugurate the first gondola on the big lake. Believe me, that was a sight! A gondola in Montreal! We got a look at it before anybody else because it arrived the week before the party and we came and watched the workers set it up on logs, so that it could slip into the water nice and easy during the ceremony. . . . We couldn't get over it! A gondola ride in the middle of Montreal! I was so excited about it I couldn't get to sleep at night. . . . All the papers were talking about the big party and there were so many people that all the streets around the park were blocked. Your father and I, and Albertine and Gabriel, who were still babies, we met there at nine in the morning so we'd have good places, even though the party wasn't supposed to start till two! I brought a big blanket and we all laid down on it, right out there in the open. . . . Ozéa and her husband came over and joined us

. . . . Oh, it was a wonderful day! Some people even hid in the bushes the night before and slept out under the stars. That gave me ideas. . . . When the rich people's calèches started arriving, the rest of us, the poor people, we got up so that we could watch them." She pointed to la rue Calixa-Lavallée in the distance. "They came that way, along Rachel, then they turned right at the path that goes to the bridge, went across the bridge (they had special permission) and got out right in front of the refreshment stand. There were hundreds and hundreds of guests with invitations. . . . The rest of us didn't have any invitations. We weren't even supposed to be on the same side of the lake as them. We were on the other side of the lake, across there, but we could see as clear as day. Everything went on right in front of us, like a show. . . . The gondola — it wasn't the same one as today — it was prettier and a lot bigger too. Like I told you a while ago, they'd put it up on logs so it could slide into the water. . . . It was up on the grass, on the hill. . . . Your father said it was dipping its nose a little too much for his liking, but he was so critical, you remember. . . . So, the ceremony started around two-thirty, three o'clock. . . . There was a fanfare that played John Philip Sousa and all the rest. . . . Speeches. We couldn't hear a thing, but we clapped all the same! Anyhow, the stage was facing the invited guests, so the rest of us could only see the backs of the people that were talking. Then, afterwards, the mayor's wife walked over to the gondola with a bottle of champagne and she hit it so hard that the goddamn bottle broke! She got quite a surprise, let me tell you, with hot champagne spilling all over her hands! But it didn't seem to bother anybody else; the guests all clapped as if nothing had happened. It takes a lot to upset those people, you know. I wanted to offer her a washcloth to wipe her hands off, but your father said she could use her dress. I think that's what she did.

Anyway, she took off her gloves — I saw that with my own eyes — and they were all wet. And just then, a worker comes up with an axe and gives the first log a good whack. I don't really know how it worked, but the logs started rolling down the hill with the gondola rolling after them. . . . We were all standing up, clapping like crazy. . . . The gondola took a dive when it hit the water — and then, it sank straight to the bottom! It just sat there with its nose at the bottom of the water and its ass in the air, the motor dangling over the grass. Maybe you can't imagine it, but that spoiled a lot of people's fun. . . . Not your father though. He got down on all fours on the blanket and started laughing like a soul in hell. I was so ashamed — it was no joke! But then, everybody else around us started laughing too, and pretty soon, the only people that weren't laughing were the fancypants on the other side of the lake. They were all holding on to their tickets that gave them a free boatride and let me tell you, their jaws dropped down to their knees. The mayor disappeared; the councillors all took off; even the wardens from the Immaculée-Conception parish, who'd been standing there during the ceremony as stiff as sticks, thawed out and went and hid in the refreshment stand. Then, all of a sudden, the gondola started cracking, like rotten old wood, and the back part landed on the grass. The motor blew up and then it caught fire. Your father couldn't take any more, he nearly bust a gut laughing. Then, the people around us started clapping again and the men were shouting all kinds of things: 'Put out the fire, it isn't Saint-Jean Baptiste Day yet!' 'Next week, put the mayor on logs!' 'Say, Mr. Mayor, reminds you of the city budget, doesn't it? Waterlogged to the neck, but with its ass high and dry.' It wasn't fifteen minutes before all the calèches had disappeared and the rich people's side was empty; the rest of us were walking around the lake to see

184

what the damage was. It really bothered me, but everybody else seemed to think it was funny, so I started laughing too. The men made jokes about it all afternoon. There was a fellow from Saint-Henri who'd brought his accordion, so it wasn't long before we had another party going. I still couldn't tell you where the beer came from, but it came and we celebrated Saint-Jean Baptiste Day a month ahead of time!" Victoire had stopped walking as she spoke. She was leaning against a tree. "You wonder how come I'm telling you all this today, out of the blue, eh?" Edouard smiled. "I guess that's the day you made me. . . . You told me a while ago that you were going to show me where. . ." "Come here. . ." She took his hand, drawing him towards a bush with buds that had already started to open. "On our way home for supper, right around now, your father said: 'Victoire, the kids are asleep on their feet, we ought to put them down on the grass and lie down for a while ourselves.' I knew what he was getting at, so. . ." She looked at Edouard for a long time. "I wasn't all that crazy about. . .but I wanted another baby and I knew it was the right time. . ." Edouard was looking down. It was the first time he'd heard his mother make any reference to sex and he was embarrassed. But Victoire went on with her story, looking back towards the bush. "Then he asked me: 'Is it risky now?' and I told him no. He didn't want any more children. I never knew why. . . . And he said: 'That's good!' And then, we made you." She walked into the grove, ignoring the branches that caught at her dress. She bent down slightly. "Right here." She turned abruptly towards her son. "I'm so bored with my life, you can't imagine! I haven't got a single blessed thing to do! I feel so useless!" Edouard ran towards her and took her in his arms. "Stay with me, son. You're all I've got now!"

185

Gérard Bleau was so badly shaken by the incident with Thérèse that he hadn't noticed it was past closing time for the playground. Very few children were left at such a late hour: a pair of five-year-old twins, who hadn't stopped squabbling all day now, continued their games beneath the vacant stare of their mother who had hardly moved since morning but merely said, from time to time, in a tired, plaintive voice: "Gisèle, my head's splitting!" or: "Micheline, câline, cut it out, or Momma's going to fling you out of the swing!"; a little boy who had spent the whole afternoon on the whirligig without getting sick was screaming now because he was alone and couldn't make it spin; a few little girls in the sandbox giggled as they dug up turds deposited the night before by some feline in search of love or simply roaming; and the trio from la rue Fabre: Thérèse, Philippe and Marcel, whom Gérard Bleau dared not look at for fear of meeting the little girl's eyes, who were playing on the big slide, uttering cries of delight that most likely could be heard all the way down to la rue Sherbrooke. The day that Gérard Bleau had spent keeping an eye on children had been fascinating for him because it wasn't his usual job. He'd agreed to replace a sick friend who had sung the praises of hours spent in the sun amidst children's cries and the singing of birds — but he missed his friend for most of the day. Gérard Bleau was a mechanic at Provincial Transport and he usually spent Saturday getting shamelessly drunk, starting at ten in the morning and drinking beer after beer, until he was sodden — no matter where, no matter how. It was the same every week. But Sunday, he'd get up, fresh as a daisy, with a song on his lips, and he'd go hunting. The women in the neighbourhood knew him well and some would come out on their balconies to watch him pass by or they'd even approach him — the darling of la rue Dorion, the Don Juan of la côte Sherbrooke. That morning, though, Monsieur Gariépy, whose house he roomed at, got up with a raging toothache, maintaining that he'd kill all the children in the park if he went to work. Monsieur Gariépy, the official playground attendant at Parc Lafontaine for nearly twelve years now, was old and ugly, but the children adored him. They called him "Grampa" and rubbed against him like selfish little cats. From May to September (weekends in May and June and every day in July and August), you could see Grampa Gariépy at his post, a dead pipe in his mouth, frowning, keeping an eye on the children, handing out punishments and rewards, as if he were the good Lord in person. Sometimes, he eyed the little girls a bit too closely, especially the plump ones, whom he called his "chubby little angels," but he never made any improper moves; he was content to walk behind them when they climbed the ladders or the slides. But, Grampa Gariépy was getting on and the prospect of spending another summer at Parc Lafontaine didn't fill him with delight. Which was why he wanted to say no when they called him the week before to say that the playground was opening on May 2 and that he should be at his post at ten o'clock on Saturday morning. He'd even talked about it to his wife, who greeted the news with a scream. Grandma Gariépy had no desire to spend the summer watching her old man hanging around the house and she insisted that he agree to work for another season. In the end, he gave in — as usual. But this raging toothache — a real one as it happened, for the stumps of Grampa Gariépy's teeth were dying in tartar and pipe juice — was the old man's salvation — for that weekend, at any rate — and Gérard

Bleau set off for Parc Lafontaine with no particular enthusiasm, even feeling some apprehension, as he'd never been fond of children, considering them to be interfering little showoffs. Not one child had come all morning and Gérard felt like running away to the nearest tavern, thinking it was too early in the season for parents to bring their children to the park to play in the dirt. But he hung around the two park benches that were brought out just for him, bored to death, cursing Grampa Gariépy's toothache. And at noon, a few mothers turned their children over to him, asking him to feed them around three and wash their faces and take them to the public toilets. Amazed, Gérard didn't utter a peep and let the women go. He fed a few children in the middle of the afternoon, but he neither washed them nor led them to the public toilets. The children who knew where the toilets were went by themselves and the others calmly went in their pants — without interrupting their play. By four o'clock, Gérard had around thirty children to look after, but using his charm (he knew he was handsome and had no qualms about using his angelic good looks), he went to see the few mothers who were there, and told them his story, asking them to take over for him. He fluttered his eyelashes and used his tenor voice and it worked — as usual. (Hadn't his own mother told him before she died: "I gave you good looks. Now, use them! If you know how to do that, you'll never have to work! Use women, let them support you, save your money — and most of all — never get married!") He was at loose ends then and the afternoon was beginning to seem twice as long. The arrival of Thérèse, Philippe and Marcel was a pleasant diversion that allowed him to focus his attention on the unfortunate little cripple, towards whom he thought his behaviour was highly charitable. He even spent a good half-hour trying to imagine a day in the life of the young invalid, but imagination wasn't Gérard Bleau's strong point and all he managed to do was envision Philippe going to the bathroom. Gérard Bleau had never been afraid of women; on the contrary, he had followed his mother's advice and quickly learned to use women, soon becoming an out-and-out charmer, sometimes spending hours at his mirror trying out new pouts and winks. It was so easy for him to conquer women that he finally tired of it. For some time, out of sheer laziness, he even waited for women to throw themselves at him. Women, yes, but little girls. . . . The erection that he got before the willing Thérèse had literally terrified him and he almost ran away, back to la rue Dorion, to his house and his bed. What he felt came quickly and violently — and he understood that he could never do without it again. The mixture of fear and sexual pleasure showed him a new source of delight, whose existence he'd never even suspected before: danger. His sex life had always been too easy for him to really appreciate it. Thérèse, with her not-so-innocent kiss of a little girl who asks too many questions, gave him a glimpse of horizons streaked with the red of shame and the black of sin, exciting him tremendously and lending an air of macabre celebration to the danger, making it an inviting secret ceremony whose absolute masters were guilt, concealment and remorse. He regretted the incident, but how he'd enjoyed it! When he finally came out of his torpor, realizing it was almost half-past five, he blew with all his might the whistle that Grampa Gariépy had lent him. The peeved mother collected her twins; the spinning little boy kicked at the whirligig; and Thérèse, Philippe and Marcel slid one last time down the boards that had been polished by the buttocks of generations of ill-fed children. Philippe, who hadn't missed the fact that the attendant was no longer looking their way, had stopped playing cripple and was just beginning to enjoy the afternoon when he heard the whistle blow. "Just when I was starting to have some fun!" Thérèse pulled up her little brother's pants, which, in the course of the day, had picked up certain colours that were undefinable and even suspect. "Philippe, when we leave the playground, you're going to have to cross your eyes again—and your legs too!" And they walked past Gérard Bleau: Thérèse, pink with joy and confusion; Philippe, limping more than ever; Marcel, both adorable and repulsive. Gérard's glance followed Thérèse for several seconds and he began to feel the same agitation, the same rush of adrenalin that shook him and left him panting, tense and wild with expectation. "Gotta find out where she lives. . ." He followed the three children and was the first one to spot Gabriel crossing the street, gesticulating wildly and running towards them. Gérard hid behind a tree. Suddenly, he was overcome with remorse. "God Almighty, am I going to spend my whole life hiding behind trees?" But pleasure came to drown his remorse and Gérard Bleau, shaken by spasms, pressed his forehead against the bark of the tree.

"You don't have to tell him about the mysteries of life! I've already told him all that!" Victoire and Edouard saw Mercedes and Richard coming towards them, hand in hand, the little boy smiling at last, his back straight and eyes bright. Edouard expected his mother to fling herself at the young woman, with her claws out, calling her a degenerate floozy, but Victoire merely held out her hand to Richard. "Did she do anything to you?" "No, we just talked. I needed to talk." "To a stranger?" "Yes. What I had to say was too serious. I couldn't tell anybody in the family." Victoire turned her back to Mercedes and pulled her grandson along by the hand. Edouard smiled at the young woman. "Thank you, Mademoiselle..." "Mercedes." "Is this your day off?" "Yes. No. Yes." They both burst out laughing and Mercedes took Edouard's arm. "I used to see you at the Pingouin all the time a few years ago...but you wouldn't remember me.... You didn't pay much attention to the women." "You used to work there?" "You call that work? Fatso Petit wasn't a boss, she was an army general! And I wasn't interested in marching in step." "So now you're...on your own?" "Yeah.... It isn't always a picnic, but at least I've got my peace of mind." Victoire was leaning on Richard's shoulder. Richard stuck his hands in his pockets. "Did she tell you everything?" He suddenly blushed, going with no transition from white to crimson in less than five seconds. "You don't want to talk about it?" "No." "Well, it's your conscience, Coco. If you'd asked me..." That was what everyone in this family always said when a child, an adolescent or even an adult, spoke to someone else. But nothing was further from the truth: Victoire would never have spoken of those things, not to anyone. She had kept her own children completely ignorant of the facts of life and she didn't regret it. (It was Paul, finally, who told Albertine of her "conjugal duty"; and it was only a week before Gabriel got married that he managed to find a priest who was sufficiently versed to give him some information. As for Edouard...from early childhood, experience had shown him more than his mother would ever know.) Just then, the sound of someone shouting made them all turn around and Philippe burst out from behind a clump of bushes, pursued by his father, who was on the verge of apoplexy. "Don't ever give me a scare like that again, you goddamn little monkey! I thought you were going to have a fit and convulsions!" But Philippe

191

was agile and he managed to get away from his father, who was now huffing like a seal. They stopped directly in front of Victoire, as if they'd been caught out in the middle of some dirty trick. Philippe hesitated for a moment, then hid behind his grandmother. She eyed Gabriel, frowning. "Drunk again!" "It's Saturday!" Her brow smoothed out. "Well, in that case..." It was undeniable — a man who worked like a slave all week to feed his family was entitled to get drunk on Saturday. "What're you doing in Parc Lafontaine, Momma?" "It's Saturday! You get drunk, I go for a walk!" She took her two grandsons by the hand and walked away. Philippe, who knew very well that he'd just escaped a well-deserved thrashing, made himself as small as he could. "What monkey business have you been up to now?" He didn't answer and Victoire sighed. "That's right, everybody stop talking to me! Cut me out of your lives, like some old dry branch, and leave me to die in my corner." Gabriel followed them, his head hanging. "He was pretending he was crippled, Momma, and I thought he was sick." "Shut up, you! I didn't ask you anything, you damn blabbermouth!" Béatrice, who was walking behind Gabriel with Thérèse and Marcel, threw herself into Mercedes' arms, crying. "Where have you been, for Lord's sake?" "I'll tell you everything later." "I looked for you all afternoon!" Betty looked at Edouard. "Clients?" "Of course not. Calm down, everything will work out fine..." "What happened at the house?" Mercedes lowered her voice. "Wait till we're alone." Marcel held out his arms to his uncle Edouard who, making a face, lifted him in the air. "If you were a little piggy, I'd say you smelled good, but you stink, goddamn it!" Thérèse was resting her head against Edouard's arm. "And you there, up in the clouds, you look like you're in love!" Thérèse looked at her uncle, shocked. And they all began to walk.

A very strange procession emerged from Parc Lafontaine: leading it was a broken-down old woman who was dragging two little boys by the hand, the first, tall, pale, bony, with ears sticking out of his head, frequently running his hand over his pants as if to erase some invisible stain; the second, short and chubby, trying to conceal a tic that made his left eye blink; followed by a visibly tipsy man, his hands in his pockets, his eyes to the ground, back bent. Next came two very beautiful young women with their arms around one another's waists, the younger one leaning against the older one's shoulder, taking refuge in her sweet soapy odour; and finally, there was a fat man who drew up the rear, with a grubby little boy in his arms and a too serious little girl clutching his jacket pocket. What made the group so bizarre was the fact that no one was speaking; everyone seemed lost in thought, almost unaware of the others' presence. They walked slowly, heading nowhere, along la rue Fabre, which was completely empty so that they could pass. They could just as well have been returning from a wedding where they'd enjoyed themselves too much, or emerging unharmed from some cataclysm. Their features were almost erased by fatigue, so that it looked as if they were coming from nowhere, from any time; a procession with no destination or meaning going down a deserted street that smelled of supper. It was six o'clock and Montreal's one hundred church bells proudly chimed the hour from on high. A man was following them, far behind, hesitant, confused, a wild look in his eyes. A fallen angel trying to tag along in a parade in which he wasn't allowed. A moth attracted by a flame he knew was fatal. At the corner of Marie-Anne, however, Mercedes seemed to shake off her torpor. We'll leave you here. We can't go back to our apartment." Victoire spoke without turning around. "Come home for supper with us then.

193

It'll be a treat for Albertine!" Mercedes turned to Edouard, who burst out laughing. He nodded. "Sure, come on. Afterwards, we can go out." Then, there was silence once again. The sun was toying with the low branches of the trees; a big ball of fire now grazing the roofs of the houses. A feeble meow that seemed to come from under a balcony a few houses from la rue Mont-Royal made Marcel start and then begin to squirm in his uncle's arms. "Plessis! Plessis! It's Plessis!" Edouard put him down and the little boy rushed over to a fence, walked around a huge dog that was licking its paw, and opened the gate. Marcel knelt at the base of the balcony. "Plessis, where are you?" He spotted the cat squeezed under the stairs, covered with dried blood. Flies were beginning to buzz around his wounds. Duplessis' heart exploded with joy when he heard the boy and he stretched out his neck, as if to hasten a caress that seemed slow in coming. When the little boy's hand was on the cat's head, Godbout leaped up and began to growl. Thérèse kicked him in the side. "Don't bark at my little brother, you goddamn mutt!" Godbout slunk away, whining, and disappeared into the lane. They had all stopped to watch Marcel, who was on the verge of tears. He picked up the cat gently, but Duplessis meowed in pain. "So much suffering! So much suffering for a caress!" Ah! the smell! The little hands that didn't know how cruel they were! And the beloved head bending over his ruined eye! At last, Duplessis was happy. Marcel got up and walked away from the lawn. Edouard looked at Victoire, who didn't say a word. She hated the cat, but she knew that Marcel loved it and she didn't have the courage to separate them at a time like this. "I want to bring him home. He's sick!" And Marcel took up the head of the procession, the dying Duplessis pressed against his heart. They walked the rest of the way in silence. They crossed la rue Mont-Royal without looking to see if any cars or streetcars were coming towards them. Victoire couldn't take her eyes off her grandson. "When I die, he won't even notice. He's so scared of me, that child! But I've never had a knack for children — especially not for other people's. I'm always too hard on them. They never come and see me. Maybe they don't even like me." She dropped Richard's hand, then Philippe's. The boys seemed to relax, as though they were somewhat relieved. Rose, Violette, Mauve, and their mother, Florence, were on their balcony, waiting for Marcel. Violette had come out on the balcony to tell the others that supper was ready, but her mother put a finger to her lips. "Wait a bit, Violette." She took out the woollen circle that her daughter had knit by mistake and turned it around in her hands. "They'll stop here." The procession drew closer. Marcel stopped in front of Florence's house. He leaned against the fence and spoke in a broken voice. "Madame, Plessis's very sick. Look after him." "Who are you talking to, Marcel?" Victoire came up to Marcel and bent anxiously over his shoulder. The little boy went on, paying no attention to his grandmother. "Take good care of him. He's my friend!" He opened the gate and stepped onto the lawn. "Don't, Marcel. There's nobody there!" But for a brief moment, Victoire thought that she saw a woman come down the front steps and move towards Marcel. Then the apparition vanished and Victoire cried out, hiding her face in her hands. "It's crazy, dammit! Crazy! If you keep up this damn foolishness, I'll end up seeing things myself!" Florence smiled sadly at Marcel. "Put the kitty down." Marcel placed him on the cement. "Come back tomorrow. I'll do what I can." Duplessis raised his head. "Don't leave me, my love!" Marcel crouched beside the cat and kissed his head softly. "Go back with the others, Marcel. Go eat your supper." Marcel smiled at the four women and walked away. Victoire started climbing up the stairs to their apartment. The others followed. Marcel was crying uncontrollably now. Gabriel took him in his arms. "The lady said Duplessis would be better tomorrow!" Gabriel kissed Marcel on the neck. "Yes, that's what the lady said." Most of all, he didn't want to contradict his nephew when he seemed so completely overwhelmed. Philippe shrugged. "Dingaling!" Florence waited until they'd all gone before she bent over the cat. She was now holding Violette's woollen circle. "Violette, you'll have to fix this." Violette ran down from the balcony and picked up Duplessis. The four women walked into the house leaving four empty chairs on the balcony.

When Josaphat-le-Violon arrived around a quarter to six, Albertine had her head stuck in the oven of the coal stove where she was basting a gigantic turkey whose skin was beginning to turn beautifully golden. "Oh, it's going to be a good little bird!" She didn't hear the doorbell ring or the fat woman shout: "Bartine, the door!" Josaphat-le-Violon came into the house, followed by his daughter, Laura, who was squeezing her legs together, nearly writhing as she walked. "Quick, Poppa, let me by! I can't stand it! My kidneys are floating!" Laura ran across the dining room without even glancing into her cousin's bedroom. "Hello, ma tante!" (She called Albertine and the fat woman "ma tante" because of the difference in age, but also because she'd been brought up in Saint-Jérôme and met the women only recently. In addition, she called Victoire, "Grandma," though the old woman was only her aunt.) She jostled Albertine as she rushed behind her on the way to the bathroom. Frightened, Albertine screamed and fell to her knees, her head almost disappearing inside the roasting pan. "Bonjour, ma tante! Sorry, I have to go!" "Good Lord, you gave me a fright! Where were you? How'd you get in?" Josaphat-le-Violon put his violin case and a big bag of groceries on the kitchen table, then helped her up. "Through the door, Albertine, through the door!" They heard the fat woman laugh. Albertine rubbed her knees. "That's no daughter you've got, it's a cyclone!" Without replying, Josaphat-le-Violon pointed to the bag on the table. "I brought you some oranges." Albertine stuck her nose in the bag and sniffed. "What nice oranges! That will make Marcel happy!" She took an orange from the bag and pressed it to her nose and mouth. "Where do they get these oranges anyway, when there's a war on?" "Lordy, Bartine, they still grow on trees!" Josaphat-le-Violon turned around and headed for the fat woman's bedroom. "I haven't said hello yet..." The onset of Albertine's good mood suddenly ended. "So...he's off to pet his fat favourite darling..." She heard loud kisses and the creak of springs as the old man sat down at Gabriel's wife's bedside. "That's right, stay glued there while I break my neck making your supper!" Her cousin flushed the toilet and came out of the bathroom, laughing. "Hope I didn't hurt you, ma tante! But I didn't push very hard. I think it was the surprise that turned your legs to jelly." Albertine was bent over again, pushing the pan back into the oven. "You're really putting on weight, Laura! If you keep on, you'll soon be as fat as your aunt!" Albertine knew that Laura couldn't bear any talk about her obesity. But she gave as good as she got, so she smiled maliciously at her aunt. Albertine stood up and rubbed her back, then glanced at her cousin for the first time. "You're due the end of June, I suppose?" Laura was sitting at one end of the kitchen table, playing with the empty ashtray. "Yup, same as my aunt!" Albertine tried to bend backwards. "Same as just about all the women on the street! I've never seen so many women pregnant at the same time!" "It's normal, it's summer. . ." "It isn't summer, it's spring." "I read an article in *Le Canada* the other day, where they said that just about everybody's born in the summer in North America because the winters are so long. . ." "And what difference does that make?" "Well, ma tante, when the cold lasts so long, sometimes you want to warm up a little. . . . And when you get warmed up, well, you know. . . ." "And they talk about that in the papers! Now I've heard everything! It's bad enough the women on the street don't even hide it when they're in the family way, now the papers talk about when they make their babies!" Expecting a baby was always somewhat shameful for the women in the city. They usually hid their big bellies under corsets that suffocated them and very loose clothes that disguised their silhouettes. Even the fat woman wore a corset during her first pregnancies, despite her stoutness. And if a woman who was "a little too pregnant" walked down la rue Mont-Royal, people looked away, as if she were some obscene, shameful object; and there was always some nervous Nelly or sanctimonious mealymouth to point out: "In the last month, women usually stay at home." And it was true. Rather than submit to the silent reproaches that they could discern in every glance they met, women stayed home for the last weeks of their pregnancy. In the end, they felt a certain embarrassment at being misshapen and jostled about by the bundle of energy, the powerful life that was preparing to leave their bodies. Crushed by a monstrous religion that forbade any means of contraception, a religion founded on men's selfishness to serve selfish men, men who held women in contempt and were so afraid of them that they had created the image of the Mother, the Virgin Mary, Mother of God, a virgin, pure and intact, inhuman creature with no will and, most important, no autonomy, who one day discovered that she was pregnant without having wished it, through the workings of the Holy Spirit (whom they dared to represent in the form of a bird! The Mother of God impregnated by a bird!), and who delivered without having to give birth, the ultimate insult to women's bodies; crammed by priests with sentences as hollow as they were cruel, in which high-flown, insulting, condescending words like "duty" and "obligation" and "obedience" predominated, French-Canadian women, particularly those who lived in the cities, felt an unhealthy shame at being pregnant, they who were not worthy (unlike that Other Woman) of bringing a child into the world without a man, their owner and master, who would have his way with them; women who, most of all, didn't have the right to shirk their "duty," their "obligation," because they owed "obedience" to the marvellous instrument of fate that had been directly provided to them by the Will of God: their husbands. In a word, the Catholic religion denied the beauty of child-bearing and sentenced women *never* to be worthy, because the mother of their God, the consecrated image of Motherhood, had been only a temporary depository, which the Child neither entered nor left. Albertine lifted the cover of the cauldron of boiling soup and began to stir the steaming liquid energetically, trying to give an impression of composure. "If they keep that up, I'll stop buying the papers!" "Just *L'Oratoire?*" "Even *L'Oratoire!* Saint-Joseph's depressing!" She replaced the cover to the soup, making as much noise as possible. "Help me set the table. I'm all by myself and I'm as lonely as can be." Josaphat-le-Violon had taken his niece's hand in his big calloused carpenter's paws and he looked at her, smiling. "Do any reading today?" "No, mon oncle. I can't seem to concentrate." "Too much commotion in the house?" "No, it isn't that. Everybody but Bartine went out. . . . But. . . it's as if I'm not in the mood to read as much as I used to. The baby's moving a lot and I'm off in my daydreams." "Still Mexico?" "No. More serious." "Mustn't do that. Acapulco Bay has always helped you go on. . . ." "But I'll never see it, mon oncle! As long as I could still think I'd get there some day, even though I knew I wouldn't, it was all right, but now. . ." The fat woman took her hand from her uncle's and fixed her hair which had fallen across her forehead. "It isn't drying the way it should. . . . I wish my dreams weren't so crazy! If I could only dream about going to the Baie des Chaleurs or Percé, it wouldn't be so bad! But, oh no! Acapulco!" "It's your Indian blood that makes you want to travel. That's normal!" "My Indian blood turned to water a long time ago, mon oncle!" "This is the first time since December that I've seen you so down in the mouth. Something happen with Gabriel?" "Of course not. . . . I'd just like to get up, mon oncle, drag myself out on the balcony, sit and look at the spring sunshine, instead of watching for its reflection in Madame Chagnon's window up on the third floor! I'm sick of dreaming about Acapulco when I can't even go outdoors and sit on my own balcony!" "Listen, listen. . . . Tonight, after supper, Edouard and Gabriel and I, we'll try and take you out. . . . It's warm enough. . . . An hour or two of fresh spring air, that'll cheer you up!" This time, it was the fat woman who took Josaphat-le-Violon's paw in her plump hands. "Can I have chips and Coke?" "Anything you want." "And will you play the 'Meditation' from *Thaïs* for me?" "I'll try."

"I never saw anybody gobble down their food so fast! Whenever I come here, the food sticks in my throat and I nearly always get sick!" "Quit moaning and groaning, Momma, and wipe the dishes!" Germaine Lauzon and her mother, Rita Guérin, were washing the dishes. At a quarter past six, the evening meal was over and the dishes were already half done. In the early days of her marriage, Germaine Lauzon had trouble getting used to the fact that her husband ate whatever was put before him in about five minutes flat, then asked for more between two loud belches and two sips of beer, but she'd finally got accustomed to it and was even beginning to take on her husband's rhythm, shovelling down meat, vegetables and bread, as if each mouthful were her last. The first time Rita Guérin came to eat at her daughter's, she said: "Poor Germaine, you got yourself a real pig for a husband. You ought to feed him dishwater — he'd never notice and think of the money you'd save!" But as the months passed, she realized that her daughter was slowly being transformed until she resembled her husband, so she said nothing more. She simply watched the two of them, the corners of her mouth betraying a slight expression of disgust. "As long as they're happy, it's none of my business. They'll turn out more little pigs and everybody'll be happy!" This was, then, the first time in a long time that Rita Guérin had allowed herself to make such a remark. But the meal at which she'd just been present (she couldn't say that she'd taken part, as she'd barely seen the plates pass) had beat all records for speed and piggishness — and Rita Guérin thought that she could still hear her son-in-law, mouth full of mashed potatoes and what seemed to be smashed peas, ask: "What's for dessert?" She almost told him the bread pudding was hidden under the potatoes, but Ernest would likely have believed her, so she held her tongue. Germaine moved her hands in the dishwater to stir up the suds, but the water was too greasy and cold. The young woman sighed: "You're exaggerating again, Momma! I've never seen you get sick here!" "I hide it, little girl! So that you won't be ashamed! You ate so fast tonight, your dessert must have tasted like soup. I'm not kidding!" She laughed at her joke and put down the stack of plates she'd just dried. "I exaggerate so much that I scare myself sometimes." Germaine stuck her hands back into the dishwater and pulled a long face. "Good thing you know you exaggerate. Otherwise, we'd have to keep reminding you and that would be a drag." Rita Guérin replaced her wet dishtowel with a clean one which she took from a drawer near the sink. "You want me to stop?" "Stop what?" "Stop exaggerating!" "Don't ever do that, Momma. I've got so used to dividing everything you say by ten, I'd get all mixed up if you ever stopped!" "By ten! Now you're the one who's exaggerating, Germaine!" "I am not! When we were having supper, how old did you say you felt?" "Four hundred and sixty." "See?" "That was a coincidence. . ." Pierrette, the youngest Guérin girl, who at eleven was too tall for her age and had a complex because her teeth were growing in crooked, burst into the kitchen, visibly horrified. "Germaine, your husband's in the radio again!" Without even taking the trouble to exchange a glance, the three women rushed into the hallway that led to the living room. "Poor girl, your husband doesn't just eat fast. As soon as your back's turned, he's up to his old tricks again!" When they got to the living room, it was too late: the odour of electricity drifted through the room and some smoke was escaping from the radio. Ernest Lauzon, a sorry sight, screwdriver in hand, cleared his throat before he spoke: "It isn't my fault! I didn't touch the wires! I just gave the tubes a little tap to see if they were working!" Germaine Lauzon pulled the screwdriver from his hands. "Good thing you put on your gloves, otherwise you'd look like a piece of toast! I can't leave you alone for two minutes! You'd blow up everything! I bet the power's off in the whole house and we'll have to go and buy fuses from Marie and they'll laugh in our faces again! This is the second time this week that you've blown the fuses, Arnest! Do you think that's smart?" "I'm telling you, it isn't my fault..." "It's never your fault! I caught you up on the ladder Wednesday night digging around in the sockets in the ceiling and now you got the gall to tell me you never touched a thing — and if there wasn't any power in the house, it's because the fuses were too weak!" She rubbed her belly. The baby had just moved and her heart contracted with joy. "If this keeps on, I'll have to ask the baby to bring you up!" Pierrette burst out laughing, followed by her mother, who put her hands in front of her mouth to hide her laughter. Ernest smiled. His finest smile. He knew that his wife couldn't resist his smile and he took full advantage of it very often, especially in delicate situations like this one. He held out his gloved hands to his wife. "I like it when you chew me out like that! You're beautiful and you make me feel important." He got up and took his wife in his arms. Rita Guérin's laughter stopped immediately. "Pierrette, sweetheart, go buy some fuses for your sister." She followed her daughter onto the balcony and sat in the rocking chair. "If they do it as fast as they eat, their nights must be long." She hummed a song from her village, tapping her foot. Germaine was sitting beside the radio. "That's a real disease, you know, Arnest. I don't know what they call it, but if it's got a name, they must be able to cure it! We're going to spend the rest of our lives just missing being burned to death!" Ernest crouched at his wife's feet and placed his head in her lap. "I like electricity." "How come you aren't working in it then? It's not too late, you're only twenty-two!" "I'm fine where I am! If I worked in electricity for my living, maybe I wouldn't like it so much..." Her husband's strange logic always amazed her. "You mean, you couldn't spend your life doing something you like?" "No, I just mean, a job's no fun, not even if you like it..." "And where'd you dig up a crazy idea like that?" "Have you got a job? No, eh? Well, shut up then! You don't know what you're talking about!" He sprang to his feet, irritated, and left the room, slamming the door behind him. Germaine was left standing there, holding the screwdriver. "Now I suppose I'm the one that'll have to apologize again!"

It was a memorable meal. The atmosphere was like the eve of an apocalypse, as if some final event or imminent catastrophe were approaching in the shadows without deciding yet whether or not to happen. The period before sitting down to eat had been a little too quiet. When Albertine saw Mercedes and Béatrice walk into the house, she thought she was dreaming, but she restrained herself. She leaned against the wall in the hallway with one hand over her heart. "It isn't true! They couldn't do that to me!" She stared at the two women without speaking to them, as if they were in a store window or a stall. She was well aware that Edouard was laughing to himself during the introductions, which infuriated her. Victoire had closed herself inside her room, where Josaphat-le-Violon came to join her, or calm her rather, as she was crying and couldn't explain why. Then Edouard, very pleased with himself, showed the two floozies around the house, opening all the doors, describing everything in a loud voice (very much the mistress of the house, in fact) beneath his sister's murderous gaze. Gabriel dragged his long face into his bedrooom. As she did every Saturday when he came home, more or less drunk, the fat woman waited for him to address her before she spoke to him. Philippe ran straight to the kitchen and began to hover around the stove, playing the fool. Richard and Thérèse sat on the sofa reading Saturday's *La Presse,* huddling together. Marcel, for perhaps the first time in his life, went and took refuge in Albertine's arms and she stood there completely stunned. He clung to his mother's shoulder and his breathing became spasmodic, as if he wanted to cry and couldn't. His mother asked if he was sick. He said no, but Duplessis was, and he was very upset. It was because of Marcel, in fact, that Albertine didn't have a fit as she watched Edouard and the two young women go from room to room, laughing, exclaiming or apologizing when they disturbed someone. She didn't want to know how or why these two creatures had turned up in her domain, she just wanted them to disappear as fast as possible. "Must be another one of Edouard's and Mama's little tricks! I know those two! They'd do anything to drive me around the bend! Me, serve those two floozies supper? Not on your life! Anyway, women like that don't eat, they drink!" Albertine sat in her mother's rocking chair, which had the place of honour in the dining room, beside the radio. She rocked Marcel, with no great hope of putting him to sleep. Suddenly, the little boy began to tremble and his forehead became wet with sweat. "Does Mommy's little angel want to go to sleep in my big bed?" Little angel? She'd called him little angel! And without even noticing it, her voice became soft and lilting. Thérèse looked down at her mother and smiled. Albertine, aware of Thérèse's stare, lowered her gaze. Marcel straightened up in his mother's arms. "Don't want to sleep. I want my supper. Tomorrow, Plessis's going to be all better and Marcel wants to feel better too." "Thérèse, Richard, get to the table! Fast!" Albertine lay Marcel on the sofa. "It won't be long. Momma's going to feed you first." Edouard, Mercedes and Béatrice had ended up in the living room. Edouard did what he could in the situation—that is to say, he went to some effort to put the two young women at ease. He looked like a fat Santa Claus, out of costume, on holiday in some hot country. "I can't offer you a drink, girls, because liquor isn't allowed in the house! By-law number six thousand and twenty-two. Not even beer! But we've got cream soda and Coke by the gross, if you want some. Unless you'd rather have a nice tall glass of chilled St. Lawrence!" The hackneyed old jokes only made Béatrice and Mercedes more embarrassed, as they began to realize that no one but Edouard was speaking to them and that they were, perhaps, somewhat out of place in this house that smelled of soup and roast turkey. For Béatrice, it smelled of Christmas and that made her sad. Mercedes finally asked for a Coke and Béatrice, a cream soda. When Edouard went into the kitchen, the two friends tried to explain things to each other, but it was too complicated: Mercedes still didn't know that the three soldiers had devastated the apartment; and Béatrice, in her eagerness to say a great deal in a short time, explained herself poorly and was growing impatient. And so, when Edouard came back with the soft drinks, he found the two women in the midst of a heated argument, Betty, on the verge of tears, and Mercedes, on the verge of exploding at her. Edouard put the drinks on the coffee table. "Listen, girls, if you got something to work out, I'll go help my sister with the supper. . . . I'll call you when it's ready. . ." He withdrew, waving at them as though they were children. They were grateful to him for letting them sort out the day's events. Josaphat-le-Violon sat beside Victoire and waited for her to stop crying, saying nothing, patient as always, his mere presence comforting his sister, and most important, pacifying her. Victoire blew her nose three or four times, then she described her vision to Josaphat-le-Violon who, to the old woman's great surprise, didn't laugh. He didn't even smile at her, but kept looking her straight in the eye as she tried to describe what she called "the first signs of madness," sometimes nodding encouragement, so attentive that he seemed hypnotized. "There's nobody in that house! I know it! I must have been worn out, I don't know. . . . Or maybe it's because Marcel thought he was talking with some woman. . . . But I saw her, just for a second, you know. . . . And I'm not crazy! Marcel. . . . Sometimes he's funny. . . . He says funny things and he does funny things. . . . His mother doesn't notice. She doesn't look after him. . . . But I watch him for days at a time, you know. I haven't got anything better to do, and I'm telling you, he's not like everybody else. Not by a long shot!" She stopped, as if she had been struck by a thought that surprised her. "Come to think of it, he reminds me of you when you were little. . ." Victoire was eight years older than Josaphat-le-Violon and it was she, the big sister whose mother was too busy, who had brought him up, surrounding him with love and attention, singing as she changed his diapers and washing him three times a day in basins of warm water that soon became the great delight of young Josaphat. He had been a secretive child, excluding others from his games as well as from his affection, constructing an imaginary world where Victoire reigned and he was a toy in his sister's hands. All through his childhood, he worshipped Victoire, who returned his affection silently, an efficient little mother who quivered at her child's slightest surge of affection. They remained very close and a strange passion developed between them, from which sexuality was totally absent, but all the other components — jealousy, possessiveness, doubt, tears, secret joys, break-ups, reconciliations — were more deeply rooted than in any ordinary love and even more demanding, always leaving them gravitating between the two poles of forbidden things — guilt and remorse — and condemning them from puberty to love one another without ever touching, for sin, in their rural surroundings, was to be found far more readily on the surface of the body (the skin!) than in the labyrinth of the spirit. (Confessing an evil thought, even a criminal one, was a trifle, but admitting to a wicked touch!) Victoire married at twenty-five, as late as possible, and being separated from Josaphat (who already, at seventeen, was beginning to be called "Violon," because of his genius for learning to play in record time on the instrument that his father had made for him, the most complicated jigs and the most daunting reels, even giving them a transcendent interpretation, marking them with his personal stamp so that some, "Le Reel des culottes à Frigon," for example, became musical pieces that bordered on masterpieces, though they were still humble enough just to make people want to dance) had been equally excruciating for her when she was leaving for Montreal (Montreal! City of the damned! Cursed city! City!) on the arm of a man that she didn't love and barely respected. As for her brother, who shouted when he learned that she was leaving: "If you go away, Victoire, I'm hanging up my fiddle! I'm taking down my axe and I'm going up to the lumber camp for the rest of my days!" Josaphat-le-Violon did, in fact, hang up his fiddle after Victoire's departure, but almost three winters of being Josaphat-la-Hache disgusted him, and rather than seek refuge in alcohol as so many lumberjacks did, secretly, he came back from the logging camp one Monday afternoon in January and threw himself on his instrument as though it were his last hope, making the hearts of the village girls tremble with the tunes that he composed and dancers' feet quiver with rhythms that were more utterly mad than before. Josaphat-le-Violon wasn't married. No one knew if he'd ever known a woman and the women he had known (Rosette Blanchette, the mayor's wife, for instance, or Mademoiselle Luce-Amanda Poitevin, the librarian, who for fifty years had ruled over a batch of one hundred and thirty-two books that were never borrowed, a donation from the Pères de la Sainte-Croix, useless like all their gifts, because most of them were incomplete, having left the printers' half-printed—hence, the good fathers' generosity, as it happens) were all unfalteringly discreet, never admitting their fault (not even—especially not—to their curé, whom they'd stopped trusting, thanks to Josaphat-le-Violon, for whom curés were a sadistic, degenerate lot) and concealing their happiness beneath perpetual smiles. Five or six of the village women, then, had kept the fiddler's mark imprinted on their faces throughout their lives and the five or six men to whom they were married had, throughout their lives as well, extolled and sung the praises and, even, paraded the unspeakable joy, the blazing happiness of which they believed themselves to be the cause, but of which they were only victims, ridiculous ganders, who, without knowing it, dragged around the biggest, the heaviest, the most comical horns in the Laurentians. Even Imelda Beausoleil, who had given him Laura in the early twenties, never said a word to a soul. She managed to conceal her pregnancy until the end and went down to Saint-Jérôme to give birth at one of her sisters', who swore on the Bible that she would raise the little girl as though she were her own, without a word to anyone. When she came back to Duhamel, Imelda Beausoleil went to show Josaphat-le-Violon a photograph of Laura. "There's your daughter. If you want her, she's at my sister's. If you don't want her, you're a son-of-a-bitch!" Josaphat-le-Violon immediately made the trip to Saint-Jérôme to embrace his daughter. He left her with Imelda's sister, where she grew up. When Laura married Pit Cadieux, a lad from Saint-Jérôme who was going to try his luck in Montreal in the kitchen of one of the big hotels, Josaphat took his daughter aside. "I want to go to Montreal too, Laura. Let me come with you and Pit. I don't need much room. My two sisters are all I've got left and they're down there..." Imelda Beausoleil never saw her daughter again. She never even spoke of her. Perhaps, in the end, she even forgot her. And when Imelda Beausoleil died, Josaphat-le-Violon wept. When he arrived in Montreal, he found his passion for Victoire intact, inviolate, hard as a diamond, but he was so much more shy. And Victoire opened her arms to him, calling him "my precious little puppy," as she had in the old days, or "my little darling boy." "Yes, I thought about you when you used to come in and say the women next door were making their jam, and every time, even if there wasn't anybody in the house, you could smell the jam...." Josaphat-le-Violon put one hand on his sister's knee. "If you see that woman again.... If you're still seeing things, Victoire, tell me about it..." "You'll put me in the nuthouse." She smiled, hoping that her smile would drive away her anxiety, as if she'd just become aware of the absurdity of her vision.... "No, but if it starts again, we'll have to have a serious talk. I've got some things to tell you.... Now come and eat. You mustn't keep the company waiting too long." When Victoire and Josaphat-le-Violon reached the dining room, everyone was at the table (Mercedes and Béatrice had been seated on either side of Edouard, who was puffed up with pleasure and chuckling like a girl), but a strange silence hovered in the room. Gabriel looked pleadingly at his mother. "Momma, Bartine won't serve the two—the guests." Albertine was, in fact, standing in the kitchen doorway, ladle in hand, with a stubborn expression on her face, an expression that gave her a porcine air. "Stubborn as a mule! She only served Marcel." Marcel was eating his soup, paying no attention to what was going on around him, concentrating on his soup spoon which he'd learned to hold properly only a few months before. Mercedes half rose. "We don't want to make a fuss. . . . If your daughter doesn't want to feed us, it doesn't matter. We'll go somewhere else. . ." "You sit down! I invited the two of you and you're going to eat! When Victoire invites people to eat, they eat!" She walked around the table and stood before her daughter. "You don't want to serve the visitors?" Albertine stood up to her mother's look, but her voice was hoarse, as if some strong emotion were stuck in her throat. "Momma, you aren't going to make me feed those two hussies! I've had to put up with enough today, if you ask me! Please don't do that to me!" She held out the ladle to her mother. "Serve them yourself!" Victoire seized the ladle with a firm, decided hand. "It's about time somebody asked me to do something around here! I'm starting to grow roots in my rocking chair! But I'm warning you, if I serve the visitors, I serve everybody!" "You can't do that, Momma, your leg!" "My leg took me all the way to Parc Lafontaine today, I think it'll take me to the stove, goddammit! Go sit down Bartine — and try and look like a human being, for the love of God!" Edouard applauded and his mother turned around and looked at him. "And don't you go thinking that you look like a rose in between two thorns, Edouard! You look more like a toad in a field of daisies!" Josaphat-le-Violon burst out laughing, followed by Gabriel — and even the fat woman, who could hear everything from her bedroom. Edouard answered his mother in the same tone of voice. "And don't you go thinking that you can serve us properly, Momma! A rickety old woman wouldn't be my choice to serve the soup!" But this time, no one laughed. And Josaphat-le-Violon's slap hit Edouard in the midst of his triumph. "Sometimes you're funny, you big lump, but don't ever make fun of your mother when I'm around!" Edouard got up, went around the table and took the ladle from his mother. "I'm sorry, Momma. Go sit down, I'll serve." Victoire took back the spoon. "Not on your life! If you've never seen a rickety old woman on her toes, watch out for your boots, little boy! I'll bet you your next pair of underpants that I won't spill a drop!" Mercedes and Betty applauded the old woman, who made a little bow to them. "Mesdames, you're about to taste the best soup in town! My daughter Albertine made it, but the recipe comes from her old mother, me myself, and in my day, I've known people that travelled all the way from Duhamel to Montreal just to taste it!" Josaphat-le-Violon raised his hand. "Me, for instance!" Victoire approached her brother and put her hands on his shoulders. Her voice, softer now, became caressing. "Him, for instance." And suddenly, everyone was struck by the resemblance between them, even the children who were silent as they looked at the superb tableau that they formed, the two of them: a couple united by so much subtle affection and so many tragic bonds that, in the end, they had the same wrinkles, the same face. From that moment on, the atmosphere relaxed somewhat. Victoire didn't spill a single drop of soup ("Edouard! You owe me a pair of underpants!") and they all ate in silence, scraping the bottoms of their bowls with their spoons and eating down to the last grain of barley. As Béatrice placed her spoon in her empty bowl, she looked at Victoire. "That's the best soup I've ever eaten!" Victoire smiled. "You'll have to tell my daughter. She's the one that made it." Béatrice took her courage in both hands and spoke to Albertine. "That's the best soup..." "Okay, I heard you! You already said so!" And Albertine slurped her last spoonful.

In the last rays of the setting sun, Ti-Lou was dying. When she felt her heart beat faster and her vision begin to blur, she straightened up in bed and stretched one arm out towards the window. "One last time. To see the sun set behind the chimneys one last time!" But a sudden dizzy spell pinned her to the pillows again. "I took too much! I'm going too fast!" The bottle that had held Doctor San-regret's drops lay empty in a corner of the bedroom. After emptying the contents into a very small amount of water, Ti-Lou had hurled the bottle with all her might against the wall that faced the window, but the bottle hadn't broken (it was mocking her, the crippled old lady thought). "I don't want to go so fast! I don't want to die with the window shut!" And for almost ten minutes, she struggled, supporting herself, at first, on one elbow and using her free arm to push with all her strength, then, gradually, unfolding the arm on which she was resting, until finally, she succeeded in sitting up in bed, her one leg half out of the covers. The bed pitched and tossed; the room was sloping dangerously towards the right. "If the whole house is leaning that way, I'll fall out the window and land on the picket fence!" Imagining her body pinned to the fence that went along the lane made her laugh. "They'll think I broke a leg and they'll look all over the place for it, but they won't find a thing!" She was bent double laughing, tears streaming down her cheeks. "Gotta keep up my strength..." She breathed deep, but her heart kept pounding wildly. The room was sloping more and more, so much so that she began to look for something

213

to lean on. She turned over, brought her leg out from under the covers, and stood on the floor. "My crutches..." Generally, Rose Ouimet left the crutches against the straight-back chair between the bed and the window, but this time they weren't there. Ti-Lou was panic-stricken as she leaned out of bed. "They aren't there! I can't get up! I'm going to die in my bed, just like everybody else!" It was at this moment that the noise began. The house suddenly filled with clicking and whispers, with strident whistling and demented laughter. It was as if corpses were being dragged into the corridor or maltreated prisoners in chains were being shoved into the cellar. "I'm imagining it! There's nobody in the house! My heart's beating too hard and my blood's circulating too fast.... My brain needs air.... *I* need air!" She leaned against the bedside table with her right hand and, with her left hand, she managed to draw the straight-back chair towards her and even turn it around so that she faced the window. Leaning on the back of the chair, Ti-Lou stood up on her one leg. She felt dizzy and her head spun, but she concentrated all the energy she had left in her arms and managed to remain standing. When the vertigo passed, she realized that the voices and noises had stopped. She sighed. "I held them off!" She pushed the chair towards the window, hopping on her one leg, then began again, until the chair was leaning against the radiator. "Have to walk around the chair..." Realizing that she'd never be able to hop around the chair, she pushed it furiously to the right. It swayed to one side, first falling onto the bedside table, then, after springing back, over-turning the monumental torchère, a lamp that hadn't been used for years and that Ti-Lou had started to hate because it was so high that she couldn't switch it on. Then, the lamp crashed into the wall. The glass globe burst into a thousand pieces and a hail of sparks began to run along the electric wire. Ti-Lou balanced on her one leg for a moment, then fell forward. She stretched out her arms and managed to lean against the windowsill. "I can't fall! This is my last chance!" She was half sitting on the radiator. She pressed her forehead against the window, closed her eyes and breathed slowly. "All that fuss over a goddamn sunset!" She opened her eyes again. Blood coursed through the sky in long brilliant streaks. "Five minutes and it'll be too late." Gathering all the strength that she had left, Ti-Lou got up, bent down and opened the window in a single motion. She stood there, resting against the window frame, arms outspread. "Ah! I'm going to go the way I lived! In the saddle, come what may!" In the dying rays of the sun that were red and orange, when all the west-facing windows in town were aflame, Ti-Lou saw all the nights of her life again: the superb ones, the ones that she willingly talked about because they were flattering, when the elite of Ottawa had crowded around her, along with the visiting elite from countries that she'd never seen, but where she'd imagined herself in black arms, or the yellow or brown or too white arms of one of its representatives whom she'd had to call: "Vôtre Grace," or: "Your Highness," or: "Monsieur le Président," or simply: "Comrade," men who were always intelligent and gallant, who showered her with presents as they told her that she was Canada's finest jewel, the only pearl ever created in the cold; and the far less glorious nights that she'd spent in hotel rooms, in the arms of drunken fat officials with fetid breath, whose requirements were as brusque as they were brief, who forgot her as soon as their hunger was appeased, sometimes even going so far as to show her to the door, calling her by the name of the thing they'd just done to her; all those nights that had ended with a humiliating douche; all the pale dawns, the hour of the wolf—but not the wanton she-wolf—spent erasing from her body the dried traces of love (love?), the odour of vomit from crowned heads, and even the shit of the great of this world. Those nights, those mornings so horrible that Ti-Lou sincerely believed she'd dreamed them. She believed that they were nightmares sprung from her own imagination; while the other dreams (a house of her own and *cailles aux raisins*) remained the truth for her, the only truth — the only acceptable bearable truth. Crucified at her window, Ti-Lou saw once more the kings, the cardinals, the presidents, generals, admirals — but she saw them with their clothes on. And when the last ray of light touched her brow, she began to howl: this lonely, crippled she-wolf remembering, before she died, all her progeny scattered to the four corners of the forest, though she was well aware this progeny knew nothing of her, that it even renounced her because she'd become useless and would die with no one knowing anything about her, a rotting carcass they would hasten to devour before it polluted the surrounding air. The howls of the she-wolf of Ottawa rang out like gunshot, rose up the maple tree in the yard and echoed all over Plateau Mont-Royal — until Ti-Lou's despair burst inside the houses, the churches, in the presbyteries where priests, being served by fat servants in love with them, ingratiatingly ate vegetable stews or boiled chicken, their heads in their plates like horses in their troughs; it even scaled the steeples of the Eglise Saint-Stanislas and made the great bell ring out once, dong! only once, one little ding for the dying she-wolf, who'd never be allowed inside the church on her final journey or be buried in consecrated ground, the bitch! Little Marcel looked up from his plate, while Josaphat-le-Violon got out of his chair and walked over to him. "Plessis's gone!" Josaphat-le-Violon took him in his arms. "No, not Plessis. Another animal. Come here, Marcel. Your uncle Josaphat's going to turn on the light in the moon." And

Josaphat-le-Violon went out on the back balcony, still holding Marcel in his arms. Rose, Violette, Mauve, and Florence, their mother, stopped eating too. Florence took the woollen ball from her pocket and looked at Violette. "It wasn't for Duplessis, Violette. You knit somebody else's death." Ti-Lou died in the saddle, the way she had wanted.

When Josaphat-le-Violon had finished "La Gigue aux sept fausses notes," he lay his instrument down on a chair on the balcony and took Marcel in his arms. "Look how beautiful it is. She's going to climb up and up and up in the sky, and then she'll climb back down the other side so I can put her out. I have to wait till she comes back down, otherwise it's too high and she can't hear the music right." "You do that every single day?" "Yup, every day. Ever since . . . well, for a long, long time. I'm the one that does the job now. The other guy, the one before me, he took off in a flying canoe and he's never been seen since . . ." "A flying canoe?" "I never told you about that?" "No." "Well, well. You should've asked me. You want me to tell you now, right away?" "Oh, yes!" "All right. Now, listen carefully. . . . Ah! It all happened a long time ago . . . such a long time ago . . . way before you were even born. . . . I was just a little boy myself, hardly any older than Richard, I don't think. I was living in the country. You know, the country. . . . I've told you about it before. . . . Out where there's not many houses and lots and lots of trees." "I know, Duhamel." "That's right. Anyhow, back then there weren't any cars, so to get from Duhamel to Montreal, it took you two days. You had to sleep over at Saint-Jérôme, and let me tell you, we thought

Saint-Jérôme was a pretty big place! Yup! It was quite a treat, spending the night at the Hôtel Lapointe! Anyhow, what I'm working up to is to tell you that Duhamel was a good piece away and we didn't know a thing about Montreal. Didn't miss it either. Anyway, one night I was taking a bucket of raspberries over to ma tante Marguerite, my father's sister. She was so poor that she fed her kids right off the table, without any dishes underneath! So, we chewed the fat a while and the time passed without us even noticing it and night was falling before I decided to head back home. It was August, I remember — and a real fine night it was! I didn't have a buggy, nothing — I'd come with mon oncle Arthur, ma tante Marguerite's husband — and I was gonna have to walk back home. A three mile walk in the dark! So, I went out on the front balcony with my aunt, and she'd've been real glad to have me stay over, but I never really liked the way it smelled in that house, so I said no. . . . You couldn't see six feet in front of you! That's the truth! I was standing there on the doorstep and ma tante was holding a lantern that shed a little light on the floor and the posts that held up the roof of the balcony. . . . But down at the bottom of the steps — nothing! I didn't want to tell my aunt, but I was a little scared. . . . I never liked the dark. . . . I'm no sissy, never have been, but all the same. . . . Like I said just now, I had a good three miles to go through the woods, over a little road where it wasn't unheard of to run into a bear, face to face, even in broad daylight. . . . And I'll tell you straight out, all alone there in the dark, the farthest I'd ever gone in the dark like that was to the outhouse! Ma tante Marguerite tells me: 'I'd let you have a lantern, Josaphat, but your uncle and your cousin Manuel took the other two lanterns and I'll be needing this one when I go and have a last look in the henhouse. . .' 'I don't want any lantern,' I tell her, 'I know my way home!' Then, to show her that I wasn't afraid, I ran down the front steps and there I was, in the dark.... It was like falling into water.... As soon as I left my aunt's lantern behind, it started getting cold...not like in the winter, no; in fact, it was as hot as the hinges of hell.... It was as if...as if, I felt cold inside.... I couldn't see a thing in front of me; my heart was ticking away like a busted watch.... When I turned around, I saw ma tante Marguerite waving at me.... The lantern was throwing big shadows that went flying out all around.... She looked like a ghost, goddamn it! I felt pretty small inside my boots, let me tell you! Then, all of a sudden, she went back inside the house and there I was, all by myself. You know how quiet...how quiet it is in the country.... How can I explain it?... When you're all by yourself in your room, lying on your back with all the lights out.... and it's the silence itself that scares you.... You're scared of the silence. But when you're outside, in the country, *inside* that silence, it isn't the silence that's scary then, it's the thousands and millions of little sounds that live in it.... That's when you realize that there's really no such thing as silence...that there's always something to hear in the silence.... I was...it was as if I was paralyzed there by the side of the road. Nothing in front of me, nothing behind, nothing alongside.... And up over my head, no moon in the sky; the sky was empty. Empty! But in the midst of that emptiness, there were sounds...all around...noises....Old leaves crackling...little branches breaking...and...things crawling over the pine needles: the padded paws of animals that you hear all the same because it's dark.... An owl hoots and you think it's a ghost; a bat flies out in every direction instead of going in a straight line, the crazy bugger! Ah! A little light...two, five, twenty, a hundred little lights! Fireflies on parade, going to look for the damned soul of a sinner to take him on his last journey! I sure wished I was somewhere else! Eventually, my eyes got used to the dark and I could see the road like a long yellow ribbon, a little paler than the rest of the surroundings.... I took all the courage I had left (about enough to fill a thimble, I think) and I set off down that road, my head scrunched between my shoulders, my eyes as wide as soup plates, my heart changing place every two or three beats.... What's that? A rat? A rabbit? A raccoon? A dog? A sheep? A wolf? A bear? What is it? I started to run.... Another parade of fireflies.... Good God, was that somebody laughing? Eh? How far is it to the house? Dumbbell, you just left! I'm suffocating.... Too bad, I'll stop! If they want to nab me, they'll nab me; at least I'll know who I'm dealing with.... Hey, what's that? I hear a sound behind me, louder than the others.... I look around and what I see is a sort of white light moving along the road.... Horses! It looks like horses coming this way! Yes, that's what it is! I'm saved! Maybe it's somebody I know! Maybe I'll be able to get into my bed sooner!... Ah! What's that? Over there!... Horses.... White ones! Loose!... You won't believe me, Marcel, but true as I'm standing here, I saw two, four, six, eight white horses running down the road, all by themselves! Eight big white horses with manes so long they looked like wings!... The horses seemed to be running as if they were on their way somewhere very important.... They were whinnying and galloping like crazy.... They came closer and closer and their hooves made the road shake. I could see them as if they'd been lit up by the moon. But there wasn't any moon. Hide! But I was too scared to get down in the ditch! They're coming closer! They're coming! They're...so...beautiful! Haaaa! They streaked past me like bolts of lightning, galloping and whinnying, their ears in the wind, their nostrils all foamy, their eyes wild.... You'd almost think

they went right through me! My hair was standing up on
my head! I had goose pimples!...I wanted to piss and I
was pretty close to doing that other thing too.... The
horses had taken the road that curved in front of me.
Then they disappeared, as if there was nothing after that
curve. I was paralyzed in the middle of the road; I
couldn't move; I was too scared of what I might see after
that curve in the road.... And I couldn't move
backwards either. I was sitting in the middle of the road
and I started howling like a kid. (I was a kid, but I never
used to howl like one. I was too proud.) You understand,
seeing things like that in the middle of the night, when
you're all by yourself in the middle of the mountains, it's
pretty scary.... You start wondering if maybe you're on
your way downhill and at the bottom of the hill, the
asylum's waiting for you.... Especially because my
mother always told me that I dreamed too much and
some day all that dreaming was going to play a trick on
me.... So, there it was, goldang it! If I'd had my fiddle
with me at least.... You know, sometimes music....
But that's something you'll understand later.... So, what
I did, my boy, was pick myself up and just keep going
.... And there was nothing beyond the bend in the road.
Walk, walk, walk....no news from the horses. I ended
up thinking that I'd really been dreaming, and then, I
started whistling so that I'd forget about it all. When all of
a sudden, I hear a terrible uproar back behind the mountain.... There was such a commotion, child, it was as if
half a dozen thunderclouds were hammering at each
other.... Then, I heard a kind of whinny, far, far away,
on the other side of the mountain.... More than
one...as if there were horses moaning somewhere on the
other side of the country.... Then, when I looked up, I
saw a sort of greyish-yellow light shining on the trees on
the mountain.... 'Is our place on fire?' And then...I

saw . . . the eight big horses coming out from behind the mountain . . . and rising up to the sky, whinnying and pawing the ground! They were pulling on chains and they seemed to be straining like I've never seen animals strain before in my life! As if they were pulling on the heaviest thing in the world. The chains dug into their skin and there was blood running all down their hides. . . . I could see their bleeding sores and their wild eyes. The eyes of animals that have gone crazy, that don't know why they hurt so much! And then . . . at the very end of the last chain . . . you could see a red ball. The moon! They were pulling the moon up from behind the mountain! It was big — nearly as big as the mountain, I'm telling you — and red! You know, like the full moon in August that's so scary. . . . The horses' blood was running onto the moon and the moon was dripping like an orange. . . . Then, as soon as the moon was up on top of the mountain, and nice and round, the chains came apart and those eight horses ran off in eight different directions, like a compass card. The full moon never looked so much like a big wicked eye. I started to cry, yelling, I didn't want the moon, that it was a beautiful full moon, but that was no reason to make the poor animals suffer like that. . . . It wasn't dark any more; it was nearly as bright as those nights in winter when the snow gives off its own light. . . . I got back on the road again. . . . It was as if I'd been hit over the head. I felt as if the moon was watching me. She was up there on my left as I walked, and she was looking at me. . . . You'd have thought somebody'd fired off a cannon in the sky and made a big red hole. . . . But. . . . I wasn't quite so scared now, because I could see up ahead of me. . . . I'd almost made it back home when, off in the distance, I heard a sort of music, like a bunch of drunks who were singing a sad song. I looked behind me on the road . . . but there wasn't a thing. But the song was coming closer.

When it was so close that, ordinarily, I'd have seen the singers, my heart was in my mouth again.... White horses a while back; now, invisible men.... I don't know why, but I looked up...maybe to check if the moon was still there (I was pretty close to thinking it was the moon that was singing) and then.... I saw a birchbark canoe come out from behind the mountain, with eight guys paddling through the sky and singing as they went.... A fiery red birchbark canoe with seams that looked like stars.... They were singing at the tops of their lungs and they were drinking from bottles of caribou.... Then, all of a sudden, the canoe stopped just above me and I recognized those eight men with their paddles, singing 'Envoyons d'l'avant nos gens,' singing themselves hoarse: there was Willy, Ti-Pet Turgeon's boy; there was Gaspar Petit — I'd seen him the night before. He had double pneumonia and he had the gall to be wandering around the sky in his pyjamas; there was big Laurent Doyon, the curé's hard-hearted brother, who worked as beadle from time to time, but only when it suited him; there was Georges-Albert Pratte, the village barber, who also worked as a dentist and got drunk on eau de Cologne, according to my mother, but maybe that's just gossip; there was Rosaire Rouleau, too, the beggar, who we hadn't laid eyes on for a good long while, who we thought might be dead; and the Patenaude twins, Twin and Twin — one Twin, with his blind eye; the other Twin, with a stump for an arm; and last of all, there was Teddy Bear Brown, the only Anglais that we'd ever seen in the village, who always claimed he was the one that turned on the light in the moon.... Every day, at the end of the afternoon, he'd disappear, and when he came back, there was the moon, pale or shining bright, full or as thin as a slice of lemon, depending on what day of the month it was.... All eight of them were as drunk as skunks and they were having so much fun in that canoe that they seemed about to fall out of it. Georges-Albert Pratte, who was a kind of relative, because he was married to my mother's brother-in-law's sister, he leaned out of his canoe and yelled at me: 'Hey, Josaphat. We're on our way to Saint-Jérôme to see fat Minoune! Want to come along?' Then, he started laughing himself silly. . . . You see, fat Minoune — well, I was still a little young to be going to see her. . . . But that's something you'll learn about later. . . . Anyhow, the whole bunch of them were having fun, that's for sure! Then, Teddy Bear Brown, he leaned over the canoe too and he shouted at me with his squarehead accent: 'Hey there, Josaphat! You want my job, old buddy? I'm sick of lighting that old moon. If you want the job now, it's yours. You and your fiddle. . . . It'll be better because I had to bark and, you know, at my age, it's un peu ridiculous, you know. . . . You want it? Oui? Okay. You start tomorrow. I'm on my way to Saint-Jérôme to see fat Minoune and if you never see me again, think about me when you play your tunes to light up my old friend.' Then, it didn't take thirty seconds till 'Envoyons d'l'avant nos gens' and the loud vulgar laughing started up again, and the canoe shot off, heading for the moon, nearly capsizing at every stroke of the paddle. Then I realized that if the horses had suffered so much that night, it was because that asshole Teddy Bear Brown hadn't done his job! So then I told myself that I, Josaphat-le-Violon. . .I'd be faithful to that moon for the rest of my life, and never again, as long as I lived, would those horses have to pull the moon out from the side of the mountain. . . . And ever since, every day, my fiddle's climbed up in the sky, and the moon can come out in peace." Marcel had fallen asleep, overcome with happiness and fear, his head filled with horses, moons, birchbark canoes and lanterns shaped like fiddles. When he was quite certain that the little boy wouldn't hear any more, Josaphat-le-Violon finished his story. "And some day, when I'm too old, some fine afternoon I'll come and see you and I'll say: 'Marcel, I'm tired.' I hope you'll understand and that you'll respect the moon as long as you live. No *chasse-galerie.* Because the moon's the only thing in the world you can be sure about." From her dining room window on the ground floor, Florence had been listening to Josaphat-le-Violon tell his story. When he finished, he bowed gallantly to her and she responded with a smile of complicity.

Laura ate her supper with the fat woman. When she saw the house suddenly filling up, she took refuge with her cousin on the pretext of a dizzy spell. "Can I stay with you a while, ma tante? I feel sick when there's too many people around.... Does that ever happen to you?" The fat woman gave her the ghost of a smile. "There's never a lot of people coming to see me all at once, you know..." "I'm sorry, you're right, you can't move and the room isn't all that big." "Sit down, Laura. You're supposed to be feeling dizzy." Laura sat on the bed, legs together, arms folded across her bosom. "And relax.... I'm not surprised you feel sick, you're wound up tighter than the strings on your father's fiddle!" Laura unfolded her arms, but her legs remained firmly stuck together. "Laura, really! Let yourself go! Lie down on the bed..." "Come on, ma tante. I'm not that sick..." "Will you listen to me, Laura Cadieux? If you want to eat like a civilized person, you're going to have to rest a little first..." So Laura lay on the bed, but still she seemed ill at ease. "Did you and your father walk here?" "Yes." "You shouldn't walk too much in your condition..." "No, that isn't what's wrong. I like

225

walking. And it's good for me.... No, I know why I'm not feeling good.... I eat too much. That's what it is. There's a reason why I'm so fat! If you could see how much I eat in a day, ma tante, you wouldn't believe it!" The fat woman burst out laughing. "Do you realize who you're talking to? I haven't got a reputation for living on lettuce, you know..." Laura raised her head somewhat as she answered her cousin. "It's different for you. I've seen pictures of you when you were my age. At least you weren't fat when you were twenty-two.... But look at me.... If I keep putting on weight like this, what'll I look like when I'm forty, will you tell me?" Laura's voice broke and her eyes began to cloud over. She lay her head on the pillow. "That's what happens when you marry a man that's a maniac in the kitchen!" The fat woman looked at Laura a long time before answering. "You don't have to eat everything he cooks, you know..." "But I like eating, ma tante! And everything Pit makes is so good!" Pit Cadieux, Laura's husband, worked as an assistant cook at the Windsor Hotel, one of the great hotels of Montreal, and his culinary talents, especially at sauces, which he never spoiled and which he prepared with unusual skill, were beginning to draw attention to him from the chef, for whom he was truly a blessing, right up to the hotel management, who were delighted that the reputation of their dining room was growing from week to week. People were even starting to come to the Windsor Hotel just for the sauces of Chef Vaillancourt, who was careful not to admit that his great specialty was, in fact, the work of some third kitchen boy he'd discovered by chance one day when everything was going wrong and he'd been obliged to ask the staff at large, with no great hope of getting an affirmative reply, the question: "Does anybody here know how to make a *sauce béarnaise*? I haven't got time and there's a bunch of fucking Frenchmen out there that won't

eat their fucking steaks without it!" Pit Cadieux timidly
raised his hand. "I'm good at sauces. I like to make them."
Without really knowing why, Chef Vaillancourt trusted
the young man who was already fat and nearly bald, who,
he'd noticed some time before, did whatever he was asked
with an obvious love for his work. Pit's *sauce béarnaise* turned out to be far superior to Chef Vaillancourt's. The
Frenchmen were overwhelmed and insisted on shaking
the hand of Chef Vaillancourt. He went along with the
ceremony and came back to the kitchen delighted. "Do
your sauces always turn out that good?" "Every time."
"Okay. Whenever I need one, I'll ask you. Where do you
come from anyway?" "Saint-Jérôme." "Where'd you work
before?" "The Hôtel Lapointe." Chef Vaillancourt nearly
choked. "You mean, you learned how to make *sauce béarnaise* at the Hôtel Lapointe in Saint-Jérôme?" "Hell, no!
You eat worse than the devil there! I learned out of books.
I'd try the sauces out at home." It was Laura, in fact,
who'd been acting as the guinea pig for Pit's experiments
ever since they met. Every Saturday before they got married, instead of taking his girlfriend to a restaurant and
wasting the little money at his disposal on frightful hot
chicken sandwiches or club sandwiches thrown together
from the week's leftovers, Pit would spend hours with his
cookbooks, then go off to do his shopping with Laura on
his arm. He bought everything himself. He trusted no
one, especially not Laura, who he knew was a little too
thrifty and might have a tendency not to buy the finest in-
gredients. Afterwards, he spent the afternoon in the
kitchen, happily trumpeting the songs of Fernandel, while
Laura went to the movies with her girlfriends, or simply
watched him work, fascinated. And when it was time to
eat... bliss. Laura and Pit looked at one another as they
ate, smiling, throwing kisses. Laura would say, "It's so
good!" And Pit would answer: "Shut up and eat!" After

227

supper, they went for long walks around Saint-Jérôme and people who met them would nudge each other. "If you ask me, they've just committed a sin, those two . . . . Or they're getting ready to." But the only sins Pit and Laura committed at the time were of a sort that would have greatly disappointed the curious. And since they'd been married, it was even worse. Their cravings for food had multiplied tenfold and they ate at every hour of the day — before *and* after making love, and sometimes even in bed. As soon as he'd become, in a way, the master saucemaker at the Windsor Hotel, a sort of frenzy had taken hold of Pit Cadieux and, at home, he began to try out every sort of sauce imaginable, from the simplest to the most complicated, dreaming of seeing his greatest successes on the hotel menu. And Laura, who was already plump, started to get dangerously fat. When she complained about her obesity to her husband, he shrugged or kissed her neck, saying: "I like you fat. There's more of you to love. And I hope the little one that you've got in the oven isn't going to look like a skeleton either!" Sometimes late at night, from the hotel kitchen, Pit would bring home cakes made with almond paste, Laura's favourite, and they would ceremoniously sit in the dining room and savour them. A little piece of cake to finish off a little glass of milk. Then, a little glass of milk to finish off a little piece of cake. Afterwards, obviously, they slept badly, but as Pit Cadieux, *chef saucier* incognito of the Windsor Hotel in Montreal, put it so well: "If you miss a night's sleep, you can always catch up on it; but if you miss a meal, it's a waste!" The fat woman wiped her sweat-covered face with a damp washcloth. "If you're that crazy about eating, don't complain!" When Gabriel came into the bedroom without saying hello to his wife or to Laura, whom he hadn't seen for months, the latter, feeling that she was in the way, struggled up from the bed, but the fat woman gestured to her not to leave the room. So Laura stayed at her cousins's side while Gabriel lay down beside her, turning his back to them. The two women remained silent for several minutes. Laura sensed that her cousin wouldn't open her mouth until her husband decided if he was going to talk, or until he started snoring. But after a while, Gabriel sighed, and when he spoke, his voice seemed faint and weary. "Sorry I didn't say anything right away. . . . I'm a little bit drunk. And I'm really down in the dumps." Laura and the fat woman exchanged a glance, frowning. "I'll take a little nap for half an hour, then I'll feel better. Bonjour, Laura. Everything all right? How about Pit?" And almost immediately, Gabriel fell asleep. All the time that she'd been lying in her cousin's bed, Laura had felt the need to confide in her: the words rose in her throat, confidences she'd held back for too long, doubts she didn't understand, that struck her more and more frequently, even when she was eating, doubts about Pit and herself. There were questions, too, that had been forming in her head for some time and which she couldn't answer; they nearly came tumbling out, like a plea, but Gabriel's arrival disarmed the young woman, who immediately began to babble the sort of trivia that fills meaningless conversations between people with nothing to say to one another. She no longer felt like sharing her confidences because there was a man sleeping behind her and men were incorrigible wet blankets where confidences were concerned. Only once had she tried talking to Pit about her doubts. Her husband stopped her cold with a gesture and silenced her questions with a word. "If you start asking questions, we'll never get out of the woods! Do like me, throw yourself into your work and stop thinking!" And though she loved her Pit — she was sure of that — the growing importance of cooking in her husband's life made her feel uncomfortable. In a way, she was jealous of her husband's work. She had no idea how to combat this state of affairs, the reasons for which she hadn't figured out. Was she annoyed at Pit because he was the reason that she was getting so fat so fast? Or was she just annoyed at how he made a living? But if Pit had been a shoemaker, she'd still have eaten as much, because, in any case, she had a natural penchant for eating well. Perhaps the fat woman couldn't answer all these questions, but just talking to someone about them would be an immense relief for Laura. Instead, though, she heard herself asking her cousin if she needed anything, or whether or not it would bother her if she had a cigarette before supper—and she heard the fat woman reply, "No, I don't need anything." And, "Yes, it'd bother me if you smoke, because it's bad for your health and the baby's too." The fat woman, for her part, was aware all this time that Laura wanted to talk, but she hadn't dared to ask any questions, telling herself that if the need was there, everything would come out by itself. While the fat woman waited, she kept the conversation going, occasionally casting a glance at her cousin that might have contained a question, but which Laura interpreted as an encouragement to gossip. And when Edouard, shouting at the top of his lungs, "Dinner's ready, ladies!" waddled through the house, trying out some ridiculous dance steps, Gabriel woke with a start, stretched like a cat sluggish with sleep, and walked out of the bedroom, rubbing his eyes. Then, Laura was even more embarrassed to be there, an involutary witness to a silent domestic scene. Her cousin patted her hand. "Don't worry, Laura. We'll talk to each other eventually, my husband and I . . ." "You're lucky. . . . I can't talk to Pit. The only thing he cares about is what's on his plate." But Laura said no more, thinking this wasn't the moment—at suppertime—to bother her cousin with problems that didn't concern her. So, the two women ate in silence, laughing when they overheard something funny from the dining room and never looking at one another, because obese people don't watch one another eat. When the meal was over, they heard, through the open window, Josaphat-le-Violon telling Marcel the story of how the moon got its fire. The fat woman wept uncontrollably. Gabriel had often told her that he'd grown up under the spell of his uncle Josaphat's legends and every time she heard the old man tell one of his stories, with their mixture of true and false, of humdrum country life and her own astonishing need for illusions and the marvellous, her heart began to beat faster, and she would be carried away with joy in the *chasse-galerie* or to the land of nuns' farts where you got the giggles and lost your memory. As for Laura, she envied Marcel; she envied his innocence, his great naïveté, and his touching credulity. "I believed it too, just like him! I wanted so badly for it to be true! If it were true, it would give us all a reason for going on!" After Josaphat-le-Violon's story, the fat woman put her plate on the bed, beside Laura. "Do you ever talk to your father? He knows a lot about things, you know. . ." "My father? He's a poet, my father. . . . He never has his feet on the ground. He says that he can light up the moon, but he walks down the street with his fly undone! How can you talk to a man like that? He makes up legends for himself; I make up problems." And suddenly, so easily it seemed almost ridiculous, Laura began to talk. Everything came out at once, the way that she'd felt it was beginning earlier; and as she spoke, she could see her problems flying away from her like birds escaping from a cage. "It feels good to talk, ma tante! It really helps!" "I can imagine."

231

"There's still time to get there before the show starts..." "I said no, Mastaï! And I don't want to hear another word about it! Next time, you'll think twice before you talk! It's fine to pull my sister's leg a little, but you didn't have to make her suffer that much!" "Gaby, it was just a joke." "I know it was just a joke! That's what makes it so awful! You never want to hurt anybody, but you always go too far, so this time, I'm going to teach you a lesson..." "If you cut me off, you'll be cutting yourself off too!" "That's exactly it — and I hope you'll feel twice as guilty." Mastaï Jodoin took the theatre tickets from his pocket and put them on the table. "Two and a half bucks shot to hell! Maybe we can give them to somebody..." "Who? The show starts in half an hour.... They'd have to break their necks to get there.... No, no. Throw them out." Gabrielle Jodoin came out of the bathroom where she'd just made herself beautiful again. She and Mastaï had been talking through the closed door while she gave her hair a final brushing. She rumpled her husband's hair and screwed up her face in distaste. "You aren't even changed!" Gabrielle was truly ravishing in her flowered dress and Mastaï felt his anger melt like snow in the sun. "We're only going to your sister's, Gaby.... And anyhow, I'm not dirty!" His voice was softer now and Gabrielle was aware of it. She held back the smile that was already beginning to turn up her lips. "Put on a shirt at least.... I'm not crazy about seeing you cross the street in your undershirt." As soon as he set foot in the house, Mastaï had the unfortunate habit of parading about in his underwear — and Gabrielle hadn't yet managed to cure him of this defect, which she and her sisters considered outrageous, but which their mother, Rita Guérin, thought was funny. She often said that her son-in-law resembled a big baby looking all over for his mother and never finding her. No one really understood this image, but Rita Guérin seemed to find it most amusing. When Mastaï put on his clean shirt, Gabrielle undertook to fix his hair with her hairbrush, something her husband particularly enjoyed. He sat on a kitchen chair, squeezing his wife between his legs and moaning with joy. He wrapped his arms around Gabrielle's big belly and assumed his little boy's voice, a voice that made Gabrielle laugh so much, and thanks to which he could get anything he wanted from her. "Your big honeybear all forgiven?" "You look too damn swell, Mastaï. I'd have to be blind in both eyes if I really wanted to be pissed off at you!" Mastaï raised his head and rested his chin against his wife's belly. "Want me to call a taxi? It wouldn't take us more than fifteen minutes to get there..." Gabrielle bopped him on the head with her hairbrush and he howled, more from surprise than pain. "You think I'm a nincompoop, Mastaï Jodoin? I told you I forgave you, but I never said I'd forgotten everything! So get La Poune and Juliette Pétrie out of your head, my dear, because it won't do any good!" Everything happened so abruptly that Gabrielle had no time to react. Mastaï literally leaped on the telephone and dialed a number. "For the love of God, what are you doing?" "Calling a taxi, ciboire! Maybe you don't want to go to the theatre, but I do!" He gave the address and hung up, grabbed the two tickets which were still on the kitchen table and headed for the door. "Go play cards with your mother and your sisters, if you want. I'll ask Germaine's husband to come and see La Poune with me!" Gabrielle ran after him. They crossed the street behind one another— Gabrielle holding her belly with both hands, and Mastaï waving the tickets in his right hand. "If you do that, you'll be sorry, my little man!" Mastaï stopped at the bottom of the outside staircase that went up to Germaine's apartment. He turned around and faced his wife. "Will you stop treating me like a child, tabarnac? And stop punishing me like a baby when I do something you don't like! I'm not a child, Gabrielle Jodoin, and you won't get me to do something by taking away my candy! My mother tried that trick when I was little and you can see where it got her! I bought these tickets because I knew it'd make us both happy, cibole! And I don't see any reason why I shouldn't enjoy myself! Okay, so I didn't treat your thin-skinned little sister with kid gloves, but that's no reason to turn it into a three-act tragedy, calvaire! I'll tell her I'm sorry and then we'll forget the whole business! I'll bet that she's already forgotten all about it! Sometimes your sister 'The Actress' is a hell of a lot less dramatic than you are!" Gabrielle sat on the steps, her head down. Her husband sat down beside her. "Here comes the taxi. Are you coming with me or should I take Ernest?" Gabrielle put one hand on Mastaï's knee. "Go with Ernest. I see what you mean, but I'm not in the mood to go out any more." Mastaï sprang to his feet, furious, and climbed the stairs four at a time. He walked into his sister-in-law's house without knocking. Gabrielle folded her arms on her knees and lay her head on them. "How do you expect me to have any fun when you get me all worked up like that?" Rose Ouimet and her husband, Roland, were walking slowly down the street towards Germaine Lauzon's house. Despite the heat, Rose Ouimet was wearing a roomy wool coat over her dress, probably to conceal her pregnancy. She jumped at the sight of her sister Gabrielle sitting on the stairs. "Good Lord, something's wrong with her!" Roland Ouimet raised his eyes to Heaven. His wife's family was grounds for wailing and the gnashing of teeth, Roland Ouimet knew only too well. After all, he had married the most dramatic daughter in the family, Rose, who saw tragedies everywhere, revelling in them constantly, watering them copiously with her tears and never doing anything to settle them. He spoke so softly that his wife didn't hear him. "Jesus Christ, another drama! You must be proud of yourself!" Just then, a taxi stopped in front of Germaine's house. Mastaï and Ernest came out on the second-floor balcony, waving their arms. Rose walked faster, leaving her husband behind her. "Just what's going on here?" When she reached the stairs where her sister was prostrate, her two brothers-in-law were coming down the steps. Mastaï walked past Gabrielle without a word and ensconced himself in the taxi, followed by Ernest Lauzon, who didn't seem to have the slightest notion of what was happening to him. Germaine Lauzon, Rita Guérin and Pierrette Guérin, in turn, came out on the balcony. Mastaï Jodoin slammed the taxi door shut and shouted: "Salut, everybody, have a nice time!" The taxi drove away. Slowly, Gabrielle got to her feet and climbed up a few steps. Rose Ouimet followed her, almost in tears. "Good Lord, what'd he do to you now?" They're all alike, the sons of bitches, every last one of them!" Roland Ouimet had remained at the foot of the stairs, watching the two women climb the stairs. He spoke to his mother-in-law, who was waiting for her daughters on the balcony. "They gone for the night?" Rita Guérin shrugged. "What do *you* think? Did they look like they were going to buy an ice-cream cone, numbskull?" Roland stepped back a few paces. "So, I'll be the only man here tonight! I can't stand playing cards with a bunch of women! Play with yourselves, I'm going to the tavern!" As his wife watched him with contempt, he began to walk along la rue Mont-Royal. When her two daughters reached the balcony, Rita Guérin took Gabrielle in her arms. "Instead of playing cards tonight, we'll sit out on the balcony by ourselves. It's warm enough. . . . Pierrette, bring out the chairs. Your sisters mustn't strain themselves." Gabrielle blew her nose noisily into the handkerchief that her mother offered her. When she'd finished drying her eyes, she sighed deeply. "The worst of it is that he's right, the bugger!"

Léopold Brassard walked into the living room without making a sound. The room was plunged in darkness. Guessing at his wife's silhouette rather than actually seeing it, Léopold approached the window, his hands in his pockets, embarrassed. Immediately after supper, without a word, Marie-Louise had gone back to the living room, to her kingdom, and attached herself to her window, without even thinking of switching on the lamps. Marie-Louise didn't hear her husband come in and she started a little when he spoke. "How come you're sitting in the dark like that?" "Is there anything worth looking at in here?" "Is there anything worth looking at outside?" She buried her head a little deeper in the lace curtain. "It doesn't bother me, what's outside. It's more interesting." Léopold put his hand on his wife's shoulder. "Did the baby kick today?" Marie-Louise freed herself, as if some disgusting animal had touched her. "Please keep your hands to yourself, Léopold! You smell of the printshop." She brought her hand to her mouth. "Why not come right out with it and say I make you sick?" "Yes, Léopold, you make me sick." "See how silly you are. . . . I was coming to get you so we could go out and sit on the balcony . . . . Everybody else on la rue Fabre is out on their balcony to celebrate the arrival of spring. . . . We're the only ones shut up inside — as usual." "Maybe they've got something to celebrate. We haven't." "Please, Marie-Louise. It's just as dark on the balcony and it's cooler . . . . In your condition. . . ." "What do you know about my condition?"

"Not much maybe, but I know if a woman shuts herself up in the dark, in her living room, it's because she's got something to hide!" Marie-Louise jerked her head towards her husband. "You said it! I've got something to hide all right!" She got up slowly, leaning on the back of her chair. "This!" Laughter burst out on one of the balconies across from them, but Marie-Louise and Léopold didn't look towards the window. They were lost in their mutual hatred, looking into one another's eyes, nearly hypnotized. Mercedes and Béatrice were coming down the stairs of the house across the street. They were followed by Edouard, who was singing at the top of his lungs, "Some Day My Prince Will Come," and throwing kisses, left and right. On the balcony, Thérèse, Richard and Philippe were laughing like little lunatics. Very slowly, Léopold looked away from his wife's face in order to glance out the window. He managed to smile. "Some people know how to have fun." Marie-Louise clicked her tongue four or five times. "That's right! Go down the stairs singing 'Some Day My Prince Will Come' and I'll laugh." Léopold walked out of the living room, his heels clattering on the linoleum. He took a folding chair from behind the door in the hallway and put it on the balcony, beneath the amused gaze of the fat man who had stopped singing as soon as he saw him come out of the house. Edouard bent over his two new friends. "Sweet Jesus, girls, the rats are coming out of their holes! The plague can't be far behind!" Mercedes and Béatrice hid behind their hands and laughed. Léopold, smiling at the sight of his neighbours in such a merry mood, took out his tobacco pouch and pipe. "I wonder what the hell he said to make them laugh like that?" Mercedes, Béatrice and Edouard were sitting on the steps like children now. Béatrice seemed impatient. "That taxi's taking its sweet time. . . . "Don't get your shirt in a knot, Betty, the night's still young. . ." Edouard took the girls by the shoulders. "Betty's like me, she likes them young!" Thérèse and the boys had come out to join their elders on the bottom steps. She dislodged her uncle and sat between Mercedes and Béatrice. "I'd like to know how come you were laughing your heads off just now." Edouard tapped her shoulder lightly. "You're too young, Thérèse, you wouldn't understand." Visibly angry, Thérèse leaped to her feet and stood with her fists against her hips. "I understand a lot more than you think, ma tante Edouard!" Edouard collapsed on the steps with laughter, while the two women nudged each other, snickering. Thérèse, who had thought that her reply was insulting, even though she didn't understand all the implications, was taken aback. "They're such dummies tonight! They'll laugh at anything!" Before sitting down again, she held her hands round her mouth to form a megaphone. "I kissed a man on the mouth this afternoon!" Her words didn't have the expected effect. Béatrice had just sprung to her feet, her nerves on edge. "There it is! There it is!" She was pointing at a taxi that was driving along la rue Fabre. "I hope we won't be too late." Edouard waved both arms to attract the taxi-driver's attention, as the driver checked addresses with a flashlight. "Anyhow, girls, Juliette Pétrie and La Poune never come on before the middle of the show. . . . They're the stars, you see, so they fix it so people have to wait for them!" When the taxi started up again a few moments later, Thérèse heard Mercedes say to Edouard, "That niece of yours is going to be a real beauty." Thérèse smiled with satisfaction. She couldn't hear her uncle's reply, however. It would have pleased her less. "She'll be a beauty all right, but if you ask me, she's going to be a goddamn monster." The taxi turned west on Gilford and disappeared with a squeal of balding tires. Edouard was leading Mercedes and Béatrice towards a destiny that none of them could guess at: a twenty-year reign of feasts and splendour for Béatrice, who until the early sixties would be the darling of Montreal's nightowls, the prostitute draped in more jewels and compliments than any other in the city's history, always demanding and sometimes perverse, well-padded when necessary, when fashion demanded it, and thin as a rail the rest of the time, a second Ti-Lou, but without the accent and, more important, without her pretensions. (Béatrice was quick to realize that, though they paid better, the high and mighty often didn't fuck too well — and she quickly began to specialize in businessmen who were less glamourous, but hornier.) Sometimes she was rich enough to give away her dresses after wearing them only once (one day she happened upon a biography of Marie-Antoinette and decided to copy her, instead of watching her outfits wilt in her wardrobe); sometimes she was as poor as the bums in Dominion Square, for whom she felt so much affection, and who returned it, though they concealed it cleverly as they waited for the next windfall, which always, even if they had to wait, would descend on them; and for Mercedes, there would be an ephemeral but dazzling career as a singer, unfortunately cut short by a fatal automobile accident that would cost her her life, sometime in the mid-fifties. In fact, in the wings of the Théâtre National, to which Edouard had an entrée, thanks to a tap-dancer recently hired by La Poune, Fine Dumas was waiting for them, a self-styled impresario for touring dancers, but in reality, an unscrupulous procuress and supplier of fresh meat to all the whorehouses in Quebec, from the sleaziest to the fanciest, from the most discreet to the most garish. Fine Dumas would appreciate immediately the inestimable value of the merchandise that Edouard was innocently bringing her, and she would take over the two friends, turning them into the crowned heads

239

of Montreal-by-night. And so it was that three plundered soldiers and a walk through Parc Lafontaine would supply Montreal with ten years of love songs and twenty years of furtive but dazzling loves. Léopold watched the scene as he pulled voluptuously on his pipe. The good smell of tobacco that made him feel so secure gradually enveloped him, and he felt himself becoming light. A few minutes later, the door opened discreetly behind him. He heard the door open, but he didn't turn around. Marie-Louise spoke in a very low voice, as if she were telling him a secret. Or a confession. "Go get the rocking chair, Léopold. It's too hot inside." On the other side of the street, Philippe, who was intently picking his nose, asked Thérèse a question that made the little girl blush. "Thérèse, did you really kiss a man on the mouth this afternoon?"

Albertine, Josaphat-le-Violon and Laura were washing the dishes as Victoire listened to the news on the radio. Albertine seemed exhausted and large drops of sweat were running down her face. "You could have left the dishes till tomorrow, Bartine. . ." "Tomorrow. . . . Don't make me laugh! Tomorrow, mon oncle, I have to start all over again. If I don't do the dishes at night, I have to get up early tomorrow and do them." "How come the children don't give you a hand? Thérèse is big enough. . ." "She's big enough, all right, but she isn't interested, as you can well imagine! Not very often, anyway. I always feel as if she's judging me, so there's times when I'd just as soon she wasn't around." "You should stop thinking that everybody's judging you, Bartine." "I'd think it even if it wasn't true! Do you think I couldn't see the whole bunch of you at suppertime? Eh? I didn't want to serve those two floozies out of principle — principle, mon oncle — but all I got for my trouble was stupid jokes and mean cracks. I got laughed at because I've got principles! So let me tell you, I'm starting to ask myself a hell of a lot of questions! If it's got to the point where you have to invite floozies for a meal to get some respect in your own house, I'd like to know what happens next!" Furiously, Albertine emptied the tea kettle that was full of hot water into the now-tepid dishwater. "Don't scald yourself now! That isn't necessary!" "And all those stupid ideas that you're filling Marcel's head with. . . . Just now, I heard you tell him that story about turning on the light in the moon. I ask you, does that make any sense? The child's four years old, don't forget, and he believes everything you tell him. Last Saturday, you told him that story of yours about the nuns' farts that make people lose their memories, and Sunday morning, he started telling me that he didn't know where his shoes were because a nun's fart had hit him during the night. Four years old, I tell you, and he's making fun of me already!" "If you had more of a sense of humour, Bartine. . ." "A sense of humour! Hocus-pocus that you can't make head or tail of that turns our kids into liars! Life's tough enough without them making up things on top of everything else!" Josaphat-le-Violon decided to stop arguing with his niece. Albertine turned to Laura, who hadn't said a word since the conversation began. "And how about you, Laura? How can you tell when your father's stringing you a line and when he's telling the truth?" Laura stopped drying the dishes for a moment. She seemed lost in thought. When she did speak, it was with conviction — and her reply required no response. "I don't really care, ma tante. In fact, I think sometimes it even helps me get on with my life, the way he spins his yarns."

Albertine plunged her hands into the boiling water. "Bon, okay. I get it. I'm the one that's crazy. Go ahead and dream, the whole bunch of you. One of these days, you'll tell me you'd have been better off with your two feet on the ground like me." Josaphat-le-Violon and Laura looked at one another and shrugged. In the dining room, Victoire had her ear pressed to the radio, as she did every evening, but she wasn't listening. The long walk that afternoon had tired her far more than she was willing to admit, and her heart was beating a little too fast for her liking. "Goddamn potato! It's going to blow up on me!" She took the shawl that was always draped on the back of her rocking chair and shivered as she wrapped it around her shoulders. "I shouldn't have served the supper either. . . . I'm too goddamn proud!" The presence of the two floozies in the house had had the effect they'd counted on: Albertine was furious, but Victoire wasn't able to derive the slightest pleasure from that fact. Usually, making her daughter angry was one of her greatest delights (it was her way of reminding Albertine that she still existed, even though she was kept away from everything that went on in the house on the pretext of her age and her infirmity), but at supper tonight, perhaps for the very first time, Victoire had felt some pity for poor Albertine as she contemplated Mercedes and Béatrice with such horror and disgust that it seemed as though she might be sick in her plate at any moment. "I'm getting old too fast. Getting soft. There's no reason to feel sorry for Bartine. She goes looking for trouble!" Marcel, who had been sleeping on his sofa for a good half-hour, stirred in his sleep and uttered a few incomprehensible words, among which Victoire thought that she could recognize "moon" and "horsey." Her vision from the afternoon came back to her. She didn't want to think about it any more. Ever. Josaphat-le-Violon had half-comforted her by making her feel that she wasn't crazy...but the old woman on the balcony seemed so gentle...and she looked at Marcel so tenderly.... And that family resemblance!... "I'm overtired, that's all! Instead of seeing things like that, I just won't go out! Ever again!" And suddenly, she was filled with all the dread of that possibility—until it submerged her and she brought her hand to her heart, thinking that she was going to die. "No! No! I don't want to stay cooped up in here! I don't want to!" Gabriel was sitting at his wife's feet. He told her about his afternoon: the incident with Willy Ouellette, the too many beers, his doubts about the war, his flight, and finally, his meeting with Béatrice. The fat woman listened to everything, stroking his head. When he finished, she spoke to him softly, almost as if she were speaking to a child, emphasizing certain words by pressing her fingers against her husband's temples or his neck, waving away his doubts as much with her hands as with her voice, slowly comforting this soul that she knew to be weak, but whom she loved so much, concealing her own problems, her own fears, in order to tend to his. At last, he fell asleep, his head on the fat woman's lap. Then she was silent and she turned her face towards the moon that had moved into her corner of the sky. Her breathing was spasmodic, as though sobs were trying to come out of her throat. She rested her head against the back of her chair. "Acapulco!" The child in her belly kicked so hard that she couldn't help crying out in pain. Gabriel awoke with a start.

Pierrette Guérin was still out of breath. She'd come running down the street to announce her good news to her best friend, Thérèse, but to her great surprise, Thérèse didn't seem at all excited. On the contrary, she frowned and grimaced in distaste. "How come you're carrying on like that, Thérèse? I give you some good news, but you look as if I'd just slapped your face!" "I don't know if your news is all that good, Pierrette..." "Oh, everybody knows you've got straight teeth and everybody thinks you're beautiful! But if you had big spaces in between your teeth like me, you'd be singing another tune!" Thérèse and Pierrette were sitting at the foot of the stairs. Pierrette was fiddling with the hem of her dress. Richard and Philippe, who didn't like Pierrette very much, had disappeared as she approached and gone up to sit in the big chairs on the balcony before the grownups came outside and took them away. "Listen, Pierrette, I think a plate's disgusting. Can you see yourself stuck for the rest of your life with this thing in your mouth that's too big for you? That you have to take out of your mouth and clean and...yuck! Just thinking about it gives me the creeps." Pierrette stopped playing with the hem of her dress and now she was looking at her friend with pleading eyes. She would have liked a word of encouragement, an affirmative nod, a friendly pat, but instead, Thérèse was doing everything possible to discourage her. "But Thérèse, at least I'll have straight teeth!" Thérèse got up, turned her back to her friend and climbed up a few steps before replying. "Anyhow, do whatever you like, because I don't want a friend with false teeth that could fall out anytime, that she sticks in a glass of water beside her bed when she goes to sleep at night!" Thérèse had often seen her grandmother's false teeth in a glass of water that Victoire kept on her bedside table, and she imagined that everyone who wore dentures was obliged to take them out in order to sleep. Abandoning her friend with no remorse, Thérèse went to join the boys on the balcony. Philippe was rocking a little too hard in his father's chair, and sometimes, the back struck against the brick wall with a thud, while Richard was falling asleep in his grandmother's folding chair. "What's she up to, your pal, Pierrette? Did she bite you with her crooked teeth?" "Don't worry, Flip, pretty soon, she won't be able to bite!" Pierrette was going home, her head drooping, when she met the dog. It was a huge yellow beast, flabby and ugly; it was following a trail with determination, sniffing the sidewalk lustfully, as though he were going to eat it, furiously sniffing the air when he smelled an odour different from the one he was pursuing, then letting out a little moan of satisfaction when he smelled it again. Pierrette, her hands behind her back, cautiously approached the yellow dog. "You're a big doggy! And real ugly too! You looking for something to eat? There's a little girl over there on the second floor. . . . I wouldn't mind if you took a couple of bites out of her . . . . She's pretty skinny, but you'd be doing me a favour!" Pierrette had come a little too close to the dog, who suddenly began barking wildly. Five seconds later, Pierrette was running up the stairs of her sister Germaine's house, throwing herself into her mother's arms, sobbing. Rita Guérin put down her Coke on the floor of the balcony. "Well, another tragedy, eh? Was that you the dog was barking at? Yes? Well, that's just too bad! How many times have we told you not to get too close to dogs you don't know? And don't wipe your nose on my dress like that! I just washed it!" Rita Guérin held out her handkerchief to Pierrette, who blew her nose loudly. "I saw you gabbing with your great friend Thérèse just now. . . . I hope you didn't go and tell her that I promised you a set of dentures. Because when I told you that just now, it was only to get you off my back. You're getting on my nerves, you and those damn teeth of yours! You're only eleven years old, Pierrette. Your

teeth've got all the time in the world to straighten out. . . .
I wouldn't get your teeth pulled at your age, it'd be
criminal! Now don't go telling anybody that I said that or
else they'll think I'm crazy! Wait till you're seventeen, like
everybody else!" As soon as Pierrette disappeared, the
dog continued on its way. The track it was following
stopped abruptly in front of a wrought-iron fence that
smelled of fresh paint. The dog walked back and forth in
front of the fence three or four times to be sure there were
no gaps that he could slip through, then he flattened
himself in front of the fence gate, his head on his front
paws in a gesture of supplication. He began to moan like
a puppy that has lost its mother. But his act was pure
hypocrisy. While he seemed on the outside to be pleading
and pitiful, ideas of carnage and murder were seething in
his head. "Come out, you goddamn cat! Come out, if you
aren't too yellow! Instead of staying inside there, being
fussed over like some lily-livered coward, try and show
me how brave you are, so I can put out your other eye
and then jump on your throat and finish you off! I have to
finish you off! I have to make sure you're dead! Otherwise, if I know you, you could get better in no time and
come back and shit all over me. I gave up my territory
tonight so I could come and settle things with you once
and for all! But it's worth it! I won't be safe till I'm sure
you're off in cat heaven or maybe cat hell, where mice and
dogs are allowed to chase you and kill you and eat you up
and then start all over again, for ever and ever!" Philippe
was leaning over the balcony railing. "Lookit, Thérèse,
that damn dog from this afternoon followed us all the way
home." But Thérèse wasn't listening. For several minutes
she'd been watching a shadow slumped on one of the
staircases on the other side of the street. At first she
thought it was Monsieur Brassard or Monsieur Poitevin,
but Monsieur Brassard was up on his balcony smoking

his pipe and Monsieur Poitevin had been in the hospital for weeks. Then, a gesture that the shadow made, the way the man ran his hand through his hair, made Thérèse's heart leap. "It's him! He followed me all the way home!" A mixture of sensual pleasure and fear ran through her body and she began to tremble. "My Lord, what'll I do? I have to tell somebody.... No...no.... There's no danger...and it's exciting.... He liked it when I kissed him and he wants more.... He wants me to do it again! Well, he'll just have to wait, goddamn him, if he thinks I'm going to jump on his neck like that.... Sure, he's handsome.... But I can be independent when I want!" Thérèse began to laugh softly and Philippe looked at her, amazed. "You think it's funny, him following us all the way home?" Thérèse smothered her laughter. "Did you see him too?" "Can't you hear him howling? But I know what he wants. He's waiting for his victim so he can kill him." Thérèse, panic-stricken, ran into the house. On the staircase across the street, Gérard Bleau was weeping.

Around nine o'clock that evening, Josaphat-le-Violon and Gabriel helped the fat woman out onto the balcony. It wasn't nearly as complicated as they'd expected. The fat woman managed to get out of her chair, and then, by putting an arm around each of the men's shoulders, she walked slowly across the bedroom, taking small steps, supported more by her will, perhaps, than by her legs. She stopped for a moment in the dining room in front of Marcel's sofa, where the little boy was asleep with his fists closed, and smiled at her mother-in-law, who was beginning to drift off to sleep in her rocking chair. "I'm going out to sit on the balcony and I'm so glad!" Victoire belched, coughed and cleared her throat. "I do believe I was having a snooze there. . . . I'd better go to bed, I think. . . . You ought to spend the night out there, if it isn't too chilly. . . . Cover yourself up well and breathe deep. It'll do you good!" Josaphat-le-Violon, Gabriel and the fat woman began to make their way slowly down the corridor. The fat woman felt as if she were dreaming. Often in her sleep, she had seen herself get up and walk — or float, rather — through the house, going into all the rooms to check that nothing had changed and kissing every member of the family, as if they were all her children. This time, though, she wasn't dreaming, and yet, the same sensation of lightness supported her on her long walk to the balcony. Everything in the house was smaller than she remembered, though. The rooms, the furniture, even the huge furnace that sat imposingly in the corridor between Victoire's room and Edouard's. The ceilings were lower too. "Maybe it's because I've got so fat. . ." Philippe and Thérèse came to meet her and they encouraged her as much as they could. "Keep going, ma tante. You'll see. It's worth it. It's so beautiful outside. . ." "Want me to help you, Momma? Is there anything I can do for you?" Albertine followed behind, grumbling: "What are you doing, going outside like that? In your nightgown! And in your condition! What will people think? They'll be calling us gypsies!" Victoire followed on the fat woman's heels, pushing her daughter from the back. "Viarge, Bartine! Leave her alone! I'd rather be called a gypsy than find her in her bedroom tomorrow morning dead of boredom!" Laura Cadieux brought up the rear, holding her belly with both hands. When they finally reached the door to the balcony, the fat woman asked for a few moments' respite. "Let me catch my breath. It's been so long since I've taken a step. . ." She stood there, clutching her husband's and her uncle's neck, but stretching her head so that she could look outside. She was so eager that her heart leaped. "It's beautiful...the leaves haven't started to grow yet, but it won't be long now.... It smells of April and May, all at once!" Inside her, the baby moved again. "It won't be long now, angel. It won't be long. Momma's finished her walk and now you can see how good it is to breathe the fresh air!" She advanced a few paces and stepped onto the balcony. Richard woke with a start and cried out in delight when he saw his mother there. He got up and huddled against her belly. "Come, sit down, Momma.... You feeling all right? You sure?" They sat the fat woman down in Gabriel's big rocking chair. "Everything all right?" "You comfortable there?" "You need anything?" "I'll get you a pillow." "A nice cold soft drink would taste good, don't you think?" Even Albertine was leaning over her. "I bought some Larose spruce beer this afternoon..." When everything was silent again, and the fat woman was able to contemplate the street as much as she liked, steep herself in the images and sensations of the early spring night, scrutinize the smallest shadowy corners, recognizing, in spite of the darkness, the faces of all the neighbours watching her from their balconies, breathe deep the promises of May, and what still remained of April, time was suspended and nothing moved. Then, very softly, as if he were afraid of breaking the spell, Josaphat-le-Violon offered to play a tune on his fiddle. Around him, the faces all lit up. "Now what should I play for you? 'Humoresque' or the 'Meditation' from *Thaïs*? Or maybe you'd like a jig or a reel..." "I asked for the 'Meditation' from *Thaïs* this afternoon, mon oncle. That's what I'd like..." Philippe ran to get his uncle's fiddle. And the "Meditation" from *Thaïs* rose above la rue Fabre, perhaps a little wheezy, but played with such sincerity that even the wrong notes transported the soul and chased

sorrow away in concentric waves. Then, Josaphat-le-
Violon played "Humoresque," which he knew and played
better, and after that, "Le Reel du pendu," and "La Gigue
à Giguère," and the rest of his country sorcerer's reper-
toire, which in just one evening, can make you forget all
the miseries on this earth and all the unhappiness in the
world. Victoire even started tapping her foot as she used
to do when she was young; and Gabriel warbled along, as
his father had taught him to do. Albertine went inside and
awakened Marcel, who thought he was dreaming, and expected that, at any moment, Duplessis would jump up on
his lap, telling him in his pussycat's language: "I'm back!
I'm back! And I'm more marvellous than ever!" Thérèse,
Richard and Philippe, the first real city generation, for
whom music was something that came out of the radio,
not from the hands, feet and mouth of people they knew,
were fascinated, dazed, transported by the sight: their
grandmother, tapping her foot, and their great-uncle, the
balcony magician. The fat woman herself launched into
"Le Temps des Cerises," as she did in the days when all la
rue Fabre would listen to her sing when she made her red
ketchup and green chowchow in the fall. On the other
side of the street, without even realizing it, Marie-Louise
Brassard put her hand over her husband's hand. "It
reminds me of back home! I don't feel as if I'm in a cage
any more!" Rita Guérin and her three pregnant daughters
came down from their balcony, followed by Pierrette, and
sat on the steps. Claire Lemieux, abandoning her fat
white whale of a husband to his beer and potato chips,
came and joined them. Marie-Sylvia put the little sign
that read: "Closed until 7:00 tomorrow morning" in her
window and walked across the street in her Saturday
dress, its freshness gone now. And suddenly, after "Heure
Exquise," which everyone sang in chorus, swaying from
left to right, the fat woman leaned over the balcony

railing and said: "Come on up! Come on! Come up and have a chat!" She looked, in turn, at Germaine Lauzon, Rose Ouimet, Gabrielle Jodoin, Claire Lemieux and even Marie-Louise Brassard, who hadn't left her own balcony. "I'm going to have a baby too, just like the rest of you. . . . Come on. Let's talk about it." The three Guérin sisters were the first to make up their minds, followed closely by Claire Lemieux. The last to move was Marie-Louise Brassard, who indicated at first that she didn't want to leave her balcony, even getting up and going into the house. But when the fat woman spoke directly to her ("Come on, Madame Brassard. You too. We don't know each other yet."), she was obliged to obey. All the same, though, when she crossed the street, she tried to conceal her pregnancy with a sweater draped over her arm. The others left the balcony discreetly, making way for the pregnant women. The fat woman's family disappeared into the house, and soon you could hear Josaphat's fiddle playing in the dining room. "Le Reel d' la Pleine lune d'été." Marie-Sylvia went down la rue Fabre murmuring: "Duplessis! Duplessis!" looking under balconies and behind fences for the outline of her cat; and Rita Guérin went back to her own balcony, dragging Pierrette behind her. Godbout and Gérard Bleau hadn't stirred. Then, from the balcony came laughter, whispers and shouts that were held back by hands placed over mouths. There were seven women. Six were in their early twenties and didn't know what was in store for them, while the seventh, who could have been their mother, explained it all to them.


Rose, Violette and Mauve were knitting. Their balcony was plunged in darkness, but their hands automatically assumed the correct gestures, the right rhythm. In her lap, Florence, their mother, was holding a sick cat whom she'd finally managed to lull to sleep. She smiled as she listened to the seven pregnant women who sat above her. Godbout suspected that something was up. Still, he searched the darkness in vain, seeing nothing. Despite that damned smell of cat that clung to the night air, the balcony remained empty, mocking him.